DANGEROUS PASSAGE

Center Point
Large Print

Also by Lisa Harris and available from Center Point Large Print:

Baker's Fatal Dozen

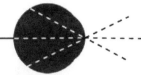

**This Large Print Book carries the
Seal of Approval of N.A.V.H.**

Southern Crimes Series • Book 1

DANGEROUS PASSAGE

Lisa Harris

CENTER POINT LARGE PRINT
THORNDIKE, MAINE

This Center Point Large Print edition is published
in the year 2013 by arrangement with Revell,
a division of Baker Publishing Group.

Scripture quotations, whether quoted or paraphrased, are
from the Holy Bible, New International Version®. NIV®.
Copyright © 1973, 1978, 1984, 2011 by Biblica, Inc.™
Used by permission of Zondervan.

This book is a work of fiction. Names, characters, places,
and incidents are the product of the author's imagination
or are used fictitiously. Any resemblance to actual events,
locales, or persons, living or dead, is coincidental.

The text of this Large Print edition is unabridged.
In other aspects, this book may vary
from the original edition.
Printed in the United States of America
on permanent paper.
Set in 16-point Times New Roman type.

ISBN: 978-1-61173-933-6

Library of Congress Cataloging-in-Publication Data

Harris, Lisa, 1969–
Dangerous passage / Lisa Harris. — Center Point Large Print edition.
pages ; cm. — (Southern crimes)
ISBN 978-1-61173-933-6 (library binding : alk. paper)
1. Women detectives—Fiction. 2. Single mothers—Fiction.
   3. Murder—Investigation—Fiction. 4. Large type books. I. Title.
PS3608.A78315D36 2013b
813′.6—dc23
                                                    2013024116

To all those seeking freedom.
May you seek and find it
in your heavenly Father.

Look at the birds of the air; they do not sow or reap or store away in barns, and yet your heavenly Father feeds them. Are you not much more valuable than they?

Matthew 6:26

Chapter 1

After another grueling weekend spent wrapping up a homicide, Detective Avery North was not about to let anything get in the way of her one nonnegotiable indulgence on her first day off in two weeks. She pulled into the parking lot of Glam Day Spa and stepped into the sultry Atlanta morning. The rest of her Monday might end up being a marathon, but she didn't care as long as she had the next hour to look forward to being pampered.

The petite, dark-haired manicurist greeted her at the front counter. "Morning, Miss North. You're right on time."

"Morning, Riza."

"You're off today?"

"Thankfully." Avery finished the rest of her iced tea while following Riza back to an open chair. "I managed not to cancel my appointment a third time. Crazy weekend."

"Then you need to sit down and relax completely. We could add a manicure? I have a new color that would look stunning with your red hair."

Avery melted into the padded chair, kicked off

her sandals, then dipped her feet into the hot, bubbly water, feeling herself relax for the first time in days. "Maybe next time."

Her feet tingled. One whole hour to forget about the leaky kitchen sink, her father's retirement party, and her mother's relentless questions about it. She closed her eyes. One whole hour to completely unwind and indulge her thoughts in something besides caterers, plumbers, and homicide cases.

Something pleasurable like . . . Jackson Bryant. Her first date with Jackson had started off with a severe case of rattled nerves that left her realizing she'd rather confront an armed murder suspect than jump back into the dating scene. By the end of the second date, she'd somehow managed to lose a corner of her heart to the handsome heartthrob, but even that hadn't been enough to lessen her surprise over the fact that there was now a third date planned for tonight.

At thirtysomething, with a somewhat moody tween and a mother whose own emotional stability was currently in question, Avery wasn't exactly Atlanta's perfect catch for a rising professional like the associate medical examiner. She wondered how many dates it would take before he started reconsidering his options—or she got cold feet.

Her shoulders relaxed. Dreaming of Jackson might be dangerous, but it might also prove to be the perfect escape. Gorgeous brown eyes that seemed to peer right through her. Dark hair, solid muscles, and an illegal amount of charm for one person—

Avery's phone rang in her front pocket. She opened her eyes and rubbed the back of her neck. She wasn't going to answer. It was probably her mother again, with more nagging questions about her father's upcoming retirement party.

Or it could be Tess. But she'd just dropped off her daughter at the middle school, so she should already be in her first-hour class.

A glance at the number told her it wasn't either of them. "Detective North speaking."

"This is Simons. 911 just received a call about a homicide. We've got an officer securing the crime scene, but Captain Peterson wants you there ASAP."

Not today, Lord. Please, not today. You know how badly I need a day off . . .

Avery glanced at her watch. She deserved this day off. Having to reschedule the eleven o'clock lunch with her mother was one thing, but missing an hour of pure relaxation was an entirely different story.

Avery pressed her fingers against her now throbbing temple. "It's my day off—"

"There's a tattoo of a small magnolia on the victim's right shoulder."

Avery's chest contracted. The recent crime

scene flashed before her. A young girl. Asian. Body discarded next to a Dumpster. And a small magnolia tattooed on her right shoulder.

They'd never found the murderer.

"Where?"

Simons passed on the address.

"I'm on my way." She flipped the phone shut and turned to Riza. "I'm sorry . . . I've got to go."

"Do you want to reschedule?"

Riza patted Avery's feet with a white fluffy towel, but Avery was already reaching for her sandals, ready to slide them on her still damp feet. "Yes . . . no. I'll have to call."

She left a generous tip on the chair, then slipped out the front door, back into the sultry Georgia morning.

Chapter 2

Avery slowed down as she approached the address Simons had given her over the phone, her gaze scanning the area for anything out of the ordinary. It wouldn't be the first time a killer returned to the scene of the crime.

The tree-lined street, with its brick buildings looming on either side, reminded her of the neighborhoods she'd worked as a rookie police officer. It was a unique mixture of mom-and-pop stores, neighborhood bars, apartment buildings, and charming older homes.

Statistically, crime might be higher in this community situated outside the ritzier golf courses and gated country clubs, but she'd always found the people friendly. More often than not, it turned out to be the combination of too many drinks or the addition of illegal drugs that turned simple disagreements into something ugly.

Like murder.

Of course, it was also the neighborhoods like this one that Mama was convinced would be the downfall of the city. She believed Atlanta's greatest attribute was its lingering pockets of old-fashioned southern charm. And everyone knew that transplants diluted that charm and added to the growing crime rate.

Avery, on the other hand, loved the diversity Atlanta offered with its collection of ethnic neighborhoods. The fact that she and Tess could spend a cultural afternoon in the city or escape to the nearby mountains on her time off was, in her mind, a plus. But someone had just lost any chance to visit Kennesaw Mountain Trail or Amicalola Falls. And it was up to her to find out why.

Especially if they were dealing with a serial killer.

A chill ran through her.

Avery pulled into the open space next to the alleyway, ten feet away from the yellow crime tape blocking off the scene. Detectives Sanders and Martin's unmarked sedan sat next to the medical examiner's vehicle and a couple of patrol cars. Already, a good number of onlookers stood gathered at the edges of the cordoned-off area. Avoiding the press would be impossible.

She grabbed her cell phone from the console, then hesitated. She should call her mother, except she'd never hear the end of missing today's meeting with Aunt Doris, who was catering her father's retirement party. She shoved the phone into her pocket. Mama would have to wait.

She got out of the car and headed for the sidewalk, where she took the clipboard from the uniformed officer standing guard at the front of the alley. She signed in, scribbling her initials and badge number.

Jackson Bryant's name had already been scrawled above hers.

She ignored the unsolicited flutter of her heart and addressed the officer. "Tell me what you've got."

"Asian female. Late teens, early twenties. The scene is secure. The medical examiner and two other officers arrived just before you did."

She nodded toward the growing number of spectators. "Make sure no one steps onto this scene without my permission."

"Yes ma'am."

The alley smelled like cheap liquor and overripe garbage. Cigarette butts lay scattered across the gravel. Green ivy threaded its way up the walls of the brick buildings lining the alley. A white Accord blocked the left side of the alley, its back taillight broken, leaving shards of the red plastic lying scattered on the ground. Determining what was evidence from this crime was going to be long and tedious.

On the other side of the Dumpster lay the body.

Avery's stomach heaved at the familiar smell of death—something she'd never gotten used to—mingling with the coppery taste of blood and the stench of the alcohol. The haunting scene from six weeks ago continued to flash before her. Even at first glance, the similarities were unmistakable. A young Asian victim, no more than seventeen or eighteen. Facedown on the ground, simply dressed in a shirt, short-sleeved sweater, and skirt. No shoes. The only difference was the copper bracelets adorning her left forearm.

Jackson finished covering one of the victim's hands in order to preserve evidence, then looked up. The butterfly-eliciting smile he normally gave Avery was missing.

"Avery." He pulled back the girl's sleeve to reveal the tattooed magnolia. "I knew you'd want to see this."

"What happened to her?"

He leaned forward and pointed to the mass of dried blood on the side of her head. "The autopsy will give us something more conclusive, but for now it looks as if she was killed and then dumped here."

Like the last victim.

Avery tried to push aside the feelings of vulnerability that swept through her. She was supposed to be the strong one who could handle anything. Except it wasn't always like that. "How long ago?"

"Not long. Rigor mortis has already set in, but I still don't think we're looking at more than five or six hours."

She pulled on a pair of latex gloves, then crouched down beside him. "So someone killed her, then dumped her here in the middle of the night, hoping to cover up their crime?"

"That would be my initial guess."

"What about the tattoo?"

Jackson pointed to the edge of the flower. "Healing typically takes anywhere from two to six weeks, so she's had it for some time."

"Any idea who she is?"

Detective Sanders leaned over her, camera in hand. "No ID, wallet, or purse was found on the body or in the car near the Dumpster. Which means, so far, we've got another Jane Doe."

"Signs of sexual assault?"

Jackson shook his head. "I'll let you know for

sure after the autopsy, but there are definite signs of struggle. She has scratch marks on her arms and left cheek."

Sanders stepped back and snapped a photo of the wall behind the victim. "I've already taken photos of the body."

"Finish photographing the scene, then I want the area swept in a strip search pattern, with each block numbered individually." Avery signaled to the other detective working on sketches. "Martin, when you're done, talk to Missing Persons and see if anyone has been reported missing in the past seventy-two hours that fits her description. Maybe we'll get lucky. Then find out who owns that car and make sure the Dumpster is searched for evidence."

She stood up. "Who called this in?"

"A guy who works at the bar . . ." Martin flipped open his notebook. "A Jeffery Vine. He was taking out the trash about six forty and found her."

"Let him know I want to talk to him once we've gone over the scene and processed the evidence. For now, we need to canvass the neighborhood to see if anyone saw anything."

Avery strode to the far end of the alley. Anger simmered as she tried to imagine what the girl had gone through the last moments of her life. Tried not to imagine if this had been Tess or one of her friends.

Pushing aside her emotions, she studied the narrow passageway, trying to see it through the eyes of the victim. Windows lined the brick walls. Trash bags and piles of empty boxes lay on the ground next to the overflowing Dumpster. There had been a fight with someone. A boyfriend? A stranger? Then someone had dumped her body here . . .

She turned around and started back toward Jackson. TV shows concentrated on the value of forensics evidence and high-tech computers, but experience had proven over and over again that it was the door-to-door grind and gathering of evidence that usually paid off with the best results. Which was exactly what they were going to do. Because her job was to ensure that whoever did this didn't get away with a senseless murder.

As with all their cases, they'd end up sifting through piles of evidence, most of which had nothing to do with the case. But all they needed was one lead. One tiny clue that would point them in the direction of the killer.

Jackson caught up with her halfway down the alley. "As soon as you're done with the body, I'll bag her and take her back to the morgue."

"Promise you'll call me as soon as you're done with the autopsy."

"Of course."

She didn't want to be there. Some cases hit too close to home.

"Hey, are you going to be okay?"

"I don't know." She shook her head and started back toward the Dumpster again. "These are the cases that always get to me. Somebody's baby, lying in an alley. Just like the last one."

"Avery."

She glanced back at him and let his sympathetic gaze wash over her.

"This isn't your fault."

Avery stopped midstride. "What if these cases are related? If I'd found the murderer of the last victim, this girl might not be lying in the back of some alley."

"Maybe, but you don't know that."

"Sometimes I can't help but wonder if I'm really cut out for this. I want to make the world a safer place, but the evil around us never stops. What did she do to deserve being murdered? What did my other Jane Doe do?"

"That's what you have to figure out." Jackson's hand brushed the back of her arm. "The reason you do this is because you have this uncanny ability to look inside a person and see why they do what they do. You look at the root cause and motivation behind the crime. In the end, you win more than you lose—and make things safer for Tess and all the other young girls out there."

"What about the next girl he murders?"

"We don't know yet if this is the work of a serial killer."

"But what if it is? What if I can't save his next victim?" The guilt still refused to dissipate, but Jackson didn't deserve to see this side of her. "I'm sorry. It was a long weekend and my mother . . ."

She missed her mother. The strong, supportive woman she used to be. Instead, they'd argued again this morning over the details of Daddy's retirement party. Lately Mama would argue with a fence post if there were no one around.

"You have no reason to be sorry." Jackson's comment pulled her from her thoughts. "I know things have been extra hard for you lately. Any new leads on your brother's case?"

They walked a few silent paces. Michael's unsolved murder had left all of them searching for answers.

"I found a discrepancy in the witness list." For months there had been nothing but dead ends. She didn't expect this latest lead to turn into anything, but like every other piece of information, it was worth following up on. She'd learned firsthand that seeing death through the eyes of a homicide detective was nothing compared to experiencing it through the eyes of the victim's family. Which was one reason she wanted to stop someone else from experiencing the unending grief she still wrestled with.

"Maybe it will turn out to be what you've been looking for."

"I hope so."

"What I said about this case is true, Avery. None of this is your fault—"

"Maybe not." Avery turned back to face him. "But we've got to find out who did this before he strikes again."

Chapter 3

Avery paused at the corner of the tree-lined street that faced the crime scene, feeling a heightened sense of urgency. Both experience and instinct told her the murderer would strike again, but after canvassing dozens of homes and businesses located near the scene, they'd ended up with only a handful of vague possibilities to follow up on, none of which seemed promising. Which meant, for the moment, they were no closer to finding out the identity of their Jane Doe . . . or her killer.

Avery reached up to wipe away the sweat that had beaded on the back of her neck. The curious crowd had long since scattered after losing interest in the yellow police tape that fluttered in the early-afternoon breeze. To Avery, though, nothing could make her forget the young girl who now lay in the morgue. This couldn't end up as another unsolved case.

Stepping over an upturned piece of concrete in

the sidewalk, she hurried to catch up with her partner, Mitch Robertson. At six foot four, Mitch hovered over most of the officers in their department. Avery, at five foot eight, felt almost petite next to him. She'd learned to trust Mitch with her life—something she'd had to rely on more times than she cared to remember. Risk came with the job, and Mitch had proven to be one of several men in her life who would do anything for her. Like her father, who still tried to treat her like a princess.

And now there was Jackson.

A smile tugged at her lips as she followed Mitch up the driveway of the next house on the block. Jackson's entrance into her life had been as unexpected as the white potted orchids thriving on the veranda despite the hot Atlanta summer.

Her mother and sister had convinced her to finally try dating again, but in the three years since becoming a widow she'd gone on fewer dates than she could count on one hand. Agreeing to go out with Jackson hadn't been easy. Dinner and a movie had simply been a way to prove to her mother that her heart was mending. Which in a way was true. While she still missed Ethan fiercely, time had begun to heal the immense hole his death had left. What she hadn't expected was agreeing to a second and then third date with Jackson. Or that her heart would actually flutter at the thought of seeing him again.

"Avery?"

She stopped in the middle of the driveway and looked up at Mitch, his expression clear that it wasn't the first time he'd tried to get her attention. "I'm sorry. My mind is—"

"A thousand miles away? I can tell."

Talking to Mitch about Jackson was out of the question. Which left room for only one thing. "This case has me rattled."

Jackson aside, it was the truth. Maybe he'd simply become the distraction she needed at the moment. They started walking again toward the porch, giving her time to shove aside any lingering romantic daydreams and start acting like the leader of her team again.

Mitch stepped onto the porch. "Hits a little too close to home?"

There might not be an excuse for her lack of focus, but at least she knew Mitch understood. Keeping the streets safe for her daughter was part of the motivation behind what she did.

"I can't help thinking, what if we were searching for Tess's killer? What if I didn't know where she was? What if I found out she was lying on a cold morgue slab, tagged as Jane Doe?"

"This isn't Tess, Avery."

She tried to shake off the chill that slid up her spine despite the afternoon heat. He was right. They weren't after Tess's killer. Tess was safe at school. She forced herself back to the present. On

21

duty in the middle of an investigation wasn't the time to be worrying about her daughter . . . or fantasizing about Jackson, for that matter. She shifted her gaze back to the porch, the scent from a fresh coat of paint still hanging in the air. It was time to pull herself together.

She blew out a sharp breath and rang the front doorbell.

The door opened an inch a moment later, its metal security chain still in place.

Mitch held up his badge and identified them. "Afternoon, ma'am. We need to ask you a few questions about an incident that happened this morning in your neighborhood."

The woman peered over the rim of her glasses at the badge. "You say you're detectives?"

She had to be at least eighty. Avery groaned inwardly. The woman probably couldn't see across the room, let alone across the street on a dark night.

Mitch nodded. "Can we speak with you for a moment, Mrs. . . ."

"Waters. Evelyn Waters." She shut the door, unlatched the chain, then opened it again. "A woman my age living alone can't be too careful, you know. And I'd invite you in, but my grandson's been doing some repairs on the house, including having the carpets cleaned, and they're still a bit damp."

"No need to worry about that, ma'am." Avery

22

caught the hint of loneliness in the woman's voice. She breathed in the smell of a roast as it overpowered the acrid scent of the paint and cleaning supplies. Her stomach rumbled, reminding her she'd missed lunch. "We need to ask you about a young woman who was murdered next to the bar last night. We're talking to your neighbors to find out if anyone saw something."

"Murdered?" Fear flickered in her eyes.

"Yes ma'am."

"I saw the commotion and the police cars this morning and wondered what had happened." Mrs. Waters tugged on the waist of her flowered dress, her brow furrowed. "When that bar went in five years ago on the corner, I told Harry it would come to no good. I couldn't begin to count how many times the police have shown up at that address. Not a lick of good, I tell you. The neighborhood's gone down ever since."

"Did you see anything last night?" Avery tried to redirect the woman's train of thought. "A strange car? Anything out of the ordinary?"

"I didn't see anything, but I know of someone who might have."

Avery glanced at Mitch. "Who would that be?"

"There's a homeless man who walks these streets at night."

"You saw him last night?"

"Last night and most every night. I have arthritis, you know, and have trouble sleeping.

23

Which is why I see him most nights. He comes up the street this way, rummages in the trash cans if it's trash day, always carrying a backpack. After that, I can't see where he goes."

Avery flipped open her notebook and jotted down the woman's information. "What time?"

"I usually see him around four or so. Never later than four thirty."

"And last night?"

"The clock by my bed read four ten when I got up, so a few minutes after that, I'd say."

"And you have no idea where he might go?"

"I used to tell Harry—"

"Who's Harry?" Mitch cut in.

"My late husband, bless his soul. He died from cancer of the bone earlier this year."

"I'm sorry to hear that, ma'am." The sooner they gathered the information, the sooner they could follow up on this lead, but the woman's words curbed Avery's impatience. The look of loneliness had resurfaced.

"Harry used to say that you could almost set the clock by Mr. Nomad. That's what we call him. I think he's been walking that same route for—I don't know—ten, eleven months. I figure he heads south to the park."

Which would put him at the crime scene around four fifteen. Their victim would have already been dead, but there was a chance he saw something. "Can you describe the man?"

"Describe him?"

"Any information you can tell us will help, ma'am."

"I suppose he's several inches taller than me, but thin." She patted her thick midsection. "Dark hair and a beard, I think."

"What about his clothes?"

"He wears this long, brown trench coat. Like Columbo. Even in the summer. My husband, bless his soul, loved that show and used to watch every rerun before he died. That and *Bonanza*. You young people probably don't remember back that far, but he loved Michael Landon. I used to tell him that too much television would turn his brain to mush, but it helped him pass the time."

"Anything else you can remember that might help us be able to track him down?" Keeping the woman's thoughts focused was almost as difficult as finding witnesses in today's murder.

"I've only seen him at night, you understand, and except for that streetlight, he wasn't much more than a shadow. But I'm sure about the beard."

A moment later, Avery handed the woman a card and asked her to call if she saw the man again, then headed back to the car with Mitch.

"So what do you think?" he asked.

"That we just received the best lead we've had all morning."

Which meant they needed to compare notes

with the rest of the team, strategize, and find Mr. Nomad.

Her phone rang, and she pulled it from her pocket. It was Jackson.

Avery turned away from her partner and pressed the phone against her ear. "I hadn't expected to hear from you so soon."

"Do you have a second?"

"Yes. Go ahead. We're just about finished canvassing the neighborhood."

"And we've finished the autopsy."

"Any information like estimated time of death?"

They'd have to wait on forensic testing before Jackson filed his final autopsy report, but there was still information that could be gleaned from the external and internal exams. And she'd take anything she could get at this point.

"I'm putting the time of death between two and four."

"Good. What else?"

"If you have time to come by, I have something I need to show you in person."

"I'm on my way." Avery flipped her phone shut and shoved it back into her pocket. "I need to drop you off at the station, then head over to the ME's office."

"And the rest of the team?"

"Compare notes with Carlos and Tory to see if there are any other leads from their canvassing to follow up on, then start tracking down this homeless guy. Another stakeout . . . another canvassing of the neighborhood . . . do whatever it takes to find him. He's the closest thing we've got to a witness. Did they find out who owns the car that was left in the alley?"

"Tory just sent me a text." Mitch glanced at his phone. "Car belongs to a Paul Adams. She's tracking him down now."

"Good." Avery climbed into the driver's seat and started the car.

Mitch snapped on his seatbelt. "So how is he?"

She pressed her foot against the brake. "How is who?"

"Jackson Bryant. You can stop pretending. I've caught that daydreamy look in your eyes whenever the two of you are in the same room. Or on the phone together."

Avery frowned. "It's nothing."

"Nothing?"

After a quick glance in the rearview mirror, she started for the station. She could always opt for leaving him on the street to find his own way back. "We've gone out. Twice. It's not like we're dating or anything."

"Sounds to me like you're dating."

Avery felt her face flush. So much for professionalism and hiding her emotions. On the other hand, if Mitch had any downfall, it was his lack of commitment with women.

"I could always bring up your dating habits."

"Don't flip this conversation back on me."

"When's the last time you had a second date? You carry around that little black book of yours like it's some—"

"I'd be careful before you start profiling me like one of your murder suspects, because I actually might surprise you. I asked Kayleigh to marry me this weekend."

Avery braked too hard at a stop sign, then caught her partner's grin. "You're serious? You asked her to marry you?"

"We even settled on a Valentine's Day wedding."

"Wow. Congratulations! Though I have to admit, I expected her to be just another name added to your little black book." Avery glanced at him before crossing the intersection. "You did burn your little black book, didn't you?"

"Apparently some of your unsolicited advice got through to me, though I believe it was your mother who told me—"

"My mother." Avery read the digital clock on the dash. Two thirty-five. She'd never called her mother. "I'm sorry. I was supposed to meet her for lunch."

"Why do I have a feeling she doesn't deal well with being stood up?"

"You clearly know my mother."

Trying to explain to her mother why she hadn't been there to help make the final decision between jumbo shrimp or bacon and tomato tartlets for her father's retirement party would be useless.

Avery pulled into the parking lot of the police station. The dull headache that started earlier this morning in her temples had spread to the base of her neck. Between mothering, her career, family, church, and dating . . . something was going to have to give.

Chapter 4

Jackson finished jotting down the rest of his notes for his official report while his tech began cleaning up the autopsy room. Avery had been right. Some cases managed to become far too personal. After eight years of working in autopsy, he would have thought that his scientific interest would keep him coming to work every day. Sometimes it wasn't enough. Some cases ended up eating at him for days, making him question why he was in this line of work.

And like their last Jane Doe case, this one might very well prove to be another one of them.

For now, his motivation would have to come from the realization that anything he discovered could help break the case and bring their Jane

Doe's murderer to justice. So far, though, he had little to report beyond time and cause of death. Now came the perpetual wait for fingerprints to be run against the system, fluids tested, and lab work results gathered. And so far nothing he'd found could help identify the body lying in his morgue.

Except the photo.

He stepped out of the windowless autopsy room and into the sunshine filtering through the narrow corridor, trying to shake the ever-present feeling of death that hung in the air. The half-dozen spider plants hanging strategically throughout the room helped remove some of the toxins the dead bodies brought with them, but even the green foliage couldn't completely erase the vinegary odor of formalin or the other foul smells he had to work with every day.

He looked up as Avery stepped into the building at the other end of the long hallway, making him thankful he'd taken the time to exchange his stained lab jacket for a clean one. There wasn't much he could do about the lingering smell of antibacterial cleaner until he could take a long, hot shower.

She traversed the hallway with no sign that she was bothered by the subtle odors drifting through from the autopsy room. Except for certain cases, he hardly noticed the smells anymore. But that didn't hold true with most people. He was still surprised he'd managed to land a third date. He rarely got this far in the dating game. The combination of discovering he lived with his grandfather—who had been recently diagnosed with Alzheimer's—and knowing what he did for a living inevitably ended up scaring off most women.

Avery was proving to be different.

She stopped in front of him, two large drinks in her hands and a tired smile marking her features. "Hey, thanks for calling me."

"Any excuse for some time in the company of a certain woman."

"Flattery will get you everywhere, you know."

"That's what I was hoping." He paused for a moment, taking in her blue eyes, strawberry blonde hair, and full lips. He hadn't been looking for a relationship when they'd first met a couple months ago, but a string of cases kept throwing them together. Finally, he'd admitted to himself that he couldn't get her out of his mind.

"I brought you a surprise." She held up one of the drinks and handed it to him. "Vanilla coke with a dash of lime."

"Just how I like it. No wonder they made you detective. You've got an eye for detail."

Her nose scrunched when she smiled. "Funny."

He took a sip of the drink, then glanced out the window. "Want to go for a walk? I've got a few minutes until my next autopsy, and besides this caffeine boost, I could use some fresh air."

"I'd like that."

Her smile tugged harder at his heart. Oh yeah. He was in serious trouble. She followed him outside into the sunlight that caught the red highlights in her hair, toward one of the iron benches outside the building. It might still be summer in Atlanta, but after four hours in an enclosed room, he didn't mind the humid air at all.

He took another long sip of the icy drink, hoping for a round of small talk before they delved into business. "Has your day gotten any better?"

Avery's smile faded. "After hours of canvassing the neighborhood, we ended up with a homeless man who roams the streets at night. At this point, he's not a suspect, but I am hoping he saw something."

"No one else saw anything?"

"Someone will turn up eventually, but time isn't on our side in this case. I need to know who she is before our killer strikes again."

He caught the worry in her eyes. If this was the work of a serial killer, the count was already up to two bodies—two that they knew of. Neither of them wanted another victim on their hands.

"There's still a chance this was simply an isolated case and not a serial killer. This Jane Doe was killed with a blunt instrument to the side of her head. It's a different MO from your last victim, who was stabbed, then dumped."

"True, but the two cases are still close enough in my mind that I can't overlook the connection at this point. Between the location, race, and age of the victims—and especially the tattoo—there are simply too many similarities."

She looked up at him, her fingers wrapped tightly around her drink, expression somber. "What if I don't catch this one and justice isn't carried out? What if this happens again to another girl?"

"Sometimes finding out the truth takes time, but you'll find it."

"I'm sorry." She leaned back against the bench and rattled the ice in her cup. "I'm really not usually like this. We're not even twelve hours into things, and I'm treating it like a cold case with no leads in sight. But I just can't stop playing out worst-case scenarios. I need more than justice. I need this man stopped, so another mother doesn't have to suffer the heartache of losing a child."

Jackson watched her expression darken and all the pieces snapped into place. Four months ago, Avery's brother, Michael, had been killed in the line of duty, leaving Avery to watch firsthand how the loss of a child had changed her mother.

"We might not be able to save them all, Avery, but we can do everything in our power to find whoever did this and stop him from ever hurting anyone again." He nudged her with his shoulder. "Or we could always think about starting our own fast-food chain and start flipping burgers together. No dead bodies, no elusive killers . . ."

As corny as his idea was, it worked. Avery laughed and leaned toward him, smelling like a bouquet of fresh flowers—a far cry from his autopsy room.

"I think I might like that."

Jackson looked out across the manicured lawns and began to relax for the first time all day. Atlanta might not be Houston, but he loved how the city seemed to rise out of the forest, its neighborhoods dotted with small parks and green landscape. On days like today, he needed the diversion of God's handiwork to settle his spirit. Adding Avery to the picture made things even better.

She was worth making time for, but finding that time to spend together the past few weeks had become far more complicated than he'd wished. Between their jobs, Tess, his grandfather, and her family, there always seemed to be something urgent pressing. And he was pretty sure she felt the same tugs on her time.

She pulled on a loose strand of her hair, a habit of hers he'd noticed. He wished he could read her mind, because his heart was pretty much already taken. All he could do at this point was hope she felt the same way.

He glanced at his watch, immediately regretting the gesture. "I'm sorry. I was hoping to prolong things, not cut it short, but I guess I should catch you up with what I found and get back to work."

"I'd like that better too, but you're right. And I've still got a mountain of work to do before heading off to Tess's swim tryouts." He caught the flicker of regret in her eyes. "Initial findings? You said you had something for me."

"Hopefully the lab will come up with something more solid, because overall I don't have much for you yet. You know the drill, it will take a few days minimum to get the results back on all of the tests we're running." No matter what his personal feelings were for her, there was only so much he could do to rush the results. "There were signs of sexual relations, though I don't think she was raped. There was no bruising."

"And the DNA."

"We'll get a match as soon as we can."

Avery shook her head. "So she has consensual relations, then the guy hits her over the head and kills her?"

"It wouldn't be the first time."

"Maybe not, but we're missing something. If it's not a serial killer, what are we looking at? Sex trade, prostitution, jealous lover, robbery . . ."

"I do have something else. I'm not sure how it will help at this point, but it is the most promising."

"What is it?"

Jackson reached into the front pocket on his lab jacket and pulled out the black-and-white photo he'd slipped in an evidence bag and handed it to her. "It's one and a half by two inches, and looks like it was cut from a photo booth strip, like the one you'd find at a mall."

"You found this on her person? We checked all of her pockets."

"We found a small, concealed pocket sewn into the lining of her clothes. It would have been easy for your people to miss at the crime scene. They're running the fingerprints we found on it right now, but it might only lead us back to her."

Avery fingered the photo. Two Asian girls smiled shyly at the camera, both wearing white traditional Vietnamese dresses. The one on the left was their Jane Doe. The second girl's face was half hidden behind a cone-shaped hat. Smiling. Happy. "Why conceal the photo? Why not just carry it in a purse?"

"That is a question I can't answer."

"Was there anything else in the pocket?"

"No, but there could have been."

"What do you mean?"

"The stitching around the edges had been ripped, as if someone had taken something out."

"During the attack?"

"Or maybe after she was dead. I don't know."

Avery stood, her mind clearly sorting through the information she'd just been given.

"You'll need to sign for the photo. I'll make sure that your team receives the rest of the evidence once we are finished processing it."

She started back beside him, toward the offices. "Thank you."

"You're welcome. By the way, are we still on for tonight? I know this was supposed to be your day off, but if you'd rather go out another time . . ."

He waited for her answer, hoping she was still up for it. He looked forward to seeing her again outside of work when they could talk about something besides murder investigations and autopsy reports.

"No, tonight should still be fine. I'm looking forward to it."

"Good. Me too." His phone buzzed. "Hang on." He quickly read through the text message. "It's from the lab. There were two sets of fingerprints on the photo."

Avery turned to face him. "Whose?"

"Our Jane Doe's and James Philips's—a man convicted for assault eighteen months ago."

Chapter 5

As long as Mason Taylor could remember, blending in had been as easy as breathing. By the age of twelve, he'd been fluent in English, Spanish, and Portuguese, thanks to his Brazilian mother who died from an overdose when he was fourteen. By the time he turned eighteen, he and his three brothers had lived in Los Angeles, Phoenix, St. Louis, and a dozen other crime-ridden inner cities across the US—thanks to his deadbeat dad.

Suburban homes with their picket fences, Little League baseball, soccer teams, and private schools had never been an option for the Taylors. They'd moved from one flea-infested hole to the next, skipping out when there wasn't enough money to pay the rent and changing schools more often than his father changed the oil on their 1972 Ford pickup.

In the process, Mason had become the perfect chameleon, learning to avoid the bullies at school and the gangs on the streets. No one remembered Mason Taylor from the class of '02.

Until the night that changed everything.

Mason wiped the beads of perspiration from

his neck and leaned back into the shade partially covering the wooden bench where he sat. Suburban Atlanta had been the last place he'd imagined living . . . and the first place he'd run to after his brother Sam's death. Piedmont Park was one of those places where he'd found the anonymity he'd craved. No one had noticed or cared about his late-night runs or early-morning study breaks. And that was how he wanted it.

Burying Sam that foggy November became not only his wake-up call but his way out. He'd stolen three hundred bucks from his father's wallet, and with his two younger brothers, disappeared to Atlanta, where he'd begged his mother's older sister to take them in.

She agreed, as long as they followed her rules. Church three times a week, no swearing or drinking, and piano lessons. He'd managed to avoid the altar calls and music recitals, but not his aunt's unconditional love and bottomless pans of peach cobbler.

She'd been gone four years now. It was days like today when he missed her most.

A woman jogged by, late twenties, short shorts, and a smile just for him. He studied her perfect figure as she passed before reining in his thoughts and forcing himself to look away as Finn approached Mason wearing his signature baggy pants, rumpled T-shirt, and a Braves cap. He dropped his cell phone into his back pocket and slid into the empty space beside Mason.

Mason shoved any lingering memories from the past aside and let his fingers drum against his thigh. Playing the part of user had become all too natural. "Wasn't sure you were gonna show up."

"Didn't know you were in such a hurry to be somewhere."

Mason shifted his weight on the bench, shrugging off the urge to finger the pistol missing from his hip. Trust wasn't something he could afford, just like he couldn't forget who Finn really was. He shoved his hand into his pocket, making sure the marked bills were still there.

He leaned forward, then back again, completely into his role. "Did you bring what I asked for?"

Finn set the package on the bench between them and took the money Mason offered. The exchange took less than five seconds.

Finn stood to leave.

"Wait," Mason began. "There's something else."

Finn raised his brow but didn't respond.

"I'm lookin' to make some extra cash."

"Selling?" Finn's voice lowered, even though the nearest jogger was a hundred yards away.

"No. Heard your boss wants drivers to transport goods." Mason added a hint of desperation into his voice. "I need this, Finn. I've . . . I've run into some serious financial trouble. I was told you're the one to talk to."

"By who?"

"One of the guys at the dock." Mason studied Finn's face. So far, Finn had no idea that Mason saving his life had been nothing more than an elaborate setup. Or that their relationship was based on lies.

"Think I owe you that much?"

Mason measured his words, knowing he had to push hard enough to motivate Finn, but not too hard that he started asking the wrong questions. "You'd be looking at ten to twenty if it weren't for me, and you know it."

Finn didn't look convinced.

Mason pushed harder. "I didn't think I'd need to remind you how I took out that cop so you could—"

"You not trying to blackmail me, are you?" Finn took a step toward the bench.

"Never." Mason weighed his options. Even at three inches shorter and ten pounds lighter, he was certain he could take Finn down if it came to that, but a fight wasn't what he was after. They were supposed to be on the same side.

Mason searched for another angle, his fingers tapping faster against his leg. "I grew up—"

"Forget the tough-boy sob story." Finn shook his head. "My connection isn't looking for some hungover druggie."

"My habit won't affect my work."

"You'd be transporting certain goods across

state lines that would require avoiding both the local cops and the Feds."

Bingo.

Mason tempered his desire to smile. This was the break he'd been waiting for. "I need the extra work, so illegal or not, I really don't care."

"If you get caught, you'll be on your own." Finn grabbed a pen from his front pocket, then scribbled on a scrap of paper. "Show up at work tomorrow as usual and talk to Owen."

"You won't regret this."

"I know." Finn handed Mason the note and started to walk away. " 'Cause we're even now."

Chapter 6

Avery pulled into the driveway of her house and parked in front of the garage. Jackson sat on the front step of the veranda, forearms resting against his knees, while he read something on his phone. She'd called to tell him she was running behind, but she hadn't planned to be this late.

Tess jutted her chin toward the house before opening the passenger door. "Guess I'm not the only one you disappointed today."

Avery bit her tongue. Arriving late to the tryouts had cost her the chance to watch her daughter swim. "I'm sorry, Tess. You know more than anyone that I can't always be everywhere I want to."

"These were tryouts. They're important."

"I know how important they are to you."

She might have missed her daughter's advancement to the next level of competition, but apologizing again wouldn't make a difference at this point. Because she couldn't promise it wouldn't happen again. Couldn't promise that the next time she headed off to a swim meet or school activity that she wouldn't get called into work. Not being able to always be there for her daughter was the hardest part of what she did.

"Emily should be here any minute." She handed the house keys to Tess, who was already gathering up her school bag, swim paraphernalia, and the deluxe pepperoni, sausage, onion, and extra cheese pizza they'd just picked up. "She's bringing a couple movies and stuff to make root beer floats."

Avery grabbed her own bag and phone and started toward the house behind Tess. At least her sister Emily was never late and always willing to help pick up the slack. But even that knowledge did little to alleviate the guilt.

Tess greeted Jackson as she climbed the front steps, then slipped into the house. Avery shot up a short prayer of thanks that Tess hadn't taken out her frustration on him.

She stopped at the bottom of the steps and shot Jackson a sheepish grin. "I'm even later than I told you I'd be."

"I was late too if that helps any."

Years of police work might have taught her to be meticulous in her cases, but when it came to her personal life, she always seemed to fall short. She caught his forgiving gaze and realized for a moment how much she missed coming home to someone. Someone who helped keep her grounded and balanced.

She sat down beside him on the porch and dropped her bag beside her. "I ended up having to stay longer at the precinct, which meant I missed Tess's swim tryouts, and then there was the issue of picking up the pizza, which took twice as long as it should have . . ."

She grasped for something else. Legitimate or not, her excuses sounded more like a cop-out. "Bottom line is that sometimes I fall short in meeting everyone's expectations."

"I'm not here to make you feel guilty. I came, knowing you'd been out working the case on your day off, and how on top of everything else this one hit close to home."

Way too close.

He shot her a concerned look. "You look tired."

"I am, but I'll be okay." Her body was used to the long hours and constant lack of sleep. It was the emotional issues that tended to take their toll on her.

"What about James Philips?" he continued. "Any luck tracking him down?"

Thanks to Jackson, she'd been able to add a mug shot of Philips to their crime board this afternoon. Unfortunately, finding his fingerprints on the hidden photo was about as far as they'd gotten.

"From the looks of his mug shot, he was clean cut. Six foot one. Two hundred pounds. He'd worked for a local community college as a history professor since 2005. Married to Laurie Philips, an elementary school teacher for seven years, now deceased. No children. Arrested eighteen months ago for assaulting the man he claimed to be responsible for his wife's death."

"A man with a record. That easily ups the odds he could have been involved in this."

"Yes, but that is where the trail ends. Philips served his time in prison, but there is no record of employment since that time, no credit cards, not even government aid. It's like the guy dropped off the face of the earth after getting out of prison. We put out a BOLO so local authorities would be on the lookout for him, but until we find him, we're stuck with more questions than answers."

"And the leads from the canvassing?"

"For the most part no one saw anything. No

suspects, no witnesses other than a possible homeless man we're trying to find. Even the parked car in the alley turned out to be a dead end. Turns out Paul Adams works at the bar. When his shift ended, his car wouldn't start so he got a ride home with a co-worker."

"I'm sorry."

She shrugged. "You know how it goes. We'll be sifting through possible evidence over the next week or two that may or may not be related to the case. What about you? Anything more from the lab work?"

"Just a few inconsistencies. She had an enlarged spleen, for one. I'm running tests, but as you said, it will take time."

"Any preliminary ideas?"

"Give me another day or two, and I'll be able to tell you more."

Avery nudged him with her shoulder. "You didn't come over here to talk about Philips, lab reports, or for that matter, listen to my assortment of excuses for being perpetually late."

He smiled down at her. "No, I didn't."

Avery started to get up, then noticed the white box with the familiar Krispy Kreme logo sitting next to him. Her stomach growled. "You brought me donuts."

"Someone told me you love chocolate and cream filled." Jackson pried open the lid of the box while Avery tried not to drool. "This is supposed to be your dessert. After you've eaten a substantial dinner."

"You actually think I have the willpower to wait until then?"

"I'm not getting into that argument, but you do have to share. I thought Tess might like one too."

"You're a smart man." She picked one up and took a bite. "Bribery just might work in her case."

Jackson laughed. "That was my plan."

His smile tugged at her heart, but also brought with it the uncertainties she wanted to ignore. Being single and dating was one thing. Being single and dating and dealing with a twelve-year-old daughter had thrust her into an entirely different ball game that she knew nothing about. Ensuring Tess was comfortable with the idea and liked the man she dated was essential. She took another bite, then ran her finger across the icing on top. Gooey . . . chocolaty . . . sticky . . . chocolaty . . . Oh yeah. A few bribes here and there certainly didn't hurt her either.

She felt herself slowly relaxing for the first time all day. For their first date, he'd brought her a red rose. By their second date, he'd somehow discovered her favorite flower was a white rose, and he'd brought her two. Simple. Elegant. She loved the fact that he was a gentleman and even a bit old-fashioned. She pressed her lips together and sighed. Something told her this guy was a

47

keeper. And it wasn't just his good taste in dessert.

"This is delicious, but we're never going to make it to dinner if I don't quickly change. Five . . . ten minutes tops."

"Take your time." He followed her across the porch to the front door. "Tess told me that next time I come by she'd introduce me to her conglomerate of pets, so that should keep me occupied."

"The donut will help too, but don't count on too much bonding tonight. She's mad at me for missing the tryouts and liable to take that out on anyone who happens to be in the same room."

"Give her some space. I grew up with a hormonal sister. Eventually I discovered she was a bit like the Texas weather where we grew up. Wait a few minutes and her mood will probably change."

Avery laughed. "You're right about that."

Solidarity between her and Tess had been the one redeeming outcome of Ethan's death. The weeks and months that had followed their loss had created a stronger bond between them, forcing them to survive what life had handed them together. It was something she prayed they never lost.

Upstairs, it took Avery ten minutes just to figure out what she wanted to wear. The pants and top she'd laid out this morning seemed too stuffy.

Three outfits later she finally settled on a green print sundress Emily had picked out with her and a missing pair of silver sandals. She hollered at Tess to see if she knew where the shoes were, then remembered she'd worn them Sunday for church and taken them off in the basement.

Avery hurried downstairs, hesitating at the top of the basement stairs to listen to Tess talk to Jackson about her pet mice. With a dog out of the equation because of their busy schedule, Tess had somehow managed to talk her into a variety of low-maintenance alternatives that now included three female mice, an African clawed frog, a hamster, and a Birman cat named Tiger.

Tess laughed at something Jackson said. Avery let out a soft sigh of relief. At least they seemed to be getting along.

In the basement that she'd converted into an office, she paused in front of the crime board she'd put together, like she'd done a thousand times before over the past four months. Each time reminding her that Michael was never coming back. Each time praying that this time, something would jump out at her so she could find his killer.

She'd studied the photos and files of her brother's case until she'd memorized every detail. Witnesses' photos, suspect photos, crime scene photos, lab reports. It was all in front of her like a jumbled collage that made sense only to her. This was truly her domain. The only place in the entire house with no trace of Tess's presence.

"Avery?" Jackson stood at the bottom of the stairs, carrying her missing pair of sandals and wearing a sheepish grin as if he were unsure that he should be here. "Tess sent me down here with these. They were in her room."

"Thanks." Avery plopped down onto her old leather couch to slip them on. "My daughter loves to borrow my stuff."

She smiled, unsure when her little girl had found time to morph into a full-fledged preteen. Or, for that matter, when *she* had become old enough to have a preteen daughter.

Jackson shoved his thumbs into his jeans' front pockets. "I came down here for another reason. I feel like I should offer you a rain check on dinner. You've had a rough day, and I know you're tired. If you need to cancel tonight, we can do this another time."

Avery hesitated. He was right. Fatigue had settled in, making part of her long for nothing more than a hot bath and a good night's sleep. But on the other hand she'd been looking forward to tonight for a long time.

She looked up at him and felt her stomach quiver. "I think I'll be fine as long as you promise not to keep me out too late."

"I think I can manage that." His smile hinted relief. "So this is how you wind down?"

He looked around the room, seemingly in no hurry to leave.

"Working on cases . . . ," she glanced at the easel set up in the far corner of the room, "and painting when I can find the time."

"Watercolor?"

She nodded. The only splash of color in the room—besides the crime scene photos—was the purple spray of wildflowers she'd started painting a couple weeks ago.

"You're good." He turned back to her. "And I've just uncovered yet another layer of a fascinating woman."

Avery felt her cheeks flush as she looked around the sparsely decorated room, trying to see it through Jackson's eyes. But while refurbishing the house had become an ongoing task—like the still-needed visit from the plumber—remodeling the basement had dropped to the bottom of her to-do list. For now, the bare room didn't hold much more than a chair, desk, some filing cabinets, and the old leather couch from her college years she'd patched using duct tape.

"I suppose this room could use some fixing up, but for now its purpose is more functional. I don't exactly have the kind of job I can leave behind when I head home, so this gives me a place to work away from the precinct."

"I don't know. I always pictured you relaxing at

the end of a hard day with a glass of iced tea and a good book."

"A glass of iced tea, yes, but a good book?" She let out a low laugh. "I don't even remember the last time I read something other than a police report. Besides, if I'm really going to unwind, I prefer a fast-paced workout at the gym, or even better, rock climbing with Tess."

Of course, who was she kidding about unwinding? Lately, between leading murder investigations, looking into Michael's death, and trying to balance her personal life, her nerves were—more often than not—strung tighter than the piano wires on Mama's polished Steinway.

Jackson stopped in front of her crime board. "You've told me you're investigating his death, but you've never spoken much about your brother."

"Losing Michael was—and still is—very personal."

She crossed the room and ran her fingers across the last photo she'd taken of Michael at her parents' home, feeling the familiar sting of sadness the memory brought with it. She'd meticulously arranged the photos beside the timeline and key points of the case. Five more boxes of paperwork sat filed away in the corner of the room. Suddenly, the threads of information surrounding her brother's death seemed too on display. She didn't even let Tess hang out down here. She started to flip the board, but Jackson caught her hand.

"Wait." He squeezed her fingers gently, sending shivers up her arm. "I know this is personal, but I also don't want you to feel as if you have to hide who you are for me. I've learned over the past few weeks what's important to you. Your faith, your daughter, family, your job—these are the things that make you who you are. And I like that. I like the fact that you go rock climbing with your daughter, paint in your free time, and loved your brother enough to find out the truth about what happened to him."

A fresh flood of tears burned her eyes. They'd buried Michael just a few months ago in the spring, and as much as she longed to go back and erase that moment, she knew she was going to have to accept what had happened. And it wasn't just the loss of Michael. Her mother's slow spiral into depression after a difficult year of loss had triggered Avery's need to make things right again. Finding Michael's killer might not bring him back to life, but finding answers would help bring the closure they all needed.

Because while Michael Hunt might have been one of their own, sometimes she was convinced that the department had given up on finding his killer. Not that they would ever admit that. Even her father's influence hadn't been enough to bring the killer to justice. Which meant that unless she could discover the truth, her brother's death would go unsolved. A murderer would go free. And her brother's name would be marred forever.

Chapter 7

Jackson watched Avery's expression flicker from grief to determination. Leading a murder investigation was one thing. Needing to find answers for the death of a family member had to have stretched her emotions to a whole other level.

She sat back down on the couch and drew her feet up underneath her. "How much have you heard about Michael's case?"

He moved to sit down beside her. "I know that two officers were killed in an explosion in a warehouse. One of them was your brother."

She fiddled with a loose thread on her hemline. "Michael and his partner, Blake Watson, had been working undercover for months, assigned to infiltrate a group suspected of dealing in arms and drugs in the area. They were making inroads, but then something went wrong. Michael's handler got a distress signal from Michael about three in the afternoon. Thirty seconds later the building blew up. They found the remains of their bodies, but no evidence of the weapons or drugs they were there to buy."

"Someone found out who they really were?"

"Presumably. The FBI was later able to match the bomb signature to a known terrorist bomb-maker. Which is why we believe Michael had stumbled onto something bigger than just a local arms dealer. So not only did someone find out who they were, they clearly didn't want them to dig any further."

She leaned against the back of the couch, lips drawn tight, and let out a slow breath. "I don't know what else you've heard, but there's more to the story than just two decorated officers killed in the line of duty. While the case is still officially unsolved, Michael is suspected of being a department leak."

Jackson gauged her expression. Clearly there was a lot of pain wrapped up in the accusations that to her must seem like betrayal by the department. He'd heard the rumors surrounding the case but had decided to ignore the media's version and wait until she was ready to tell him herself. "I thought everything was still inconclusive."

"The department knew someone was peddling lists of informants in return for large sums of cash. Some of it was intelligence gathered by Michael in several key undercover operations that had given him access to information that potentially could be worth something to the right person . . . if he'd wanted to sell it."

"So things point to your brother, and he is the one blamed for the leak."

"They also found a laptop hidden in the apartment where he was living while undercover that contained what the department has only described as sensitive information. But evidence can be planted."

Jackson caught the frustration in her voice. Fear of someone's betrayal was often harder to accept than death. He'd experienced that first-hand. He pushed back his own cloudy memories of his mother's infidelity. "I take it you have a theory?"

"Yes, though no one has bought into mine."

"What do you believe?"

"If you go through all the evidence—and believe me, I have—there is one person who can be linked to almost every incident, but the department doesn't agree."

"Who is that?"

"Michael's handler, Mason Taylor. I might have known Mason for a long time and thought of him once as a friend, but I knew my brother better. I know beyond a shadow of a doubt that Michael wasn't the kind of man who would sell out for money."

He sat quietly beside her and waited for her to continue. With the department on the "other side" and her family ready for closure, there weren't a lot of people she could turn to.

"This list of accusations is another reason it's been hard to let go of Michael. To listen to the rumors and the lies being spread about his character. Things that I know aren't true." She reached up to rub her temples. "Something about today made me relive Michael's death all over again. I guess it's because I've spent weeks on our last Jane Doe case, and all I ever came up with was a pile of dead ends with every suspect and every witness. Facing the same situation again with our latest victim just rubs it in, and reminds me of my brother's case—another unsolved crime."

"It's hard when so many of the pieces are out of your control."

"My family seems to think my determination to find the truth about Michael's death has become more of a vice than a help. That it's dragging out the grieving process for all of us, when instead it's time we accept what has happened and simply let him go."

"Something you're not ready to do."

"No."

Jackson searched for something to say. "My grandfather would quote Lincoln right about now. 'It has been my experience that folks who have no vices have very few virtues.' "

Avery's smile surfaced again. "I like your grandfather already. Tell me about him."

"He's a Civil War buff who actually remembers stories *his* grandfather told him about fighting in the war," he began, willing to let her guide the conversation. "He's quirky, smart, and managed to raise me since I was twelve."

"Your parents? Were they a part of the picture?"

Jackson paused. They'd talked briefly about their past over their first two dates, but he had enjoyed their slow pace of getting to know each other. Because while many of the scars from his childhood had—for the most part—healed, even time hadn't completely erased the sting of his mother's abandonment. "My mother decided early on that a family was too much responsibility, and she'd rather be out partying. Eventually she left us for good. My father loved my sister and me, but couldn't handle being a single parent. He worked as a commercial fisherman, which meant lots of time at sea, so I can't really blame him. It was the only thing he knew how to do. He eventually sent my sister and me off to Texas to live with our grandparents. Right after I started college, while my grandmother was still alive, my grandfather's job transferred to Atlanta."

"Do you ever get to see your father?"

"He came to visit every Christmas, and eventually we became close after college. He died in a fishing accident about five years ago."

"I'm sorry. I'd like to meet your grandfather someday."

"I'd like you to meet him. He was recently diagnosed with Alzheimer's, which, as you know, is the reason I moved here to Atlanta."

She caught his gaze, her eyes full of question. "You'd want to know the truth, wouldn't you?"

Jackson only had to consider her question for a brief moment. "Yes. I'd say that your brother deserves more than an obituary in the newspaper. Your family deserves—you deserve—to know the truth."

"That's what I want to give him. I'm just looking for closure. For proof he was innocent like I know he was. And for answers for my family and for me." She shook her head and grinned. "How did we get so serious?"

"It's been one of those days that reminds you just how vulnerable each of us really are." He reached out and grasped her fingers. "Are you still hungry?"

"Yes, though a part of me is content just to sit and talk."

"Me too." He loved the blush that crept up her checks, the way she ducked her head as if in doing so she could hide her most intimate thoughts. The way she bit the edge of her lip when she finally looked back up at him.

He could get used to coming home to her every night. He loved his grandfather, but being with Avery beat listening to nightly tales of Abraham Lincoln and William Sherman by a long shot.

From the first time they met, he was drawn to her fiery spirit—and now her vulnerable side. He'd never met anyone so focused. She knew how to throw herself completely into an investigation while somehow still managing to not let the day-to-day tragedies of the job harden her.

He laced their fingers together and rubbed his thumb across the back of her hand. He was close enough that he could breathe in the sweet scent of her perfume. Close enough to kiss her. He tried to read her expression as he reached out to brush her hair from her face.

A moment before he leaned forward to act on his impulse, he felt her tense and pull back. Her gaze dropped.

"Avery, I'm . . ." He stopped short of saying he was sorry. He wasn't sorry for wanting to kiss her. Or sorry for wanting her to be a part of his world.

She stood up and walked toward the basement window. "I wanted to be ready for this." The setting sun filtered through the glass, casting a soft light across her face as she turned back to him, but he couldn't read her expression. "I thought I was ready for something more to develop between us."

"And now?"

"Today, I missed lunch with my mom along with my daughter's swim tryouts because of a murder investigation. I know you are looking for more than just a casual dating relationship, but the bottom line is that I don't know if I have enough of me to give right now."

"I know your life is full, and I'm certainly not trying to demand more of you." How did he fight for her without pushing her away in the process? "But neither of us are walking into this blindly. We both know what it takes to make a relationship work. And while I realize it's too early to know where our relationship will end up, all I know how to do is be honest with you. I miss coming home to someone. I miss someone to share my heart with, to wake up to, and snuggle with in front of the fireplace at night."

"Which is exactly the problem. I'm not sure I can be that person you want."

"Maybe you're right. Maybe you're not that person, but I had hoped we could at least see if it were possible."

The heartache he'd experienced over losing Ellie resurfaced. There had been so much loss coupled with her death. Marrying his college sweetheart had seemed perfect. They'd planned to start a family, giving him a chance to become to his own children everything his parents had failed to be.

But none of that had ever happened. The

January after their summer wedding Ellie was diagnosed with cancer. Nine months later he lost her forever.

He glanced back up at Avery. Tonight wasn't about Ellie, or even his past. It was about the fact that he was falling in love with that woman standing in front of him. She was the complete opposite to Ellie in many ways, but maybe the real problem lay in the fact that the two of them had reached different places in life. While he was ready to commit to a relationship, she clearly wasn't.

"Maybe I'd better go." Jackson took a step toward the basement stairs, hoping she'd say something to stop him, while not wanting to push her in a direction she wasn't willing to take. "I'll keep you updated on any new developments in the case from my end."

"Thank you." Avery wrapped her arms around her waist. The professional tinge in her voice was back. "I appreciate all your help."

Jackson headed up the staircase, wishing he could take back the past few seconds. Wishing she'd say something—anything—to break the tension that had just settled between them. And hoping he hadn't just managed to push away the best thing that had come into his life in a very, very long time.

Chapter 8

Avery yawned, then snuggled closer against Tess's shoulder. Jackson had been right. Somewhere between slices of cold pizza and Emily's root beer floats, Tess had decided to forgive her for missing the swim tryout.

Forgiving herself for what had happened between her and Jackson had proven to be far harder.

Tess and Emily had talked her into watching one of their favorite renditions of the Cinderella story, *Ever After*. It was a movie she'd already watched a dozen times, but tonight it had taken the first half of the movie just to settle her mind. By the second half, she'd hardly been able to keep her eyes open.

Emily echoed her yawn from the other side of the couch as the final credits rolled. "I don't know about you ladies, but I'm going to have to call it a night."

"You're not the only one." Avery nudged Tess with her elbow. "You'll never be able to get up for school if you don't go to bed now. Six will be here before you know it."

Tess groaned and took Avery's hand, making her wish she could freeze the moment so she could hold on to it forever. It wouldn't be too long before the boys started calling, independence completely set in, and her tween was ready to fly the coop. She wasn't sure she'd ever be ready.

Avery squeezed Tess's hand, then helped her off the couch. "Go get ready for bed. I'll come say good night in a minute."

Tess hugged her aunt and stumbled toward her bedroom, already half asleep.

Emily started helping Avery clear off the coffee table littered with the remains of microwave popcorn and lemonade cans. "Thanks for letting me hang out tonight."

"You know how much Tess loves having you here, and so do I. And besides, I'm the one who should be thanking you. You saved me from having to help her clean out the mice cage. There aren't very many things that really bother me, but mice . . ." She exaggerated a shudder.

"Those mice are adorable." Emily dumped the cans into the recycling bin in the kitchen and laughed. "You know, I'm not sure I'll ever understand you. You work at crime scenes and attend autopsies but can't stand the sight of a harmless little mouse."

"They're not adorable, they're creepy." Avery grabbed a washcloth for the counter and got it wet. "She's lucky to have you as an aunt, and not just because you're willing to help clean out animal cages."

"And she's lucky to have you as a mom."

Familiar pangs of guilt jabbed afresh. "I'm not sure how much credit I deserve. I've been working far too many hours."

"Don't even start with the guilt act. Besides, I hardly think you have to worry about that. It does her good to spend time with Mom and me. She loves it and so do we. And you're always there when she needs you."

Avery finished wiping down the counter. Being a single mom had always been someone else's struggle until one day it had been thrust upon her and she'd had to deal with it head-on.

Emily picked up her purse. "You know I try not to be the nosey sister, but you never said anything about what happened with Jackson, or why you didn't go out."

Avery rubbed the back of her neck, trying to erase the lingering headache. She'd have to take a couple more aspirin before she went to bed. "We were going to, but my day didn't exactly go as planned. I was given a new case, which meant I missed lunch with Mom, missed Tess's tryouts. Trying to add a new relationship into the mix . . . I don't know. I just don't see how it's going to work."

"So you panicked?"

"I didn't say that . . . I'm just not sure there's going to be another date."

"You're not serious, are you? This guy is perfect for you. Smart, incredibly good-looking . . ."

Avery raised her brow. "Then why don't you ask him out?"

"Very funny." Emily crossed her arms, clearly not impressed with her excuses. "What happened tonight, Avery? What really happened?"

The last thing she wanted to talk about was Jackson. How he'd almost kissed her. And how she'd panicked. She looked down at the floor. There was a stain in the carpet. How long had it been since she'd had it cleaned? Six, eight months? She made a mental note to call the carpet cleaners.

"Avery? What happened?"

"You want to know what happened? A girl was murdered. We found her dead behind a Dumpster. No ID. She's nothing more than another Jane Doe for now."

"Wow. I'm sorry."

"Some cases are tougher than others. This is one of them."

"Listen, I really am sorry, but what does any of that have to do with Jackson? Because I also know how important it is for you to have a life of your own outside work."

"I know, but I can't lose focus on this case,

and Jackson is turning into a distraction."

"He's become a distraction, so you're not going out with him anymore? You need a few distractions in your life. That's a good thing, Avery." Emily paused for a moment. "Sometimes . . . sometimes I wonder if you don't use your work, your fixation with Michael's case, and even Tess as an excuse to avoid getting involved in a serious relationship again."

Avery swallowed hard. "What if I'm simply not ready for something serious? He tried to kiss me."

Emily's eyes widened. "You sent him home because he tried to kiss you. That makes a lot of sense."

"He took me by surprise."

"Which means what now?"

"I don't know. We left things up in the air."

"He left things up in the air, or you left things up in the air?"

"That's not fair—"

"Just answer this. Is he really an unwanted distraction, or does he make you feel vulnerable?"

Avery rubbed her temples and sat down on the couch. The last thing she wanted right now was a heated discussion about Jackson. "Emily, it's late—"

Emily sat down beside her. "You might be able to fool Tess, Mom, and even Jackson, but not me."

"What are you talking about?"

"I know you, Avery. Maybe better than you know yourself sometimes."

"Oh, really? You know what it's like to stand over the body of a girl who's just been murdered, knowing she might be alive today if you'd closed a case and put a killer behind bars?"

"Stop using your work as an excuse to guard your heart. Besides, you're the good guy, remember? This wasn't your fault."

"Maybe not, but I have enough on my plate to deal with right now and today made that perfectly clear. Between my cases, Tess, Mom . . . being vulnerable, as you put it, isn't an option."

"And why not? What you feel over that girl's death is normal. And think of what you've lost over the past few years. You know what it's like to lose both a husband and a brother. You've seen and experienced loss not just from a cop's point of view, but from a family that's lost a lot." Emily reached over to give Avery's hand a quick squeeze. "Which is why you're good at what you do. But what about your own life? Every ounce of energy you have is poured into Tess, work, and the rest of your family. You deserve happiness again. I just don't want you to give up on Jackson because you think you're too busy, or even more importantly, because he makes your heart feel again."

"This coming from the woman who just broke off her engagement?"

"I don't regret for a minute breaking things off with Charlie. But he's an entirely different story."

"True." Avery had agreed with her sister's decision to call off the wedding, but that didn't change anything about the way she felt about things between her and Jackson.

"What happened with Charlie doesn't mean I'm going to run if I ever find the right guy, and neither should you."

"I don't know, Em. Even if I wanted to pursue a relationship, I honestly don't know if I have the emotional energy for someone else in my life right now."

Emily shook her head. "I don't buy that. Call him tomorrow. Tell him you were wrong, and that you're ready to cash in that rain check for a third date."

"Emily." Avery threw one of the pillows from the couch at her.

Emily grabbed it before it fell to the floor. "You better watch it, sis. I may be younger, but I can still take you on."

"I'd like to see you try."

"Seriously." Emily threw the pillow back at her. "When's the last time you worked on one of your paintings, went rock climbing with Tess, or went to the gym for a really hard workout?"

"I don't know . . . a few days . . . a week."

"That's what I thought. I'm not a psychologist,

but you know as well as I do that you work in a very high-stress job, which means you need something to help you relax when you come home, and I'm not talking about working on Michael's case in the basement."

Avery folded her arms across her chest. "Are you done?"

"Almost. Jackson makes you smile. I've seen you around him. And I just want you to be happy. Think about what I said. Promise?"

How could she argue against something part of her wanted so badly? "Promise."

"Good. Then I'll see you sometime tomorrow."

A moment later, Avery shut the door behind her sister, then proceeded to make sure the house was locked. She shut the door to the basement and flipped off the rest of the lights in the house. No matter what she did, she couldn't shake Emily's words. The house was quiet, but snagging a few minutes of downtime never lasted long. Turning off her mind was impossible.

The stack of photo albums she'd put together over the years sat in their normal spot. Like painting, scrapbooking had become another way to indulge in her creative side.

She pulled out the top album and flipped through it. Even with Ethan gone, life had had its high moments and times of healing. She'd been assigned to a homicide team while Michael moved into the narcotics division. Tess had turned eleven, and they'd managed a family trip to Disney World.

She stopped at a photo of Michael and her father and carefully pulled it out of the album. She'd forgotten about this picture. They'd gone out to Bone's to celebrate her father's promotion. Michael had looked so much like Daddy. When he chose to follow in his father's footsteps with the police force, no one had been surprised. Serving family and country was a Hunt tradition.

Until he decided to work undercover. Mama had hated it from the very beginning, especially the lack of communication. She couldn't stand the hazards of the position. But Michael was good at what he did and never looked back. His last undercover assignment had been the worst. It had dragged on for months and been a strain on the entire family, but Michael kept insisting he was close to taking down his target.

That day never came.

Avery flipped the book shut, keeping out the photo of Michael and her father. She pulled a copy of the photo Jackson had given her out of her back pocket. The two girls smiled up at the camera, happy and carefree. There had to be a clue in the photo. An answer somewhere in the middle of the limited evidence they'd turned up.

"Mom?" Tess's sleepy call broke through her thoughts from the other room.

Avery set the photos on the nightstand and went down the short hallway to Tess's room.

The soft glow of the nightlight cast a shadow against Tess's face. "You never came to say good night."

She lay in her bed surrounded by pink ruffles and stuffed animals. She'd asked for a new bedspread for her next birthday. One that wasn't so pink and frilly. The stuffed animals would no doubt be next to go.

"I thought you weren't sleepy."

Tess yawned. "Just a little."

Avery sat down on the bed and ruffled her hair. "I really am sorry about missing your tryouts today."

"I know."

"Do you know how much I love you?"

"Not as much as I love you." Tess reached up and gave her a big hug. At least she wasn't too old for hugs and kisses. Not yet, anyway. "You okay?"

"Yeah, why?"

"I thought you were going to go out on a date tonight."

"I was, but I got a new case today and, well, . . . as you know, the day ended up being kind of crazy, so we called it off." It was as close to the truth as she wanted to get.

"He's nice. I introduced him to Freddie and Hammy and the mice."

"He told me."

"So do you like him?"

There was no use denying it. "Yes."

"Then you should go out with him again."

"Really?" Was she the only one resisting this relationship? "You sound like Emily."

"She's right." Tess's eyes were starting to droop. "If you like him, there's no reason not to."

Avery hesitated. Tess made it sound so simple. Girl meets boy, girl falls in love, they get married, live happily ever after. Maybe that did happen. Sometimes.

She searched for an excuse but came up empty again. Maybe they were right. Just because she felt pulled in different directions by all of her responsibilities didn't mean she didn't deserve to find happiness again. Still.

"Relationships aren't always that simple, Tess."

Tess shrugged, then closed her eyes as she lost the fight to stay awake.

"I'll see you in the morning, sweetie. It'll be here before you know it."

Avery kissed her daughter on the forehead, listening to the steady rhythm of her breathing while watching the rise and fall of her chest.

What if it were Tess lying on that cold morgue slab, tagged as Jane Doe?

Unanswered questions swirled around her. Fatigue, both emotional and physical, settled in.

Hidden photos meant secrets, but what? And what really happened that night when her Jane Doe took her final breath?

Avery switched off the bedside light on the nightstand, then curled up on the bed beside Tess. Time was ticking. She had to find out the truth before the killer struck again and another family was ripped apart.

Chapter 9

By seven o'clock the next morning, Avery had already eaten blueberry waffles and fruit with Tess, dropped her off at school, and made it in to the office. By the time her team assembled, coffee was simmering beside a box of day-old pastries, and she'd already downed her second cup.

She stood in front of the crime board, whiteboard marker in hand, the urgency in the back of her mind all too real. The first twenty-four hours after a murder were always the most critical, but with a possible serial killer involved, they needed to find him before he struck again. Throwing a Jane Doe into the picture made their job even tougher.

Avery rested her hands on her hips. "Let's start with our potential witness, Mr. Nomad."

Mitch leaned back in his chair and stretched his long legs out in front of him. "We have confirmed statements from several witnesses that most nights he walks through the neighborhood, but there was no sign of him last night."

"So at least we know our Mr. Nomad is real. Tory, anything on the magnolia tattoo?"

With her exotic model looks and part-Asian heritage, few people took Tory Lambert for a computer geek and white-collar crime expert. But it hadn't taken long for Avery to notice that Tory was far more than just a pretty face. Which was why she'd requested Tory join her team. Smart, diligent, and always on top of things, in the past five months, she'd become an integral part of the homicide division.

"Carlos and I hit every tattoo parlor in the area." Tory looked up from her computer. "Just like in the last case, the flower design is too generic and impossible to trace."

"It could have been one of these do-it-yourself kits," Carlos added.

"Carlos would know."

Avery raised her brow at Mitch's comment, then turned back to Carlos. "You have personal experience with do-it-yourself tattoo kits?"

"No. What I do know is that they're pretty impossible to trace if you buy them off the internet."

"Trust me, he has personal experience," Mitch

threw out. "Show them, Carlos, or if you don't want to, I'll be happy to."

"Show us what?" Tory asked.

"Carlos has a *Cars* tattoo—a sparkly *Cars* tattoo at that—on his right ankle."

Leave it to Mitch to always lighten the mood.

Avery pressed her lips together. "Isabella?"

Carlos nodded. "You try saying no to a three-year-old wearing a pink fairy costume and princess crown, armed with a bag of temporary tattoos."

"Give the guy a break, Mitch." Avery folded her arms across her chest. "Not only does Carlos have a sparkly tattoo on his ankle, he probably only had four hours of sleep last night."

"Three hours to be exact. Chloe might have just turned four months, but she still doesn't sleep more than three hours at a time. Funny how I thought detective work was tough. Parenthood is going to kill me." Carlos rubbed his chin, then looked straight at Mitch. "Though I imagine when Kayleigh sees my copy of that little black book of yours, she's going to want to kill you as well—"

"You seriously didn't." Mitch sat up.

"Remember that long, boring stakeout back in June?"

"You copied my black book?"

Carlos shrugged. "You were sleeping. It was lying on the floorboard."

"And you couldn't just leave it alone."

Carlos's smile broadened. "Oh, I knew I'd need some leverage one day."

"Sleep or no sleep, I'd watch your back if I were you, Mitch." Avery laughed.

Eight years in the marines as a military interrogator had taught Carlos James Dias how to handle an investigation. And apparently, Mitch as well.

She cleared her throat. "Now, boys, back to our investigation. What about James Philips, and don't give me another dead end—or wisecrack, for that matter, Mitch."

"Not another dead end, just nothing new. Yet," Tory offered. "The bar next to the crime scene has a video camera on the street. We're planning to go through the footage this morning. Hopefully we'll get lucky."

"Good." Avery let out a sharp breath of air. "Listen. We're looking at a possible serial killer, which means that time isn't on our side. Let's make some progress today."

Her phone rang and she fished it out of her pocket. "Detective North."

As soon as she finished the conversation, Avery shoved her phone back into her pocket and grabbed her keys off the desk. Maybe their luck was about to change. "Mitch, you're with me. They've just identified our Jane Doe."

Thirty minutes later, Avery parked her car in

front of the Sourns' two-story home. The stacked-stone exterior and perfectly landscaped yard set right behind the golf course easily added up to a million-dollar price tag. This was a place that might actually impress Mama.

Mitch let out a low whistle as he exited the car. "What I wouldn't do for a paycheck that could afford this place."

"Then you're in the wrong line of work." Avery matched Mitch's steps as they made their way up the stone steps leading to the front door. "I knew this address was upscale, but this wasn't at all what I was expecting when we found the body yesterday. Her clothes, hair—nothing about her fits this upper-class profile."

Avery knocked on the door, tapping her foot on the welcome mat. She took a deep breath. The only thing worse than finding a dead body was having to inform the family of their loss.

A woman in her midfifties with olive skin and dark hair opened the door.

"Mrs. Sourn?"

"Yes." The woman's eyes narrowed.

Mitch held up his badge and identified them.

"We understand that you called in a missing person report for your niece."

"Yes. Tala." Mrs. Sourn pressed her hands against her chest. "Did you find her? When she didn't come home, I . . . I didn't know what to think."

Avery searched for the right words. Telling a family member they'd just lost someone was never easy. First of all, Mrs. Sourn was going to need the support of friends or family. "Is there anyone else in the house with you?"

"No, but please . . . tell me where she is."

"Would you mind if we came in and sat down for a few minutes?"

The woman blinked, confusion filling her expression. "No. Of course not."

She stepped aside, allowing Avery and Mitch to enter the foyer. Inside, the expensive décor matched the exterior of the house. A chandelier hung above them from the high ceiling. Oh, yes. Mama would love this. But as much as she might wish it, this was no social call to one of Mama's friends.

Avery sat down next to Mitch on the offered couch filled with plush, colorful cushions, while taking in the baby grand in the corner and the expensive artwork hanging on the walls.

Avery pulled out the photo of Tala and handed it to the older woman, who had taken a seat on the other side of the coffee table. "Is this your niece?"

"Tala . . ." Mrs. Sourn grasped the photo. "Yes. That's her. She told us she was going out with friends."

"I truly am sorry, but your niece was found murdered yesterday morning."

"Dead?" Mrs. Sourn stood and turned to face the long wall of floor-to-ceiling windows overlooking the green, taking the time to compose herself before turning back to them. "I thought maybe she'd gotten into some trouble, but . . . I can't believe that. Who would murder her?"

"That's one of the reasons we're here, ma'am," Mitch said. "And what we intend to find out."

Mrs. Sourn sank back into her chair. "I'm sorry. I just don't understand."

"Where is your husband?"

"He . . . he's meeting with a number of overseas clients. He told me this morning that I wouldn't be able to reach him."

"He went in to work, even with your niece missing?"

"We never imagined anything like this happening." The woman's fingers gripped the arms of the chair until her knuckles turned white. "I told him not to worry. That she'd probably spent the night with a friend. I decided to let the police know just in case, but I was so sure that she'd be home by now."

"When was the last time you saw her?"

"We ate dinner together Sunday night. She left right after we finished."

"She has a car?"

"No, someone picked her up."

"Who?"

"I don't know. Tala was a very private person."

"Tell me about your niece."

"Like I said, she was a quiet, private girl. Didn't have many friends." Mrs. Sourn cleaned her glasses on the hem of her shirt, then slid them back on. "She never caused us any problems."

"Did you try to call her?"

"Her cell phone . . . it must have been dead. I never got through."

"You said she didn't come home," Mitch said. "Was that normal?"

"No. She was a good girl. Cheerful. Responsible."

"Was there a change in her behavior?"

"She'd been moody the past few weeks, but not enough for me to really worry. I should have worried. I should have said something and tried to talk to her."

"How long had your niece been living with you?"

"Just a few months, since she graduated from high school. She planned to take some time off, then start college in January."

"I'm going to need a list of her friends with their phone numbers. Anyone who might know where she was Sunday night."

Mrs. Sourn slowly shook her head. "I'm not sure I will be a lot of help with that."

"Why not?"

"She'd made a few friends since moving here, but she didn't bring them here, and I didn't ask.

She was over eighteen. I felt as if she had the right to live as she pleased. I could show you her room."

Avery nodded, then stood. "That would help."

Tala's room was located on the second floor, elegant like the rest of the house, but simple. A few scatterings of personal things filled the room. A stuffed frog on the bed, high school diploma hanging on the wall, and a jewelry box. Neat. Spotless.

Avery ran her fingers across the top of the built-in desk next to the window where a row of romance and mystery novels sat. "You mentioned a cell phone, what about a computer?"

"Tala wasn't into computers or electronic things. She reads a lot and watches TV. As for her cell phone, I assumed she had it with her."

Avery made a mental note to get a trace going on the missing phone as soon as they left. "Did she work?"

"No, like I said, she was planning to start college in a few months. My husband and I had agreed to take care of any financial needs she had."

"That's very generous of you."

"She was family. We didn't mind."

Avery pulled the second photo from her pocket. "This photo was found on her body. Her face is partially hidden, but do you recognize the other girl?"

Mrs. Sourn adjusted her glasses. "I've never seen this photo. That is Tala, but the other girl . . . no. I don't recognize her."

"So you've never seen her before?"

"No." Mrs. Sourn handed the photo back to Avery. "Like I said, Tala was a private person. She tended to avoid the camera."

"What about her parents?" Mitch asked.

"Her parents were killed in a car accident about six months ago, which is why Tala decided to come live with us."

"Where was her family originally from?" Avery asked.

"Vietnam."

"Does she have other family either here or in Vietnam?"

"Distant family, but Tala lived in the US her whole life. She didn't even have a passport."

Avery and Mitch followed the older woman out of the room and back down the stairs to the living room. "Any brothers or sisters?"

"No. She was pretty much alone in the world. My husband and I felt sorry for her and believed the least we could do was let her live here."

They stopped in the middle of the living room, and Avery caught the older woman's gaze. "Mrs. Sourn, I do need to ask you, where were you Monday morning between two and four?"

Mrs. Sourn sat back down in her chair. The reality of the situation had begun to sink in. "I was here with my husband. He can verify that."

"I have one last question for now, Mrs. Sourn. Your niece had a tattoo on her shoulder. What can you tell us about it?"

"The tattoo . . ." Mrs. Sourn's fingers grasped the edges of her chair. She shook her head. "I don't know. I think she had it when she moved here."

"So you don't know when or where she got it?"

"No, I'm sorry."

Avery pulled a business card from her pocket and handed it to the older woman. "Thank you for your help, Mrs. Sourn. We'll be in touch again soon, but if you think of anything else that might help us find Tala's killer, please call."

"Of course."

"We will need to speak to your husband as well. Do you know when he'll be available?"

"He told me he'd be home for dinner."

Mrs. Sourn didn't move from her chair, her face pale.

"Are you going to be all right, ma'am?" Mitch stepped forward. "Can I call someone for you?"

"No. I . . . I'll be fine."

Avery nodded at Mitch. "Then we'll see ourselves out."

Outside, golf carts buzzed along the green in the distance, a world away from the stench of death and loss.

A few moments later, Avery gripped the

steering wheel as she drove out of the neighbor-hood with Mitch beside her.

"What do you think?" he asked.

"She seemed genuinely upset."

"And afraid. Nervous," Mitch added.

"Why wouldn't she be?" Avery wasn't sure she should defend Mrs. Sourn, but she had been on the receiving end of a call like they'd made today. "The woman just found out that her niece was murdered. I remember after Ethan died, I couldn't stop thinking that if death could take him, then why not my parents, or my sister . . . or Tess. The thought tormented me for weeks."

"You could be right, but I still think we need to dig deeper."

Avery nodded. "I agree. I want you to go with Tory and talk to the husband. He might be in meetings all day, but we need to know if their stories match, and if you can get any new information out of him."

"So you think Mrs. Sourn knows more than she's saying?"

"If she is involved, she's quite an actress."

"And there's still the matter of the tattoo. That isn't exactly insignificant. The exact same tattoo and crime scene setup as the other girl." Mitch turned up the air conditioner in an attempt to get rid of the humidity that hung in the car. "I know you don't believe in coincidences any more than I do."

Mitch was right, but they needed more pieces before they could put the puzzle together. Which meant that for now, finding out the identity of their Jane Doe had left them with far more questions than answers.

Avery's phone rang, and she pressed the receiver on her steering wheel. It was Tory.

"We found our homeless man."

"Where is he?"

"Here at the station. Officers picked him up twenty minutes ago."

"His name?" Avery asked.

"You've probably already guessed. It's James Philips."

Chapter 10

Avery slipped into the interrogation room behind Carlos, dropped a file onto the table, then set a cup of coffee in front of their Mr. Nomad. At least the man finally had a name. "Mr. Philips. How are you doing this morning?"

He clasped his hands together in front of him, ignoring the coffee, while rocking his body back and forth. "You can call me Bear."

"All right, Bear. I'm Detective Avery North and this is Detective Carlos Dias." She sat down across from him in one of the metal chairs. "Would you like to take off your coat? It's warm in here."

They might have the air conditioners running, but interrogation rooms always tended to be on the warm side, and the man's long coat couldn't be comfortable.

He fiddled with one of the black buttons. "I'm fine."

"Okay," Avery said. Carlos took a chair on the far end of the table. Captain Peterson stood behind the two-way mirror. "Do you know why you are here?"

Bear's gaze stayed fixed on the table in front of him. "I mind my own business, don't bother anyone, but now you bring me here because I don't have a home."

"You're not here today because of your living situation." Avery worked to soften her voice. She was used to playing the role of good cop, but that didn't mean she was convinced the man was innocent. A witness to a crime was one thing. Finding one's fingerprints on a victim's murdered body quickly moved a person from witness to suspect.

She leaned back in her chair, watching Bear's body language. Fingers tapping against the table, the continued rocking, refusal to make eye contact . . . He might not have killed Tala, but he was definitely hiding something. If she could help the man relax, they might get more out of him.

"How long have you been living on the streets, Bear?"

"I don't know. Six, seven months . . . maybe longer." He spoke quietly, still avoiding any eye contact.

"I can't imagine how difficult it must be for you. Do you have any family or friends?"

He gripped the edge of the table with his fingertips. "My parents have both passed away, so there was only Laurie—my wife—but she is dead too."

"I'm sorry, Bear. I know how hard it is to lose someone you love very much."

"I loved her. I don't know why she had to die."

"Sometimes we lose people we love. Sometimes it's hard to go on with life. Tell me, Bear, do you ever stay at a shelter?"

"Yes."

"Which shelter?"

"The one at St. Martin's. They have good food."

"They do have good food," she agreed. "What is your favorite meal there?"

"The turkey. Thursday is turkey day, like Thanksgiving." He was starting to calm down. The rocking had stopped. He loosened his grip on the edge of the table. They needed to keep him talking. They'd made his rights clear, but if he asked for a lawyer, it was over.

"I like turkey too, Bear. I need to ask you some questions about a young woman who was killed."

"Why?" Bear shook his head. "Why was she hurt?"

"We don't know, that's why we need to ask you these questions," Carlos said. "It's very important that you tell us the truth. We found her in the neighborhood you walk through every night."

"I don't know anything."

"Bear, Detective Dias just told you that it was very important that you tell the truth. We know that you saw her."

Bear started rocking again and didn't respond.

"What can you tell me about these letters?" Carlos opened a folder and pushed two letters across the table. They'd been folded into thirds and placed in white envelopes. Tory was already working on the translation of the letters that had been handwritten in flowery Vietnamese. "Are these yours?"

Bear ran his fingers across the paper, his features strained as if he were trying to remember something. "No."

"We found them in one of your bags." Carlos pressed harder. "We need to know how they got inside your things."

"I told you. They aren't my letters."

"We understand they aren't yours, Bear. That is why it's very important that you tell us why they were in your bag." Avery leaned forward, making sure she kept her voice low. "There's a girl who's dead, and it's our job to find out who killed her."

Bear stared straight ahead.

Avery leaned in closer. "Bear, I need you to answer my question. Telling us will help us find the person who hurt this young girl. You want us to find who hurt her, don't you? Just like with your wife. Tell us why the letters were in your bag."

"I found them."

"Good. Can you tell me where you found them?"

He pushed them toward Carlos. "I don't remember."

Carlos dropped the letters back into the folder. "We have reason to believe that these letters belong to the girl who was murdered. Can you tell us anything about her? We know you saw her Sunday night."

"No." He shook his head, his fingers tapping again against the metal table. "I told you, I mind my own business and don't bother nobody."

Carlos swung out of his chair and stood up, still holding the file. "This young woman I told you about, we found her murdered. Do you understand what that looks like? Someone murdered her, and we know you saw her that night."

"I didn't murder her."

"But you saw her." Carlos slammed the file back onto the table. "You touched her."

Bear's hands shook. His fingers knocked against his coffee cup and it tipped. Carlos caught it before the liquid sloshed over the edge.

"Tell us what happened, Bear." Carlos let go of the cup, still pressing for an answer. "We need you to tell us, because when you lie, it makes us believe you're hiding something."

"I . . . she was laying in the alley. Every night I go by that alley. I never saw her there before."

Good. They were making progress. Avery touched the edge of the file. "She was there because someone killed her. We want to find out who killed her. Did you kill her, Bear?"

"No. I didn't hurt her. I didn't hurt anyone."

Avery tried to read the man's expression. Fear. Panic. "But you've hurt people in the past, Bear."

"Only once. That man . . . he hurt my wife."

Avery weighed each word, not wanting to cross the fine line that pushed a suspect too far. But not pushing enough would give her nothing.

"I'm sorry about your wife, Bear." Avery couldn't help but wonder what had gone wrong. Two years ago, the man had been a professor at the local community college. Then he'd lost everything. Had anyone even noticed? "I know you must miss her very much, but right now I need to know about the girl from Sunday night. What can you tell me about her? Someone hurt her, and it's my job to make sure that the person who did it is brought to justice."

Bear clasped the table with his fingers again. "She . . . she was laying on the ground. By the Dumpster in the alley. I . . . I thought she was sleeping, but she never woke up. I tried to wake her up."

"What time was it?"

"Time?"

"What time was it when you found her, Bear?"

He looked at his watch and slowly moved his fingers around the dial. "One o'clock. Three o'clock. Four. Four thirty." Bear looked up at Avery for the first time. "It was four thirty."

"Good, Bear. You're doing good."

"What did you do when you found her?" Carlos asked.

"I didn't hurt her."

"What about her purse?"

"There wasn't a purse. I never saw a purse. Just a sweater."

Avery struggled to put the pieces together. What had the girl been doing out in the middle of the night without a bag or money? "Are you sure you didn't see a purse, money, a telephone, or identification?"

"Yes." Bear's gaze dropped again to the table.

"Bear? What is it?"

"I was trying to save her. To see if she could breathe, but . . . her hands were cold."

"Is that when you found the letters?"

He nodded. "There was a pocket. Hidden inside

her shirt. I was only trying to save her. I didn't hurt her."

"And you found the letters inside the pocket?"

"My wife liked to write me letters. Not . . . not computer letters . . . not emails. She wrote me letters on pretty paper."

"Handwritten letters?"

"Yes, like the letters I found. I couldn't read them, but they smelled like perfume and reminded me of my wife."

Carlos took a step toward the table. "What else was in the pocket, Bear?"

"There was a picture."

"Tell me about it."

"There were two girls in it. Pretty girls wearing white dresses."

"There was something else in the pocket, wasn't there?"

Bear avoided Carlos's gaze. "No."

"I think you're lying to me." Carlos dropped a key onto the table in front of him. "Can you tell me about this?"

No response.

"We found it with your things."

Bear simply shrugged.

Carlos wasn't ready to give up. "You've been to prison before, and I'm assuming you don't want to go back. But if you refuse to cooperate . . ."

"It's a key to a storage unit."

"What's inside it? We're waiting on the warrant

right now, but helping us will help your case."

"My wife . . . they're Laurie's things. I paid two years up front after she died. Put all her personal things in storage, because I-I couldn't deal with them."

"We know you've been there recently." This time Avery dropped a photo in front of him. "The storage unit surveillance places you there at nine thirty Monday morning."

"Why did you go to the storage unit?" Carlos rested his hands against the table and leaned forward. "I think you found something on the body."

"I didn't hurt her."

"Maybe this will help jog your memory. We also found a receipt in your things from a nearby pawnshop, dated Monday morning for the sale of a ring. Forty-five hundred dollars. Tell me where you got the ring, Bear."

"There was a ring in her pocket."

"What kind of ring?"

"Blue sapphire. 18-karat white gold. Diamonds. Expensive."

"How expensive?"

"Custom made. Worth ten, maybe twelve thousand dollars. My father was a jeweler. He taught me what to look for. But she was already dead. She didn't need the ring."

"Or you killed her for the ring." Carlos's voice rose. "Forty-five hundred dollars will go a long way for a man who's been out of work the past year, and since we didn't find the money on you, we're assuming it's stashed in the storage unit. Is that right?"

Bear said nothing.

"We have your fingerprints on her photo. Her letters in your bag, your own confession that you were there . . . Everything points to you."

Bear slammed his fists against the table. "I didn't hurt her."

Avery signaled to Carlos. "Bear, we'll be back in a minute."

Carlos followed her down the narrow hallway toward their offices. "What do you think?"

"I don't know. He's clearly adamant it wasn't him, but he's got motive, means, and opportunity, so I'm certainly not ready to take him off our list of suspects. But if he's telling the truth, the only crime he committed was selling stolen goods."

Which unfortunately was a crime that far too many got away with. Pawnshops were supposed to send daily reports to the police on what they'd bought, but the department was weeks behind in updating the database of identified stolen goods. The cracks in the system meant that often stolen items were long gone before they made it into the system. But selling stolen goods was a far cry from murder.

Mitch and Tory were back from their interview

with Mr. Sourn and were now working at their desks.

"What else were you able to find out about the Sourns?"

"Nothing out of the ordinary." Mitch leaned back in his chair. "They've lived in Atlanta for the past twenty-five years. Started Sourn Import and Export back in the late nineties."

"What do they import?"

"Mainly things from Asia. Furnishings, home décor, gifts, and accessories. They have a warehouse in northeast Atlanta, as well as a store open to the public."

"Arrest record?"

"Nothing on record other than a couple traffic tickets, though their business has been under investigation in the past for tax fraud and money laundering. No arrests were ever made. I'm looking into that now."

"Good. And Mr. Sourn? What about your interview with him?"

Tory shrugged. "Basically, he was cooperative. Seemed a bit distracted, but also appeared to be genuinely upset about his niece's death."

"Alibi?"

"Said he was asleep at home with his wife. Last time he saw Tala was around dinnertime Sunday night. She went out with friends and never came home."

"That matches his wife's story."

"What about the Sourns' friends?"

"Several knew that their niece was living with them, but none of them had met her yet." Tory clicked on her computer. "I've been researching their business holdings and found something interesting, though it's probably nothing."

"I'm taking any lead at this point, no matter how slim."

"Their import/export business isn't the only place they earn their money." Tory handed Avery a printout. "They've invested heavily in dozens of nail and hair salons across the Midwest."

"Any red flags on Tala's diploma or other documents?"

"So far, everything I've dug up has been aboveboard. And I've finished translating the letters."

"Anything?"

"They're letters from a friend . . . maybe her sister? From what I can tell, there doesn't seem to be anything significant about the letters themselves except sentimental value."

They were back to far more questions than answers. "So Tala keeps a couple letters, a photo, and an expensive ring—something Mr. Philips just confessed to taking—in a hidden pocket in her sweater. Why? Then our Mr. Philips finds her dead body—or kills her—and takes the letters and the ring, but leaves the photo."

"Maybe I can answer that." Tory leaned back in

her chair and smiled. "I saved the best for last. I don't think our Mr. Philips is as innocent as he's trying to appear. There are no traffic cams in the immediate vicinity to the alley, but the bar beside it has a camera set up."

"You've got footage of the alley?"

"Unfortunately, no, but there is one at the entrance. It picked up James Philips walking out of the alley, away from the murder scene."

Avery shook her head. She needed something more. "That just proves what we already know. He's confessed to being there and we have his fingerprints on our dead girl."

"Oh, there's more. Mrs. Waters told us that she saw him the night of the murder about four fifteen."

"Right. That's about the same time he just told us in the interrogation room."

"But here's where things get interesting. The video catches him leaving the alley not once . . . but twice."

Avery smiled. Now Tory had her attention. "Twice."

"The time stamp verifies that he was there at four thirty. But he was also there two hours earlier, exiting the alley."

"Two hours earlier? That would place him there around the estimated time of death."

"Two twenty-four, to be exact. Which means at four thirty, our Mr. Philips had already been there."

"But why return to the crime scene?"

"That I don't know. But we know that, one, he's not telling the complete truth, and two, while we probably can't narrow down the time of death any further, Mr. Philips was there during that window."

Avery's mind began to spin. "Did the cameras pick up anyone else exiting the alley?"

"Not during our time frame, but if Mr. Philips isn't our killer, they could have exited from the other side of the alley. There were no camera angles on the other side."

"Good work." The pieces were finally starting to come together. Avery pulled out the receipt from the pawnshop. "Tory and Carlos, I want you to find me this ring. I want to know why Tala was hiding it. Maybe it was the Sourns' and they'd turned in a claim to their insurance or filed a police report on it recently. Mitch, see if you can find any connection to James Philips and the murder of our last Jane Doe."

Tory pulled her bag out from under her desk, then paused. "So you think Tala stole the ring from the Sourns?"

"That's something I intend to find out." Avery grabbed her car keys off her desk. "Which is why I've got a couple more questions for Mrs. Sourn, then I'll be ready to go another round with Mr. Philips."

Chapter 11

"Mrs. Sourn. I appreciate your willingness to speak to me again." Avery sat on the same place on the couch as her last visit, this time without Mitch.

The paleness in the woman's features hadn't left her. "You know I want to do everything I can to help find my niece's murderer."

"I need to ask you about a ring." Avery handed Mrs. Sourn a photo of the ring they'd gotten from the pawnshop. "Do you recognize this piece of jewelry?"

Mrs. Sourn fingered the photo. "I . . . yes. My husband had it custom designed. How did you get this photo?"

Avery ignored the woman's question for now. "When was the last time you saw the ring?"

"I don't know . . . two . . . maybe three months ago. I wore it to a dinner party with friends back at the end of April."

"So you didn't know it was missing?"

"No." Mrs. Sourn set the photo down on the coffee table between them. "I assumed it was still in the jewelry box where I normally keep it."

"We traced the maker's mark on the ring to Hannah Celeste."

"Yes, she's one of the best designers in the area. I fell in love with her work several years ago and always wanted one of her pieces. When my husband surprised me with it for one of our anniversaries, I was elated."

"Where do you keep the ring?"

"In my bedroom."

"It's worth over ten thousand dollars. Why didn't you keep it in a safe?"

Mrs. Sourn's gaze shifted to the floor. "My husband would agree with you, and now I suppose he was right. He always said we should keep my jewelry in a safety deposit box, but it seems silly to own beautiful pieces and then keep them locked up, never wearing them. I have a few things locked away, but most of it I keep here in the house."

"Where, exactly?"

"On my dresser in an old jewelry box that used to belong to my mother."

"So, potentially anyone who was in your house could have had the opportunity to steal the ring."

"I suppose."

"Like Tala."

Mrs. Sourn shook her head. "I can't imagine her stealing from me. Where did you find it?"

"Tala had the ring with her."

"Are you telling me she stole the ring from me?"

"It would appear that way."

"I just can't believe that." Mrs. Sourn reached up and rubbed the back of her neck. "And the person who killed her . . . do you have any leads?"

"We're questioning a potential suspect right now."

"So you might have found her killer—"

"It's too early to know at this point, but thank you for your help, Mrs. Sourn." Avery stood. "I promise we will be in touch."

An hour later, Avery slid the picture of Tala across the table in front of Bear. Features swollen and pale . . . the photo was haunting. "Mr. Philips. You've been lying to us, and this time I want the truth."

So far he hadn't asked for a lawyer, and she had no intention of giving him the chance until she got what she wanted out of him.

"This is Tala. The girl you found in the alley Sunday night."

Bear turned away as if trying to escape the memory.

Avery pushed the next photo in front of him. "This is our Jane Doe."

Carlos stood and walked around the table to the other side of Bear. "Six weeks ago, we found her dead beside a Dumpster. Just like Tala."

"I—"

"Please let me finish. Two girls dead. Similar

MO." Carlos leaned closer to Bear, but kept his voice soft and nonthreatening. "They both died a horrible death that neither deserved."

Avery pulled the third color photo from the folder and placed it between the pictures of the two girls. "Here's another picture."

Bear tipped his chair back and pushed away the photo. "That's my wife. Why are you showing me a picture of my wife?"

"I think you know why. It's interesting, isn't it? All young, pretty, Asian . . . and they are all dead. Your wife's case was never solved, was it?"

"You know it wasn't, but I didn't kill my wife. I would never—"

"Here's the problem, Bear." Avery kept her voice even. Tight. "We can already tie you to Tala's death. There's no question about that. And as for the other girl and your wife—"

"I didn't kill my wife. I didn't kill those girls."

Avery noted the pain reflected in his eyes and wanted to believe him, but no matter how much sympathy his manner evoked, the evidence was telling a different story.

"What do you think a jury will say when they learn that your fingerprints were all over the victim's photo found on her body? You've admitted that you stole not only her letters from her, but a ring worth over ten thousand dollars. And if there were still any doubts, there's the camera footage that puts you at the scene not once, but twice. And the first time is during the projected time of the murder."

Bear flinched.

"Did you think we wouldn't find out?" Avery leaned in closer. "Why did you lie about that, Bear? Why did you lie about the fact that you had been to the scene not once, but twice?"

"I . . . I don't know. I wanted the letters and the ring, but the picture . . . I wanted to give her the picture back."

"But it was too late. You'd already killed her—"

"No."

"Bear, we've got motive, means, and opportunity. All the things we look for to convict killers. Three cases, all similar, one killer. How do you think that looks to us? How do you think that will look to a jury?"

Avery waited for his answer. Linking all three crimes might be a stretch at this point, but he didn't have to know that.

"It looks bad."

"Yes, it does." Carlos leaned against the end of the table. "And no matter how you've been living these past few months, you're a smart man. We only want to find out the truth, but you can see how this looks to us. You and your wife got into a fight one night about money or maybe she cheated on you. Things were tense between the two of you, and something snapped."

"No."

Avery studied his reaction. Shoulders hunched, head in hands, elbows on knees. What they had to determine was if he was upset simply over the loss of his wife or if he was feeling guilt. Her department hadn't handled Laurie Philips's case, but she'd reviewed the evidence that had surfaced in the file. James Philips had always been the number one suspect. Lack of evidence was the only thing that had saved him, but there were still plenty of people who had worked the case who believed James Philips had killed his wife. And none of them could ignore the possibility that he'd killed again.

"Isn't that what happened, Bear?"

"No. I didn't kill those girls, just like I didn't kill my wife. I loved my wife. When I lost her, I lost everything. Why would I kill again when I know how horrid it is when you lose every-thing . . . everyone you've ever loved."

"You killed again?"

"No." Bear started rocking back and forth in his chair. Frustrated. Agitated. Right where they wanted him.

Carlos sat down in his chair and pushed the photos back in front of Bear. "You killed your wife, but that wasn't enough, so you killed these girls, one at a time. You lost control in your marriage, lost control of your job, which meant you were out of control professionally. In killing them, you wanted the world to know that you could still be in control. They were helpless. You are not."

"No." Bear's shoulders slumped.

"Then why did you take the ring?"

"You said it. I have nothing left. I lost my job after Laurie's death. People thought I killed her. Even when I wasn't arrested for her death, people looked at me every time I walked by. The courts might have let me go, but the world still saw me as guilty. When I saw that ring, it was my chance. In the end, everyone would win. The owner would get the insurance money, and I would sell it and go somewhere far away."

"Not everyone won."

"I want a lawyer now."

Carlos glanced up at Avery, then looked at Bear. "You'll get your lawyer, but that doesn't change the fact that we're placing you under arrest for the murder of Tala Vuong."

Chapter 12

After a long day of more waiting for test results and performing another, more routine autopsy, Jackson was ready for a break. Philips was in jail, awaiting arraignment without bond, but some of the evidence still niggled at Jackson. In his mind, it wasn't all neatly tied up like it should be. Having a low-key evening might free up some new thought processes for him. Even a few minutes of grocery shopping had helped clear his head.

Jackson hung three plastic sacks of groceries on his arm, then fumbled to open the front door of his grandfather's house. Like Papps, the house was beginning to show its age. He'd already replaced the gutters and painted the outside, but the to-do list seemed never ending. With summer here, the lawn needed to be mowed and the shrubs clipped, but that would have to wait until his next day off. As for some of the larger repairs, all he could do was tackle them one at a time.

Papps met him in the entryway of the one-story ranch-style house wearing shorts and an old Atlanta Hawks T-shirt. "Did you remember my . . ."

Jackson waited while Papps searched for the word.

". . . the bologna I asked for?"

"Yes, and the peanut butter. Sorry I'm so late. You caught me just in time when you called. I was getting ready to check out." Jackson crossed the worn yellow shag carpet through the living room and into the kitchen, where he set the grocery bags on the counter. "I still don't know how you can stand the combination."

"It reminds me of a time when things were simpler."

"Whatever you say, Papps."

Jackson chuckled as he watched his grand-father open the jar of peanut butter so he could make his peanut butter and bologna sandwich, and felt a wave of nostalgia sweep over him. His grand-father might have been born Henry Andrew Clay Bryant, but Jackson had called him Papps as long as he could remember. And he had become the only father figure in his life he could remember as well.

He watched his grandfather spread a thick layer of the peanut butter onto a slice of white bread. "That isn't exactly a healthy dinner. I told you I'd bring you something from the deli. They have some great salads and homemade soups."

"Bah. When you're eighty-five, who cares. I don't intend to spend the rest of my days eating rabbit food." He slapped on a couple slices of the bologna, topped the whole mess with another slice of bread, then took a bite. "What are you eating?"

"Somewhere in these bags is a roast beef on sourdough with a side salad."

"Rabbit food, I tell you. Your grandmother forced me to eat that stuff for fifty years."

"I suppose after fifty years of eating lettuce and carrots you have the right to rebel." Jackson grabbed the canister of Pringles Papps had asked for and shoved it into the pantry. "Within reason, that is."

Papps pulled out the Pringles and popped off the lid. Jackson went back to putting away the groceries. He'd learned long ago that arguing with Papps never worked. If anything, it only made him more determined.

"What about that girl you told me about? What was her name? Red hair, feisty, charming . . ."

"Did I use those words?"

"Maybe not feisty, but since you've yet to introduce us, I have to make up my own descriptions." Papps held up a Pringle. "But let me warn you, you marry her and she'll have you eating that salad without the roast beef sandwich on the side."

Jackson laughed. Why was it that his grandfather forgot what day it was, yet could remember details about what had been said weeks ago? "Her name is Avery, and yes, I suppose she is a bit feisty. As for your not meeting her yet, she works, remember? She's a homicide detective who's probably busier than I am. Though, at this point, I'm not so sure things are going to work out between us."

"And why not? If you ask me, it's time you found yourself a woman—working or not—and settled down. I'm not going to be around forever, you know."

"Maybe not forever, but I still intend to enjoy your company for a long time."

Jackson finished putting the groceries away before joining his grandfather in the living room with his dinner, but thoughts of his grandfather's deteriorating health—and the possibility of losing Avery—had put a damper on his appetite.

Papps sat down in his faded olive-green recliner and set up a TV dinner tray in front of him. Jackson loved his grandfather, but sometimes the nightly ritual felt like a scene from the '50s.

"Where's the remote, Jackson?"

Jackson settled into the recliner's equally faded twin and unwrapped his sandwich. "It's right beside you, Papps."

Papps grabbed the remote from the cluttered end table and flipped on the television before muting the sound. "When I was a young man, it wasn't so complicated. You met a girl who struck your fancy, you took her someplace nice for dinner, got to know her, then asked her to marry you."

Definitely the '50s.

"I find it hard to believe that a relationship between a man and a woman could ever be that simple." Lately, something always seemed to get in the way. "What about your book? Did you and Maggie get a lot done today?"

"Changing the subject?"

"Yes."

Papps balanced the remote on the stack of papers next to him, then took another bite of his sandwich. "That woman you hired for me talks too much. Every day, I hear about one of her ailments. Today it was her bunion."

"At least the two of you have plenty to talk about." His grandfather's memory gaps continued to widen, but keeping his mind as active as possible had seemed to help slow some of the symptoms. Hiring someone to stay with him while Jackson was at work had been out of the question, according to Papps. Hiring someone to transcribe the book he'd always wanted to write had worked. "Besides, at the rate the two of you are going, the book will be finished by Christmas. Then you'll have to start on the sequel."

The book had been Jackson's idea. Four generations ago, Papps's own grandfather had fought in the Civil War. Papps still remembered stories told around the dinner table as a young child. Jackson's goal was for him to get as many stories as possible down on paper before he forgot them. Which, from the way things were going, wasn't too far off.

Papps turned the volume back on—loud—then switched to the national news channel.

Jackson sent up a silent prayer of thanks for his food and took a bite of the thick roast beef while Papps watched repeats of the same news stories he'd probably been watching all day. His stomach growled and he took another bite of the tender meat. Maybe he was hungry after all.

Jackson studied Papps's familiar profile while the TV blared. Thin, white hair, face creased with age, bifocals slid halfway down his nose . . . Jackson might have struggled with his decision to make the move from Houston to Atlanta, but the day he found out that his grandfather had gotten lost one afternoon and couldn't remember how to get home had been the clarifying moment.

The solution had turned out to be a challenge, but besides his sister, his grandfather was the only family he had, and his grandfather needed him. Which meant he didn't regret his decision. But watching his grandfather slowly lose more and more of his memory had been harder than he'd expected. Some days were simply better than others. At least today seemed to be a good one.

Papps took the last bite of his bologna sandwich, grabbed the remote, and switched off the television.

"You off to bed already?"

"Might as well." Papps grunted. "I've seen that same news story a dozen times today, because those flashy reporters wouldn't know a good story if it hit them in the noggin. Those producers think we all suffer from brain damage and don't notice."

Jackson chuckled. "Grams used to tell me it

was watching too much television that would give me brain damage."

"Except when it came to those silly soap operas she insisted on watching."

Jackson took another bite of his sandwich. For Papps it was the same routine every night. Dinner in front of the television, complaints about news commentators and the direction the world was taking, then off to bed no later than eight. Of course, by four in the morning he'd be up again, puttering around the house, looking for something he'd lost, or trying to remember how to use the coffee machine. Which was why Maggie had become such a blessing. She never seemed to mind coming early or staying late if Jackson had to work, or if he had plans to go out. Though it wasn't as if his social calendar was booked. Avery had been the first person in a long time to make him want to change that.

"What about you?" Papps dug into the tube of Pringles he'd set next to his chair. "Are you about finished for the night?"

"No, not yet. I need to go over some of my autopsy notes."

"You've got a new case?"

"A young girl I did an autopsy on a couple of days ago. I'm waiting on some of the test results, but there are still some questions I need to answer."

"Like how she died?"

"No. The cause of death was the easy part. The rest, though, is like a puzzle. I'm just trying to sort out the pieces."

An enlarged spleen could mean a number of things, from mononucleosis to leukemia to a bacterial infection. His job was to perform the autopsy and investigate any inconsistencies. Avery's job was to decide if what he discovered was relevant to her case.

"I'm no medical expert so I can't help you with this one, but I don't have any doubt that you'll figure it out."

"What did you work on today?" Jackson asked the question, enjoying the conversation.

"Martha Ruth Noble." Papps held up a photo of a woman from his stack of papers. "Martha was your . . ." He shook his head. The blank look was back.

Jackson waited for him to continue. If he jumped in with the answer, it frustrated Papps. If he waited too long to help, Papps would end up just as frustrated. Sometimes there was simply no way to win. But he was determined to enjoy every conversation they had in the meantime, because the day was coming when Papps wouldn't remember his only grandson's name.

"That's okay. Go on."

Papps held up a second photo, this time of a Civil War soldier. "Anyway, she put on a uniform and enlisted in the Confederate Army."

Jackson's brow furrowed. "That's the same woman?"

"She went into battle as a man." Papps stared at the photo of Martha Noble, now with a fake mustache and soldier's uniform. "Right alongside her male comrades. And apparently they didn't find out. At least at the beginning. I was able to get hold of some letters she'd written from a cousin of your father's. She ended up dying from marsh fever along with most of the men in her company, and her true identity was discovered."

Jackson looked up from the photo. "What's marsh fever?"

"Today we call it malaria. Back then they thought it was caused by breathing in poisonous swamp gases. They think that a fourth of the men—and women—involved in the Civil War died from it."

"How long ago was malaria eradicated from the US?"

"Back in the 1940s? Maybe the 1950s. Somewhere in there. The US might have been successful in getting rid of it, but I've read it's still one of the top ten killers in low-income countries."

Jackson stood up, his mind spinning. Why hadn't he considered this before? Maybe there was no connection, but then again . . . Avery hadn't mentioned that Tala had traveled overseas, but maybe she had. "I think I've been looking in the wrong place."

"What do you mean?"

"My case. The one I'm working on right now. You might have just given me another piece of the puzzle."

Every test he'd thought of had come back negative. Nothing to explain the enlarged spleen. But what if they weren't considering every possible angle?

"I've got to make a phone call."

"To your lady friend?"

"Not yet. First I need to test my theory."

Chapter 13

Avery and Tess stepped out of the humid Georgia air into the Hunt family's two-story house in suburban Atlanta. Avery shivered and pulled her slate-colored cardigan tighter around her shoulders. She'd learned to adjust to the temperatures in her mother's house years ago by wearing a sweater in the summertime and shedding a layer or two in the winter.

Mama met them in the foyer, looking as if she were on her way to a sit-down dinner at the upscale Park 75 and not their weekly family meal. Just like the house, with its gold trim crown molding, damask wallpaper, and flashy chandeliers, Claire Hunt's taste in clothes had always bordered on ostentatious.

But it was Mama's scowl that registered in Avery's mind more than the silky teal dress and strappy high heels she wore. How long had it been since she'd seen her mother really smile? Seen her really happy?

"We set the table for five but weren't sure you would show up." Mama's patronizing tone matched her scowl as she kissed Tess on the forehead. At least someone was on her good side.

"I said I was sorry." Avery swallowed her frustration.

She'd already called to apologize for missing Monday's lunch, but tonight wouldn't be the last time she was reminded of her blunder in etiquette. Instead of trying to argue the point, she simply handed her mother the present she'd wrapped in silvery-blue paper and a shiny bow. The photo she'd found of Dad and Michael would be a perfect addition to the photo collection at her dad's retirement party, as well as help pave the way toward a bit of forgiveness. At least she hoped so.

"I brought you a peace offering."

"Don't think this will make up for your skipping out on our lunch meeting with Doris. I had to endure an hour and a half of that woman's constant babbling, sampling of high-calorie dishes, and comments about how her business is booming."

Avery set her purse down next to the door. "Maybe you should just be happy for her, Mama."

"Happy for her? She told me I should let her finalize the menu on her own. Apparently her tastes are superior to mine. I should have fired her right on the spot."

A wave of panic struck. There was no way they'd find another caterer at this late a date. "You didn't fire her, did you?"

"Emily talked me out of it."

Avery let out a sigh of relief as her mother slid her thumb across the end of the present and undid the tape. Maybe a reminder of Michael had been a bad idea.

Avery pressed her fingers around the present. "Why don't you open it later. I promise it will more than make up for my not being there."

"All right, but before you leave tonight, I want you to look over the finalized menu as well. It shouldn't take you too long."

Avery forced a smile, wishing she could ignore the familiar feeling of being jerked in yet another direction. But as much as Mama drove her crazy, she was Avery's mother and Avery loved her.

Her dad walked into the room. "Let her be, Claire."

"Dad's right, Mom." Emily was right behind her father, wearing an adorable rose-colored pleated top and skinny jeans. "Hey, sis."

Avery mouthed "thank you," while Emily took

the present from Mama and set it on the entrance table before leading her toward the dining room.

"I don't need you ganging up against me too, Emily."

"Nobody's ganging up against you, Mama."

Avery let out a short sigh. Saved by her sister, she was off the hook. For now.

Her father hugged Tess before she scrambled off toward the kitchen.

"She's hungry. Apparently she forgot her lunch today and had to beg leftovers from her friends."

"She'll enjoy dinner then. Your mother made her favorite." Her daddy gathered Avery in his arms and kissed the top of her head. "Don't be such a stranger. I've missed you."

"Things have been busy at work."

Her father let out a low chuckle. "I can't say the same for here."

Avery caught the longing in her father's eyes behind the laughter. She'd never thought the day would come when he'd actually stop working. He'd been on the force for four decades. How did one simply walk away from their life's work?

They walked slowly toward the dining room arm in arm. "How's that Jane Doe case going that you're working on?"

"You know about that?"

"I still have my connections—I'm not completely out of the loop."

"So it would seem. You always did have a

knack for getting the information you wanted. Our Jane Doe now has a name, and we were able to get a warrant for a suspect and arrested him yesterday for her murder. We can't tie him yet to our last Jane Doe case, but I'm hoping we end up closing both cases in the next few days."

"So you think he killed both girls?"

"We'll see, but the crime scenes are too similar for there not to be a connection." Avery stopped in the doorway of the dining room where Mama, Emily, and Tess were putting the food on the table. "What about you, though? How are you doing with your retirement?"

"Is it that obvious?"

"Yes."

"Two weeks, five days, and three hours, give or take."

"Don't tell me it's that bad."

"Your mom has me working on the guest bathroom. Tomorrow we're hanging wallpaper. It's gold with a white swirly pattern. You'll love it."

Avery laughed. Her dad always made her laugh. "Sounds like fun."

"On the good side, my golf swing has never been better."

"We'll have to play a few holes one of these days."

"Since when do you play golf?"

"Since when do you hang wallpaper?"

"Touché."

In the dining room, the table was set to perfection with Mama's favorite dishes—the ones that included a reproduction of some famous eighteenth-century flowery design. No doubt the spaghetti, garlic bread, vegetables, and green salad would be just as perfect. Avery slid into her chair next to Tess, then placed the cloth napkin onto her lap. Dinner had always been a formal affair.

As soon as the prayer ended, the questions began.

"I've been meaning to ask you something, Avery." Her mother took a spoonful of buttery green beans, then passed the bowl to Tess. "When are you going to bring that boy over I hear you've been going out with?"

Avery silenced a groan. "You sound as if I'm in high school, Mama."

"You know that's not at all how I meant it. I'm just curious, because your father and I haven't met him."

Avery poured some vinaigrette onto her salad and took a bite. It was so easy for her mother to make her feel as if she were transported back to seventeen, when her father had to meet and approve of every boy who looked at her with even the slightest glint of interest in his eyes.

She rested her fork on the edge of the salad plate. "It's only been two dates, Mama. It's not as if we're getting married. And it's certainly not time to meet the family."

"What's wrong with him?"

"Nothing's wrong with him." Avery looked at Emily, then at Tess, wondering which one was the traitor. Both looked completely absorbed in their piles of spaghetti.

"Then when's your next date?"

"I'm not sure there's going to be another date."

"Why not?"

"Because it's . . . complicated. We both have busy jobs, family, responsibilities . . ."

"When your father and I got married, he was a rookie officer working nights and weekends most of the time. And there were times when his forty-hour week turned into fifty or sixty hours if it was a particularly tough case."

"Mama—"

"The point is that we loved each other and made it work. Is it easy? Of course not. But when you love someone, it's worth the extra work."

"I agree, but like I said, it's been two dates. Relationships take time to develop."

"Is your hesitation because of losing Ethan?"

Avery shoved a forkful of spaghetti into her mouth to avoid answering the question. Apparently no subject was off limits in this family.

"I just want you to be happy again."

Avery managed to swallow her bite. "Who says I'm not happy?"

"You're my daughter, and I can see the loneliness in your eyes."

Avery bit back a snarky response. "You know I'll always miss Ethan, but I have Tess, you, Daddy, and Emily, a career I love, friends, and a church family. I don't have to have a man in my life to make me happy. Isn't that right, Emily?"

"Of course." Emily coughed and pressed her napkin against her lips. "Sorry, I—"

"You don't sound very convinced." Mama turned to Emily. "Does that have anything to do with a certain new schoolteacher I've heard about?"

Emily's eyes widened. "Tess!"

Tess's cheeks turned red. "I just mentioned that there was a new math teacher who was extremely good looking. I never mentioned that you agreed to go out with him, or—"

"Tess!"

Tess dropped her gaze. "I'm sorry."

Avery pressed her lips together and tried not to smile. While she hated seeing Emily on the hotspot, it did help her own case.

"What about you, Tess? Any cute boys in your classes this year?"

"Grandma!"

"Why don't we change the subject for now, ladies?" Her father helped himself to the garlic bread.

Avery decided to follow her father's lead and took another slice of bread. The one thing no one could fault Mama with was her cooking. Even Avery had to agree that it was worth the extra workout the calories required.

"I saw a segment about your Jane Doe murder on the news," Emily threw out.

"Word travels quickly in the media." Avery glanced at Tess. Discussing cases was something she didn't like to do, especially at the dinner table and in front of her daughter.

Tess twirled her spaghetti with her fork. "It's all right, Mom. It's not like I've never seen a murder victim or I don't know what you do at work. Besides, I'm twelve now."

"You've seen a murder victim?"

"Just on TV. Not a real one. All I'm saying is that I'm growing up."

"When did that happen? The growing up part, I mean." Avery tugged off a piece of the garlic bread, dipped it into her spaghetti sauce, and grinned at her daughter. Twelve years old and all grown up. She really wasn't ready for this.

"And who knows. I might even decide to follow after the family profession and become a police officer . . . or a captain."

Avery grinned at her father. "She'd make a great captain, wouldn't she, Dad?"

"Or a teacher," Emily said.

Avery's phone rang. She slipped it out of her pocket, knowing how much her mom hated any kind of technology at the dinner table. To be honest, so did she, but with an open case, she didn't have a choice.

She muted the volume and checked the caller ID.

Jackson.

Her heart flipped. While she knew she'd have to speak to him again eventually, she wasn't sure she was ready.

"Go ahead and take the call," Emily said. "If we get done eating before you're done, I'll help clear the dishes and leave the washing to you."

"Thanks, sis." Avery left the table and slipped into her dad's study in the front of the house to take the call. "Jackson . . . Hi."

"Avery. I hope I'm not calling at a bad time."

"No, it's fine." She stared at the cherry wood desk and bookcases that gave her father's office that cozy feel, and tried to ignore the tension between her head and her heart. "I'm having dinner with my parents. It's a weekly— sometimes bi-weekly—tradition when I'm not working."

"So it is a bad time."

"In a family of police officers, this is the norm, not the exception."

"Good, because I have some new information on your case."

"After a day of dead ends, any news will help. What is it?"

"That's part of the problem." He hesitated.

"What I have doesn't back up the information you have so far."

"Okay." Avery rubbed her temple with her free hand. Wouldn't you know, just when everything started to come together, evidence would arrive to blow it all apart. Maybe their latest break in the case was too good to be true after all. "We could meet somewhere. If you have time."

"I don't want you to feel uncomfortable."

Avery forced herself to focus. They were both adults and letting this hang between them wasn't going to work. "No, it's okay. I . . . I need to talk to you about something too."

It wasn't right for things to stay awkward between them. Whatever their personal relationship, they still had to work together. She pressed her lips together before suggesting a café near her parents' house.

"I know the place," Jackson said. "Will thirty minutes give you enough time? An hour?"

"I can head out there right now, actually."

Her father appeared in the doorway as Avery flipped her phone shut a moment later. "You okay?"

"Yeah, it was Jackson."

"So that's why your face is rosier than normal." He reached out and touched her wrist. "Just as I thought. Rapid pulse."

"Daddy."

"Why don't you just admit that you've fallen head over heels for the guy?"

"Because I haven't."

"Really?"

Avery dropped the phone into her pocket and frowned. She'd never been able to fool her dad. She took a deep breath and tried to sort through her feelings. Just because her heart might want one thing didn't really change anything. Dating him meant one more person to please. One more person who would demand her time. Even if she wanted to give it to him, she wasn't sure she could.

You might be able to fool Tess, Mom, and even Jackson, but not me . . .

Avery winced at the reminder of her sister's words. Maybe the person she was really trying to fool was herself.

"Avery?"

She looked up at her father. "Sorry."

"Your mother would like to know if you want coffee with your peach cobbler."

"Do you think she'll forgive me if I skip dessert? Jackson has some new information on the case he needs to talk to me about. I'm going to meet him for coffee."

"Hmm . . . skipping dessert for a date with Jackson Bryant? When I was on the force, a phone call typically worked just fine." Her father smiled. "But I think you're safe, though you might owe your sister for doing the dishes."

She grabbed her purse and opened the

front door. "It's not a date, Daddy. It's work."

Her father followed her outside and onto the porch. "Call it what you want, but when two people meet for coffee, and they have feelings for each other, I call it a date."

"You're impossible, you know." Avery took a step toward the stairs then stopped. "Can I ask you something before I leave?"

"Of course."

"You spent the past forty years building a career, a marriage, raising a family, being active in church, and even volunteering at the shelter." She leaned back against the white porch rail, trying to formulate her thoughts into words. "How did you balance everything you did without losing all of us in the process?"

Her father's brow furrowed. "That was my worst fear, I think, that I'd make it to captain but lose my family because I was too busy. I don't know, Avery. It was hard, and to be honest, more often than not, I felt as if I was failing."

"Failing?" In spite of a stressful job and all his responsibilities, she'd always known her father was there for her.

"Because I was gone a lot, and even when I was home, there were phone calls, interruptions, officers stopping by. I worried constantly that you and your brother and sister would think you weren't the most important people in my life. That anything I achieved career-wise wouldn't be worth it in the end because I missed out on what was most important. Family, simply being together."

"I always knew I was your princess." Avery shook her head and smiled. "When you were working, I always imagined you out there saving the world, and I was so proud of that. We thought we were the luckiest kids alive."

"I happen to know Tess feels the same way about you as well. I see you worry about her, though. Worry about being a single mom and the added responsibilities."

"I love my job, but I don't ever want Tess to lose out because of my decisions." Expressing her feelings out loud helped to sort through the jumbled mess of emotions. "And now with Jackson . . . I know he wants to be a part of our lives, but I just don't know if I'm ready to let someone else in."

"I've found that when you pray a lot, then fill your life with people you love and things you believe in, there's often more room inside your heart than you realize. Say no to what you have to, but do what you were called to do. Follow God. Love family. Pursue justice. And maybe in the middle of all of that you'll find that there's some unexpected room for someone else in your life."

"Thanks, Daddy." She reached up on her tiptoes and kissed her father's cheek. "I love you."

"I'm not sure how much I helped—"

"You did. You always do. I still don't have all the answers, and I don't know about Jackson, but maybe that's okay for today."

"One day at a time. That's all you have to worry about."

"I guess I'd better go." Avery stopped on the top step. "Just explain to Mama that I had to go out for a little bit, and you can leave out the word 'date' while you're at it, please."

Her father chuckled. "As long as I get your helping of peach cobbler."

"It's all yours—this time only. I'll be back to pick up Tess in an hour or so."

Her father's smile widened. "Take your time, princess."

Chapter 14

Agreeing to meet Jackson in person had been her first mistake. Splurging on a dish of banana pudding with a thick layer of meringue on top had been her second. The only way she could justify the extra calories was knowing she'd missed Mama's peach cobbler. There might be something therapeutic about eating comfort food, but even banana pudding—and her father's earlier words of wisdom—wasn't helping her sort out what she felt about the man sitting across the table from her.

Because Jackson Bryant always managed to do funny things to her heart. So far, she'd yet to convince herself this was all business—thus the mistake.

Ten minutes of small talk had proved that her heart had no intentions of letting go of the handsome forensics expert. He sat across from her, looking as awkward as she felt.

She took a deep breath as Jackson signaled the waitress for the spoon she'd forgotten to add to the ice cream sundae she'd just served him. Maybe they should just get down to business.

Avery took another sugary bite before plunging ahead. "You said you had something to tell me regarding the case."

"Yes. I . . ." He looked up at her, his sundae apparently forgotten for the moment. She tried to read his expression. Longing? Desire? Disappointment? So much for her background as a behavioral specialist. Maybe she'd never know. "I found some discrepancies in one of the lab tests when compared to what you told me about the victim."

Avery took another bite of her dessert. Maybe this was worth the extra splurge after all. She would concentrate on the business and hope her heart figured out how to handle being around Jackson. "I'm listening."

"I told you that the internal exam revealed that the spleen was enlarged."

"Yes."

"While it may or may not be significant to the case, that fact has continued to bother me."

She laid her spoon down. "Why would it bother you?"

"All the tests we've been running have so far come back negative. Mono, bacterial infection, leukemia, everything. I'm still waiting on a couple of other test results, but at this point, in looking at all the evidence combined, I'm not expecting any of them to come back positive."

"So do you have any clue as to the significance?"

Jackson smiled. "I didn't until I talked to my grandfather."

"The Civil War buff I still need to meet."

"Yes." Jackson leaned forward, clearly in his element. "Something he said got me thinking. During the Civil War hundreds of people died from what they called ague or marsh fever. Today we call it malaria."

"I vaguely remember reading about that in history class, but what does that have to do with my murder victim?"

"Think about it. What if the information you have from the Sourns isn't correct? What if Tala had been out of the country within the past six months? That would mean I was looking for the source of the enlarged spleen in the wrong place."

Avery tried to process the new information. "It's possible, but why would they lie about her travels? It's something I considered, but so far everything they said they've been able to back up. All of Tala's documents—driver's license, high school diploma—everything checks out."

"I realize that, but think about it. First of all, malaria has been wiped out in the States."

"Right." She toyed with her spoon, trying to follow his train of thought. So far, she didn't like where he was going.

"I went ahead and tested her blood for malaria and it came back positive. Which means that Tala had to have recently contracted the disease outside the United States."

"How long ago?"

"Due to the incubation of the strain, which is longer than most, I'd say between six and twelve months."

Avery paused.

"So Mrs. Sourn lied. Even with everything that they handed over to me."

"There's a good chance the documents are fake. Good fakes, if they got past you, but fakes. Either way, they're clearly hiding something."

A sick feeling spread over Avery. She'd been ready to place a possibly innocent man behind bars and wrap up her case when clearly all the pieces were not put together yet. "Tell me this.

Why would they lie about her travels? It doesn't make sense."

"I just give you the facts, ma'am. You get to sort them out." He dug his spoon into his sundae and smiled. "What now?"

"We'll proceed carefully. Not only are we going to have to figure out what else they're lying about, but we're going to have to recheck all the documents and evidence, see if we can find Tala on any flight manifests over the past year, and dig a whole lot deeper into the Sourns." She pushed aside her empty dessert dish. "I probably should go. Tess has school tomorrow morning, and I clearly haven't solved my case."

Jackson finished up the last couple bites of his sundae and signaled to the waitress. "I'll take care of the bill and walk you to your car."

Outside, the humid air hung like a wet blanket. Avery had no doubt they'd figure out the truth behind Tala's murder eventually. It was her heart she was worried about at the moment.

Jackson walked her toward her car. "You said you had something you needed to talk about?"

Avery pressed her lips together, wondering how to put off the inevitable. The last thing she wanted was to allow what had happened to hang between them. "It's complicated."

"Try me."

I've seen you around him. And I just want you to be happy . . .

Emily's words rattled inside her head. The truth was, her sister was right. Jackson did make her happy. She'd begun feeling emotions she'd thought she'd lost forever, because he made her feel as if she were living again. Really living again.

God, I need you to show me what to do. To show me how to open up my heart again and make this work.

"Does it have to do with the case?"

She followed him across the parking lot lit by two yellow streetlights. "No. It's a bit more . . . more personal."

"Shoot."

"About the other night at my house. I'm sorry—"

"Please. You don't have to apologize. I shouldn't have pushed."

"No. It wasn't your fault."

Avery stopped beside the driver's side door of her car. Traffic whizzed down the busy street behind them, but all she could focus on for the moment was the man standing in front of her. Six months ago his dark brown gaze had caught hers for the first time and taken her completely by surprise. Funny, charming, smart . . . and she'd managed to let him in. At least partway.

"I'm not usually this tongue-tied."

The streetlight caught his smile. "I've noticed."

"It's this whole dating thing. I get pressure from

my mom, sister, even co-workers who think I'll be happier if I have someone in my life."

"What do you think?"

"Honestly, I'm not sure."

"We could call this whole dating thing off, Avery. If you're not ready. I'll still work with you on cases without anything changing professionally."

Except it *would* change everything. How could she pretend that her heart didn't do a little dance every time she saw him? Was she really willing to do that?

She tried to read his expression. Maybe she'd read him wrong. There were plenty of men who looked at a third date as nothing more than a third date. It's not like it came with a marriage proposal. And a kiss didn't always come with strings attached.

She had to ask. "Is that what you want? To keep our relationship strictly professional."

He shook his head. "No."

The breath she was holding escaped. "Me neither."

She looked down at her sandals and painted purple toenails that still needed to be redone. So much for not being vulnerable. So much for not allowing herself to be pulled in yet another direction. But maybe that was okay.

"So what's next?" He stood in front of her, content, it seemed, to wait for her answer.

"The other night I panicked."

"We both know what it's like to lose someone we love. I understand if you're not ready."

"It's not that. At least for the most part. It's true that dating again after so long sometimes feels . . . awkward, but it's more than that." She searched for the right words to help him understand. "Do you ever have a million excuses not to do something you really want to do?"

"Explain."

"I have a daughter, a family who expects me to come for dinner a couple nights a week, a job tracking down murder suspects that fulfills me but requires a lot from me, and an active church family who has seen me through some really rough times."

"Are you trying to give me an excuse to walk away?"

"No, but sometimes I feel as if there's not enough of me to go around. *Most* of the time there's not enough of me to go around. I think that's why I panicked."

"And I've become another distraction."

"Oh, you're a big distraction." Daydreaming at work had pushed him into that category weeks ago.

Jackson shoved his hands into the front pockets of his jeans. "So what are we going to do?"

Avery drew in a deep breath. Running away wasn't going to solve the problem. "We both know what it takes to make a relationship work."

"And what do you want out of this relationship?"

"I don't know where this might lead, but for now, I'd like to explore a relationship. Together."

Jackson smiled at her confession. "There are a lot of things I want to learn about you. And while I don't know if things will work out in the end either, for now I'm content to get to know each other better and see what happens."

A car pulled into the empty slot behind Jackson. He took a step toward Avery to get out of the way. She looked up at him. He was close enough she could see the shadow of a beard across his jawline. Close enough for her to regret not letting him kiss her the other night.

A man emerged from the driver's seat, slammed the door shut, and set the alarm before walking away.

It was just the two of them again.

Jackson had yet to move.

Avery's heart thudded. All thoughts of crime scenes, autopsy reports, and murder suspects vanished. And all that remained was the realization that here was a man who cared for her and wanted more out of their relationship. Maybe being vulnerable wasn't so bad after all.

She drew in a deep breath. "So where do we start?"

"Did you have something in mind?"

She'd pushed him away. It was up to her to pull him back. "My father's retirement party is Friday night. It's not the ideal third date, but I still need an escort."

His smile widened. "It would be a shame for a beautiful woman to have to arrive alone."

"Yes, it would."

"Then I think something can be arranged. Anything else?"

She nodded, enjoying the way he flirted with her. The way he looked at her. And the way she felt when he looked at her. "What about where we left off the other night?"

"Are you sure?"

Avery nodded again, leaned into Jackson's arms, and kissed him.

Chapter 15

Avery took the steps up to her parents' front porch two at a time, savoring the myriad of feelings she thought she'd lost forever. If she didn't know better, she'd swear she was floating on air. The hum of the katydid's song buzzed through her thoughts. *He loves me, he loves me not . . .*

She paused at the top step and breathed in her

mother's sweet-smelling jasmine. Giving herself permission to feel again wasn't easy. Finding someone she wanted to take that risk with was even harder. She didn't know if in the end Jackson would be that one, but what she did know was that she couldn't help but wonder if he was thinking about her right now. Wondering if his thoughts of the case had been smothered like hers by these crazy emotions. And if he felt the same way about the long, breathless kiss they'd just shared in the parking lot. Jackson might be a huge distraction, but for the moment she didn't care.

She stood in front of the etched-glass front door, the amber glow of the inside lights punctuating the darkness, and smiled. After Ethan's death, her mother had insisted she and Tess move back home, but she in turn had insisted on staying in her own house, knowing if she didn't strike out on her own she wouldn't have been able to completely recover from her loss. In the end, she'd never regretted her choice. The compromise to her mother had been for Avery and Tess to come to family dinner once or twice a week. But for herself, knowing she could make it on her own had been an important step to finding her place in the world. And now she'd just taken another step forward.

Movement on the other end of the porch caught her eye as she twisted the door handle. She squinted in the darkness, noticing for the first time the familiar squeak of the two-seater swing. "Mom? What are you doing out here?"

"Nothing, I just . . . It's a beautiful night."

"Yes, it is." If you ignored the humidity and mosquitoes. Her mother hated both.

"How was your date?"

"It wasn't a date, Mom. It was work. Jackson and I were discussing details about my case."

Avery bridged the distance between them. She wasn't ready to tell anyone she'd agreed to go out with Jackson again. Or that she was afraid she'd completely lost her heart after that kiss. A smile teased the edges of her lips again. It was a feeling she needed to explore on her own.

She smiled, hoping her mother didn't notice the flush she knew lingered on her face. "I just came to pick up Tess. I'm sorry it's so late."

"It's fine. You know we love her being here. She's inside playing chess with your father."

"Mama?" Avery sat down on the wooden swing and let her heels rock back and forth. "You've been crying."

"It's nothing." She turned her head away, letting the shadows envelope her face. "I just needed some fresh air."

"Maybe, but something's wrong." Avery took her mother's hand, unconvinced. The last time she'd seen her mother cry had been at Michael's funeral. "What is it?"

She noticed the framed photo lying in her mother's lap. She closed her eyes and slouched against the back of the swing. The rhythmic squeak of the hinges creaked above her. How could she have been so foolish? She'd imagined Mama would cherish the photo, but it had only ended up hurting her. "I'm sorry. I didn't mean to upset you. I knew you were looking for a good picture of Dad and when I found this one . . . I knew you wanted Michael to be there. At the time it seemed perfect."

"It's not that. The picture is perfect." Mama ran her finger across the image of Michael and smiled. "I'd forgotten about this photo, but I remember the day. Your father had just been made captain. We were all so proud of him, but Michael especially. He took us out to dinner at that Chinese restaurant to celebrate."

"Ming Chang's."

"Yes. Your brother loved that restaurant. Always insisted that we order half a dozen different dishes and share them."

"And use chopsticks."

"I never did get used to those ridiculous contraptions." Her soft laugh competed with the sounds of chirping bugs that filled the humid air. "That night was significant to me in many ways."

"How?"

"I was proud of your father, for one. Making

captain was a huge step in his career, and one he'd reached toward for a number of years. But it was more than that. It was also seeing Michael all grown up after all we'd been through. It was a miracle to me."

"Michael could be a challenge when he was younger."

"That's putting it mildly."

Avery smiled at the sound of laughter in her mama's voice. It had been so long.

"There were days while he was in high school that I honestly didn't think any of us would survive. He was always trying to push the boundaries, trying something new and often foolish. He nearly drove your father and me crazy. And yet in the end—thanks to the good Lord—he managed to harness all that teenage rebellion and anger and make something out of himself."

Avery reached for her mother's hand and clasped it. "He was a good cop. A good man."

"I still miss him so much. I wake up in the mornings, and sometimes, for a split second, I forget he's gone. Then it hits me that it wasn't a dream. That he's gone, and he's not coming back. It happens over and over, this deep ache inside me that won't go away no matter what I do."

"Loss is never easy, Mama. It takes time to heal."

Her mother looked up and caught Avery's gaze.

"I know I'm not myself. I know it's not fair to you or your father. To Emily and Tess. I just don't know how to get rid of the emptiness that consumes me. It's as if a part of me died, and I don't know how to live again. Sometimes I'm not even sure I want to live again."

"Sometimes . . ." Avery hesitated. How long had it been since her mother had opened up to her? "Sometimes I feel as if I lost you when Michael died. We all want to help you through this. You have to believe that. We love you."

"It just hurts so much."

"We all hurt. We all miss Michael."

"It wasn't supposed to happen this way. Children aren't supposed to die before their parents do."

"And women aren't supposed to be widows at twenty-nine. But we can't change any of that. Death is a part of life whether we're ready for it or not."

Avery's memories surfaced, and with them her own sharp feelings of loss. Three years had helped to numb the pain, but its sting had never completely vanished. Sometimes, when she least expected it, the wounds of losing Ethan reappeared like it was only yesterday when she first heard the news.

I'm sorry to inform you, Mrs. North . . . there's been an accident . . . Your husband is dead . . . his car flipped . . .

"You still miss Ethan, don't you?"

"I always will."

"Oh, Avery. Sometimes I forget how much you've gone through. Losing Ethan, having to raise Tess as a single mom, working full-time. I don't know how you do it."

"I've had a lot of help."

Her mom wiped at the ring of mascara under her eyes. "If only your father could see me now."

"Daddy loves you."

"I know. I don't deserve him." She shook her head. "He . . . he wants me to make an appointment with the counselor at church."

"You didn't tell me that."

"I haven't gone. Claire Hunt isn't supposed to need counseling." She waved her hand toward the house. "I've worked my whole life to make sure I have the perfect house, the perfect family . . . the perfect life. Stepping into a counselor's office would be admitting I've failed."

"No one has the perfect life. No one can avoid hurt. All we can do is take things one day at a time, and if we need a little help in the process, then what's wrong with that?"

Her mother shook her head. "How did you deal with Ethan's death? How did you come to the point where you wanted to go on with your life again?"

"I had Tess, which meant I didn't have a choice

other than to get up every day and do what I had to do. I had to work, cook, create some sense of normality in a world that had shattered into a million pieces. It's just in the past year, though, that I've started giving myself permission to live and be happy again."

Memories of Ethan surfaced as she continued sharing. "I remember lying on my bed at night and reading from the Psalms over and over, trying to find some reason to keep going. 'When I walk through the valley of the shadow of death, I will fear no evil, for you are with me . . .' God has never left you. Neither have any of us. And a few weeks of counseling can't hurt. I went."

"I'd forgotten that." Mama pressed the picture against her chest. "I'm afraid to start feeling again. I just . . . I don't think I can."

"One day at a time, Mama."

Her mother nudged Avery with her elbow. "How did you get to be so wise? It seems like yesterday that you were Tess's age. Full of questions. Then there were the boys who started hanging around. I didn't think your father would let you out the door, until eventually Ethan came and swept you away. You made a good choice. And I know that if you do find love again, Ethan would be proud of you. I'm proud of you."

"Thanks, Mama."

"What about that Jackson? Don't tell me there's not a glow in your eyes after seeing him tonight."

"I like him—a lot—but I guess we'll all have to wait and see how it turns out."

Avery laid her head on her mother's shoulder and felt a peace spread over her she hadn't felt for a long time. She had her mother back. If only for the moment.

Chapter 16

Late morning, Avery stopped in front of the vending machine at the end of the precinct hallway and hesitated, wishing life were as simple as choosing between a candy bar and a bag of chips. Just when she thought the case was neatly wrapped up, it had somehow managed to blow wide open. The DA was now doubting the evidence to move forward with the arraignment for James Philips, even though they still needed more evidence on the Sourns for their possible involvement.

"Hey, sorry I'm late." Carlos dumped his crumpled fast-food bag into the trash can beside the vending machine. "Clarissa needed me to go with her to take Chloe to the doctor, and you know how backed up things can get sometimes at the clinic."

"It's okay. The Sourns just arrived and are

waiting in interrogation room one." As far as she was concerned, letting them—and their lawyer—sweat a bit was a good thing. "How is Chloe?"

"Thankfully, it doesn't seem to be something serious. Because she was a preemie, the doctor thinks she's not producing lactase well enough."

Avery shoved her quarters into the machine, forgoing the junk food, and pushed the button for bottled water. "That would explain her constant crying and not sleeping well."

"And my not sleeping well."

Avery laughed. "I'll be honest, I'm glad those days are behind me. It does get better eventually, I promise."

"Let's hope those days come sooner rather than later." Carlos shoved his hands in his front pockets. "You ready for this?"

"I don't know. I'm worried we don't have enough leverage to convince them to talk, and worried that even if they want to talk, their lawyer won't let them say anything."

Avery grabbed her water from the slot and shot up a quick prayer for clarity of mind . . . and for the truth to be revealed.

Inside the interrogation room, the Sourns sat at the rectangular table with their lawyer, Ryan Blackburn. Avery had hoped to do the interview without a lawyer present, especially one like Blackburn, who made ten times as much as she did and was happy to ensure she knew it.

She studied his expression that was too smug, too arrogant, and far too confident.

She took a seat across from them, set her water on the table, and plastered on her best smile. Carlos stood behind her, ready to play the game. "Mr. and Mrs. Sourn, I want to thank you for coming in and talking with us today. I know that you just recently received the news regarding the loss of your niece, and I am very sorry."

"Thank you." Mrs. Sourn nodded while kneading a tissue between her fingers.

"We are doing everything we can to find her killer," Avery continued, "but there are several discrepancies we need to clear up."

Mr. Sourn took his wife's free hand. "Finding our niece's killer is our priority as well. We're happy to help in any way we can."

"Good." Avery looked down at her notes. "You both told us that Tala had been living in your house since graduating from high school. Her diploma and driver's license are from her home state of Arizona."

"Yes, that is correct," Mr. Sourn said. "Is there a problem?"

"Actually, we've discovered a couple discrepancies. The first one has to do with the autopsy. The ME who worked on her case found that Tala had an enlarged spleen. Now this could mean a number of things, from mononucleosis to a bacterial infection, or even cancer, but everything he tested for came up negative. Until he tested her blood for malaria."

Avery caught the look of surprise in Mr. Sourn's expression. "Malaria?"

"The test came back positive."

He shook his head. "I don't understand."

"We didn't either at first. Because what makes this interesting is that malaria hasn't been a problem in this country for over fifty years, meaning that Tala would have needed to travel overseas—to a place like Vietnam—to have contracted the disease. But you told me that Tala didn't have a passport."

Mrs. Sourn shook her head. "I . . . I didn't think so."

"According to the US Department of State's Passport Records," Avery said, "there is no record that your niece ever applied for a passport."

"Which is why we started digging deeper and discovered a second problem." Carlos took a step forward and dropped a copy of Tala's high school diploma in front of the Sourns. "For starters, I applaud whoever worked on the execution of these documents. We almost didn't catch it, but Tala never went to high school . . . at least not in Arizona. She was using a laundered identity."

Mr. Sourn looked to his wife. "That's not possible—"

"It's clear what's going on here." Mr.

Blackburn interrupted Mr. Sourn. "My clients are the victims here."

"The victims?" Avery's gaze widened.

"Tala told us—"

"You don't have to say anything else, Mrs. Sourn."

"It's fine." Mr. Sourn held up his hand. "We just want to get to the bottom of this. We believed Tala was our niece. If we had had any idea her paperwork was fake, we never would have let her live with us."

Avery tried to swallow her frustration. "You are telling us, then, that you had no idea that Tala's documents were fake."

"Do you know how many people have fake licenses in this state alone?" Blackburn shook his head. "You can buy kits online that make authentic-looking IDs used for underage drinking. Some of the easiest to use are sold right here in Georgia. Tala . . . or whoever she was . . . arrived three months ago on my clients' doorstep, claiming she was the niece they hadn't seen for years, and now it's clear that she must have been involved in some kind of con."

"So now your clients are the victims?" Carlos asked.

"That is exactly what I'm saying. She stole a ring worth over ten thousand dollars and carried fake documents. What else could it be?"

"There is another possibility to this scenario."

Avery wasn't ready to let things go. "Your clients were harboring an illegal immigrant. If we bring charges against them, they'll be facing some stiff penalties."

"My clients are innocent."

"And a girl's been murdered. Have you already forgotten?"

"Robbed and murdered by some homeless professor, I was told."

"The new evidence brought forth by the ME casts doubt on his guilt."

"Which is your problem, not mine, and certainly not my clients'. If Tala Vuong—or whatever her name really was—were still alive, she'd be the one who would be charged—for possession of fraudulent identification documents, for posing as the Sourns' niece, and for theft. We've heard enough." He signaled to the Sourns. "If you need anything else, Detective, you may contact me directly."

Avery stood, fighting to control her anger. "Then let's hope you're right, because if you're not, the next time we sit down in this room, I won't just be talking to your clients about harboring an illegal alien. I'll be talking to them about obstruction of justice."

A minute later, Avery slammed her file folder down onto her desk, her head still spinning.

"Avery."

"I blew it. I should have seen it coming.

How did they become the victims in this situation?"

"Just because they won round one doesn't mean they're going to win the war. If you ask me, they're guilty, and everyone in the room knew it."

"But we can't prove it."

"Yet. They're already running scared."

"None of this adds up." Avery ran her hands through her hair and slumped back down in her chair. "We have nothing to hold them on and no other suspects."

"Which is why it's up to us to find evidence that puts a hole in their story."

Avery looked up at the knock on her door. Captain Peterson stood in the doorway, clearly unhappy.

"I listened to your interview outside, and I'm getting concerned about another case blowing up in our face."

"Things just keep getting better and better."

"You accused the Sourns of harboring an illegal alien."

"The evidence I have points to that possibility."

"I was under the impression that everything had already been wrapped up, and that the DA set an arraignment for James Philips."

"Last night, the ME came to me with new evidence from the autopsy that places doubt on James Philips's guilt."

"You're certain of that?"

"Yes. Enough for me to move Mr. and Mrs. Sourn—no matter what they say—from grieving uncle and aunt to the top of my suspect list."

"That's pretty strong. Isn't it possible that they really were the victims here?"

"That is a possibility, but I'm simply following the evidence."

"We just need to make sure this goes down by the book. Robert Sourn has been under investigation for money laundering in the past, but we never could prove he was involved. He ended up making the department look bad, something none of us want to happen again."

Avery nodded, hating the politics that managed to entwine themselves in every case. "I'll be careful, but if we don't find out the truth soon, we're going to end up with another victim."

Chapter 17

Avery took a bite of the fish taco from one of the food trucks strategically placed around the city. Thankfully, Atlanta's battle against the roving gourmet vehicles had finally come to an end and the trucks were able to sell their food. Some of her best meals had come from mobile vendors. Besides that, there was nothing like street fare when in the middle of a stakeout or, like today, another long day of canvassing.

"This is delicious."

"No kidding." Mitch started on his second chicken burrito as they stood beneath the bright green umbrella that blocked the afternoon sun for the truck's patrons.

She took another bite. It was almost enough to lighten her sour mood. Almost. Constant dead ends always left her irritated, and this case was hitting more than its share of brick walls.

They'd begun going through the Sourn neighborhood house by house for the second time, and once again they'd turned up nothing. Several neighbors thought they recognized Tala, but no one remembered speaking to her. How was it possible that she'd lived in that house three months and no one even knew her name?

Avery took a sip of her iced tea. What happened to good, old-fashioned neighborhood cookouts and the welcome wagon when one moved into town? Apparently community solidarity had gone the way of cassette tapes and typewriters.

Scrunching up the paper wrapper from her finished taco, she tossed it into the trash and waited for Mitch to finish his lunch before they headed out again. Despite Jackson's findings, punching holes in the Sourns' story had ended up being more of a challenge than she'd anticipated. Not only had their story never wavered, a search of flight manifests and border control posts confirmed that Tala—as Mrs. Sourn had told her—had not traveled overseas. Which meant they were no closer to finding out who the young woman really was than they were two days ago.

While waiting for Mitch to finish, Avery watched the dozen people standing in line for their lunch. Moms with strollers, a jogger, three men dressed in suits and ties. The smell of exhaust from the passing cars mixed with the scent of grilled meat from the food truck. "I have to say, I don't get this."

Mitch frowned and finished swallowing, clearly not happy with the interruption. The man took his food way too seriously.

He wiped a spot of sauce from his chin. "Don't get what?"

"We're missing something. The Sourns continue to insist that Tala was the one lying, but it's as if Tala never existed, except for the fact that her body is lying in the morgue. We have her fingerprints all over the house and her room, but the neighbors have never spoken to her. She has a positive case of malaria, but never left the country. We have a forged driver's license and a high school diploma, but no friends or phone numbers of friends. No one who remembers any detail about her. Did she jog in this park here in the mornings, take the dog for a walk every night? Did she watch action-adventure films or prefer crying over old movies? I just don't understand how someone could have existed, yet have been so completely invisible."

The only scenario that made sense was that Tala had been in the country illegally. It gave the Sourns motivation to lie and explained the laundered documents. They just had to find a hole in their story.

"Living in anonymity these days isn't as unusual as you think," Mitch said. "People spend more time on the internet than they do face-to-face with friends. They live their lives through reality TV, online video games, or places like Facebook."

They started the three blocks on foot back toward the Sourns' plush neighborhood. The heat hung heavy in the air, but at least she'd get in a bit of exercise today. "I don't know."

"My cousin's a prime example. He lives in his parents' basement, most of his friends are online, and he's known to most by his avatar name, Zytan. He works at home as a graphic designer, so there's no commuting, no hanging out with friends by the water cooler or lunch with co-workers. If he goes out, it's to grab fast food or to watch a movie. If he does actually show up at one of his real friends' houses, they play video games or watch a game, but he certainly doesn't call and chat with his buddies on the phone."

"Maybe you're right, but there's got to be more.

I have friends who work at home, but they have an email address, Facebook, they take the trash out and wave to their neighbors. Even though your cousin lives in his parents' basement, tracking down friends who knew him wouldn't be that difficult."

"True."

"If it weren't for her body in the morgue, and the handful of documents we have, I'd have a hard time proving Tala even existed."

"We've still got more canvassing to do. Maybe we'll get lucky."

Avery lengthened her steps to match Mitch's long stride as they reentered the exclusive community of two-story homes, each worth at least a million-plus, with its surrounding golf course. Except for the lawn mower buzzing a few houses down, the neighborhood was quiet. She studied the sign on the side of the lawn service truck. Hiring someone to mow your lawn meant you didn't spend time outside doing your own landscaping.

She looked down the street in the other direction. A black sedan pulled into a driveway. The garage door opened with the push of the button, securing the driver inside, where he would probably spend the rest of the day locked away inside the comfort of the air-conditioned home. Once the weather cooled, he might hang out on the back porch surrounded by a fence tall enough that none of their neighbors could see him. It had been built purposely for that reason.

No barn raisings or hunting parties for the men.

No quilting bees for the women.

Nothing requiring them to work together.

Maybe Mitch was right. It was possible to be invisible in the middle of a community.

"Have you ever thought about how much life has changed over the past hundred and fifty years, and how much we've lost?"

"Lost?" Mitch chuckled. "A hundred and fifty years ago, they had no cable TV, no cars or airplanes, no internet, no fast food . . . I must be missing something. What have we lost?"

"We have everything we need at our fingertips. We've lost that true sense of community where we rely on each other for our very survival. Instead we live in communities where they lose a young girl and no one misses her."

They walked up the long drive. Avery rang the bell, then took a step backward. A little boy, no more than five, finally opened the door.

Avery bent down, pressing her hands against her thighs. "Hi, I'm Detective North. Is your mommy or daddy home?"

The boy's eyes widened. "You're a policeman?"

"Yes, I am."

His smile faded. "Am I in trouble?"

"Not that I know of."

"Teo?" A young woman behind him tried to pull the boy back into the house. Asian, like the boy, late teens, maybe early twenties.

"Wait, please—" Avery started.

"Teo, *vui long!*"

Teo stood his ground and didn't budge from the still-open door. The young woman spoke a few more words, then glanced behind her as if she wasn't sure what to do.

Teo didn't seem to care. "I want to be a policeman when I grow up."

"I'm sure you would make a very fine officer." Avery took a step forward and identified herself to the woman. "Do you speak English?"

The young woman shook her head. "No. No English."

"I'm helping her learn. She can say hello, good-bye, how are you—"

"I'm sure you make a wonderful teacher, Teo. Is she your mother?"

"No, her name is Malaya. She takes care of me when my mother is gone."

"Is your mother here now?"

He shook his head. "No, she had to go shopping."

"I have a picture I would like you and Malaya to look at. I need to know if either of you know this girl. She died, and we are trying to find out what happened to her."

Teo made a quick translation and Malaya

nodded. Avery handed the girl a copy of the photo they'd found on Tala's body.

Malaya studied the photo, then shook her head, but not before Avery caught the brief flicker of recognition in her eyes.

"She says she's sorry, but she doesn't know the girl. I don't know her either."

"Is she sure? It's very important."

Teo repeated the question to her and Malaya shook her head again, insistent. Avery shoved back her frustration. Without more evidence, there was nothing more she could do for the moment.

She pulled out her business card. "One more thing. If you or Malaya remember something you think might help me, please call me."

Teo took the card and stepped inside before Malaya slammed the door shut, leaving Avery and Mitch alone on the front porch.

Avery started down the drive toward the next house. "I think she recognized her."

"Maybe. There was definitely fear in her eyes, but it could be that she was simply afraid she was going to get in trouble for letting Teo open the door to a stranger."

"Or it could be something more. Not every person who can't speak English is here illegally, but after she saw our badges, I'm pretty sure she didn't want us there."

She started up the next driveway beside Mitch

and watched a landscape crew pack up their tools, load them into their truck, and drive away down the empty street. She didn't want to run off on tangents not supported by evidence and forensic findings, but neither could she ignore the way the pieces of the puzzle were coming together.

"There's a connection somewhere here, Mitch. No one knew Tala, which means that it's possible she was living in a situation no different than a prostitute kept under the radar by her pimp. And now this girl, she was clearly frightened by something."

Mitch shook his head. "I know where you're going with this, but most of the people in this neighborhood pay their employees to cook for them, watch their children, clean their houses, and mow their lawns. It's economics, not exploitation. And it certainly doesn't mean they're all doing it under the table by using illegal immigrants."

"I'm not concerned, right now anyway, about other people's employees and whether or not they're here legally." Avery turned to him and caught his gaze. "What I'm worried about is one dead girl, and the possibility of more murders."

Chapter 18

Malaya tried to breathe, but the air wouldn't reach her lungs. The living room started closing in on her. She leaned against the wall for support, but all she could see was Tala's face. They'd killed her. Just as they'd promised. She and Tala had been warned, but Tala hadn't listened and now she was dead. There was no way out. Why couldn't she have seen that? The scarred man on the boat had been the first to threaten them, and now they had come for her.

The voices replayed over and over in her mind. *If you try to escape, we will kill you. And do you know what the police do to undocumented workers?*

"Are you all right, Malaya?"

Malaya managed a smile for Teo. "Let's not tell your mother about the police, okay? You know how they've told you never to answer the door. She might get angry with you. And neither of us want your mother angry."

The boy's eyes widened. She hated scaring him, but what choice did she have?

"Are you hungry? I think it's time for a snack."

Teo nodded, his smile back. She'd learned quickly that a few sugary treats went a long way in getting him to do what she wanted.

"I think there are some cookies left. Why don't you grab a couple and color for a while."

Malaya wanted to learn English, but no English was spoken to her in this house except for what Teo said to her when they were alone. She'd convinced him that it would be their secret game, her trying to pick up words and phrases. One day they would surprise his parents.

Except she knew their reaction wouldn't be one of surprise. It would be one of anger. But she didn't plan to end up like Tala.

Malaya held the card the police had given her. She should throw it away. If Teo's mother found it, she would want to know where it came from. She could burn it, but if Teo found out, he was bound to ask questions and tell his mother.

She peeked through the window. She couldn't see the man and woman with their badges anymore, but she couldn't help but wonder, why this neighborhood? Had they somehow linked Tala back to this neighborhood and Malaya? Could Tala have lived in this neighborhood and Malaya hadn't known it? But how could she know? She'd been kept isolated and the rules had been clear. Clean and cook during the day, and keep Teo occupied. She wasn't allowed to go out or use the phone or answer the door. The beatings she'd received had been enough to remind her they were serious.

Not that it mattered. Who would she talk to if she did run away? If the police were after her, and she couldn't communicate with the outside world, there was nowhere to run.

"Malaya?"

She spun around, sliding the card into her pocket. Mrs. Chu stood in the middle of the kitchen, her face etched with a scowl. Malaya's heart pounded. How had she missed the sound of the garage door opening?

"Why are you just standing there? I'm going upstairs to rest. I expect dinner on the table by six."

"Yes, ma'am."

Fatigue swept over her. Sixteen-plus hours of work a day, sleeping on a mat in a corner of the garage. Two days ago, Mr. Chu had beaten her for breaking a dish and left a bruise on her rib cage where Teo wouldn't see it. Most of the time they left her alone, because they knew that threats were just as effective as physical abuse. She knew what they could do.

Malaya began chopping vegetables. Teo sat quietly at the end of the bar, eating his snack and coloring. She scooted the cutting board closer so she could see what he was doing.

"What are you coloring, Teo?"

He held up a picture of a racecar and started describing it in Vietnamese.

"In English, Teo." She lowered her voice. "Tell me the words in English."

"This is a car. This car goes very fast. Very far."

"Car. A fast car."

A car that could travel very far. Back to another world? Longing swept over her as she cut the rest of the carrots and tossed them into the salad bowl. She wished she were home, watching her mother fix dinner in their small kitchen while their father entertained them with stories of what had happened at work that day. Laughter around the dinner table had been as abundant as the rice growing in the surrounding fields. They had thought they were giving her a chance to better her life. Instead, she'd become a prisoner.

But what if there were a way out?

Malaya started chopping harder and dismissed the thought.

Her gaze shifted briefly to the front door. She slid her hand inside her pocket and felt for the card again. There had been a hint of kindness in the woman's eyes. Malaya might not have understood anything the woman had said, but the card she'd given her held a phone number. What if she heard her story? That she'd been told she would have all the necessary papers. That her family had paid the required fee to bring her here. What if she told her what they had done to her? How she didn't want to be here. Wasn't America supposed to be the land of freedom and opportunity?

What if the woman understood?

Tala's face surfaced, and for a moment, Malaya thought she was going to be physically ill. She stepped back from the counter, her hands shaking.

"Are you okay, Malaya?"

She nodded, eyes closed until the nausea passed.

Her thoughts were foolish. The police were not an option. Running was not an option. Praying for a miracle hadn't worked.

But she would find a way out. Somehow.

Chapter 19

Hearing the words "Mama just fired the caterer" couldn't have come at a worse time. This morning the DA had dropped charges against Philips and released him. The rest of Avery's day had been a string of long, unproductive dead ends and frustration, and now the high hopes she'd had that everything was running smoothly for tonight's party were effectively dashed.

Avery hurried into the large rectangular reception hall that could hold two hundred guests comfortably and forced herself to take a deep, calming breath. It didn't work. With barely an hour until the party started, she'd spent the entire twenty-minute drive wondering how in the world she was going to have time to save the party, run home and change, and be ready for Jackson to pick her up at six.

The rivalry between Doris Lincoln and Claire Hunt was legendary. Or at least it had been. Aunt Doris had left behind petty rivalries to become one of Atlanta's top caterers. It was Mama who had changed into someone Avery hardly knew anymore. And for all of Avery's experience in fixing things, she'd discovered that sometimes even her best efforts weren't enough.

She glanced at her watch. Fifty-eight minutes and counting. She'd never make it.

Inside the hall, she wove her way past round tables covered with white cloths and gold trim. They matched the black-and-gold shimmering centerpieces that were just masculine enough that her father wouldn't raise his eyebrow when he saw them. The head table held pictures of Thomas Hunt throughout his career, from rookie cop to captain of the precinct. Despite her father's avoidance of cameras, they'd been able to gather a glowing testimony of forty years of service.

Leave it to her mother. Everything was perfect.

Or so she'd thought until her sister's frantic phone call.

Emily entered the hall from one of the side doors. "Avery, I'm so glad you came."

Avery drew in another breath. "I managed to get away, but honestly, Em, I don't have time to deal with a family emergency right now."

Avery took in her sister's very vogue, very vintage party dress she'd probably picked up at some suburban thrift shop. On her, the deep purple fabric with its fitted waist and flared skirt looked fabulous. So classic. So Emily.

She, on the other hand, was still wearing her semi-stylish gray slacks with a matching jacket that covered her Glock, and a pair of very functional shoes. Sensible maybe, but not exactly party attire. And it certainly wasn't what she intended to wear on her third date with Jackson. Yet, somehow, she was supposed to work on leads in order to track down a killer, solve a family crisis, and still manage to find time to go home and change into the party dress she'd bought last month on a rare shopping trip.

The way things were going, she had no idea how that was going to happen.

She tugged on the open front of her jacket. "As you can see, I'm still officially on duty with a murder investigation going on and certainly not ready for the party. So please tell me that I misunderstood what you said and that Mama didn't fire Aunt Doris."

Emily grabbed Avery's arm and headed for the kitchen. "Oh, you heard correctly."

"How did this happen? No one in their right

mind fires the caterer an hour before the party starts."

"I tried to talk sense into her, Avery, but Mama won't listen to me. Guests are going to start arriving soon, and if we don't negotiate some sort of truce between the two of them, there will be no party for Daddy. Or at least nothing for our guests to eat, and somehow I don't think that's going to go over very well."

"What do you want me to do, Emily? This isn't a murder investigation—not yet anyway—it's more like a hostage situation, with tonight's menu on the line."

"The biggest question is, how are we going to explain the situation to the guests if things aren't worked out in the next hour?"

Avery hesitated in front of the swinging door leading into the kitchen. "If this party is so important to Mama, how did it ever get to this point?"

"They got in a heated argument, and before I could calm either of them down, Aunt Doris started loading the food back into her van. She's in there right now, sending her workers home and taking back the food they brought."

Avery should have known it would end in disaster. Only her mother would have the gall to fire the caterer—family or not—minutes before her father's retirement party. Putting her mother and Aunt Doris in the same room had clearly been a recipe for calamity.

"Tell me exactly what happened."

"All I know is that Daddy showed up and started talking to Aunt Doris. Mama accused Aunt Doris of flirting—which, in Mama's defense, she was." Emily lowered her voice. "After three divorces, I think Aunt Doris is as jealous over Mama's ability to keep her man as Mama is over the fact that Aunt Doris is a successful businesswoman. Needless to say, in the end, they both said a few things they shouldn't have."

A crash sounded in the kitchen.

There was no use denying the inevitable. Avery took a deep breath and strode into the industrial-sized kitchen, quickly assessing the situation. Both women looked at the door and froze.

Mama stood in the middle of the room, balancing a three-tiered cake in front of her. Aunt Doris stood over a dropped silver tray of tartlets that had smeared chocolate and peppermint across the tiled floor and her white shoes.

Trying to compose her thoughts, Avery eyed a serving cart filled with savory tarts, shrimp, and mini quiches, and felt her stomach grumble. Lunch had been hours ago. She found herself debating whether she should pull out her gun for emphasis or simply grab one of the quiches and squelch her appetite.

She opted for the authoritative voice she used on suspects trying to get away from her. "Mama, please set the cake down on the counter before you drop it."

Mama hesitated, then surprisingly, complied. "She's threatening to take my cake."

"Aunt Doris, will you excuse my mother and me for a moment?" Avery held up her hand. "But stay in the kitchen . . . please."

Avery led her mama to the other side of the room, out of earshot of Aunt Doris. "The party starts in less than an hour. What is going on?"

"She made a pass at your father."

"I'm sure she was just being friendly."

"Trust me, she was being more than just friendly."

Avery watched out of the corner of her eye while Aunt Doris began wiping the chocolate from her shoes. At least she wasn't making a run for it. Not yet, anyway. "Mama, you need to apologize."

"Apologize? You can't be serious."

"I'm sorry, but if we're going to come to some sort of truce in the next few minutes, someone is going to have to swallow her pride. This is Daddy's retirement party. I know you want it to be special. You've put so much work into it, and this is not how you want things to end. Please apologize, and I'll try to work something out before the entire party is ruined. The two of you used to be friends—"

" 'Used to' being the key words here. I'm not

going to apologize, Avery." Her mother looked up at her. Fine lines around her eyes had deepened into dark shadows. Her mother had aged a decade in the past year. "You should have seen the way she looked at your father, putting on her southern charm and airs like she owned *him,* not just a catering business."

"Mother, you're family. Don't you think this feud has gone on long enough? I might never know exactly what happened between the two of you, but I do know that you used to be best friends."

Her mother's gaze shifted to the floor. Avery had no doubt that if she had her way, the secret would go with her and Aunt Doris to the grave. "I'd like to see you talk some sense into her, Avery."

"Fine. I will."

Avery approached the large metal island, avoiding the smeared filling and stopping just long enough to pop a bite-sized quiche into her mouth. She allowed her taste buds to appreciate the cheesy bite, swallowed, then faced her mother's longtime friend turned adversary.

Medium frame, slightly plump, too-heavy makeup, perfect upswept hair—thanks to L'Oreal's Café Noir coloring—with an extra dash of southern charm thrown into the mix. Charm that curdled when you got on her bad side. "Aunt Doris. I understand that there's been a disagreement between you and my mother, but—"

"Darling, your mother's been difficult for as long as I can remember, but lately . . . the woman has become impossible."

"I understand that she fired you, but with less than an hour until the dinner, it seems prudent for both of you to come to some sort of truce."

"She fired me? She didn't fire me. I quit. And it all boils down to jealousy."

"Jealousy?"

"I've tried to get along with that woman, but it would take Mother Teresa herself to forgive and forget at this point."

Avery took in a deep breath. Rule One: find out what the hostage taker wants.

"Aunt Doris, I know that my mother can be a bit . . . demanding at times, but we need to come to a compromise." Avery managed to swallow any remaining pride. "Tell me what you need to resolve this situation."

"Honey, there is nothing you can do to rectify this situation after what your mama said."

Rule Two: establish goodwill. Ask for concession.

If it worked in hostage negotiation, surely it would work between two grown women.

"How about this. If I promise that she'll stay out of the kitchen during tonight's party and allow you to run the catering side without any interference from her, would you agree to stay?"

"And why should I?"

Rule Three: make the hostage taker realize that noncooperation is impracticable.

"Think of it this way. You don't want word getting around that you walked off a job . . . or that you were fired, for that matter."

Aunt Doris set down the tray of pink shrimp sitting in a ring of ice she'd been holding. "I will need some sort of . . . compensation."

Rule Four: never allow a hostage taker to get the upper hand.

Avery tried to ignore the rhythmic pounding in her temples. She was going to have to scratch that rule for now.

Rule Five: ask questions.

"How much?"

"I will need a 10 percent increase in my bill for . . . for emotional strain."

Emotional strain? Really. Aunt Doris always had been somewhat of a drama queen.

"Fine."

"Now listen. I've spent the past twenty years building up my business. I won't have Claire Hunt—family or not—bring it down in one night, especially over a falling-out that has its roots in a college homecoming ceremony."

Now there was a clue worth following up on. Southern rivalry might be fine on the football field, but not in the kitchen.

"I understand. Do we have a deal?"

"You're not going to make me regret this, are you?"

Avery stooped to pick up the fallen tartlet tray and set it on the counter. She was already regretting it. "No ma'am."

Now to face Mama again.

"Mama. Aunt Doris has agreed to stay on one condition." She'd deal with the other condition later, even if it meant the tacked-on fee came out of her own pocket. "I need you to leave the kitchen . . . for the rest of the evening."

"Why would I do that? That woman will ruin everything—"

"Mama, please, I don't want to hear a word about 'that woman.' She used to be your best friend. She'll stay if you stay out of the kitchen."

"I will not—"

"Mama." Avery felt her teeth grind. "You need to be out there with the guests anyway, not worrying about whether or not there's enough shrimp or ice."

Mama took a step forward, but Aunt Doris had already slipped out the back door, presumably to bring in the rest of the food she'd whisked away earlier. "So on top of trying to steal my husband, she's skimped on the shrimp as well?"

"No, Mama, of course not. It was just an example."

Avery's phone went off, saving her from further

explanations. She glanced at the caller ID before taking the call.

Jackson.

The way things were going, their third date was liable to turn into another disaster. Her simple black dress was still hanging in her closet. She'd never make it.

It rang a fourth time and she answered the call, hoping she didn't sound out of breath.

"Jackson . . . hi."

"I had to stop by the precinct to drop some things off, and they told me you left in a hurry. Some family emergency. Is everything okay?"

Avery decided to play it down. "A few last-minute issues regarding tonight's party have come up, but I think we've been able to sort them out."

"You're not going to have to cancel on me again, are you?"

She didn't miss the hint of concern in his voice.

"No, of course not, it's just that . . ."

She could have him meet her at the party.

No. She could still make this work.

"Listen, I am running late, but I'm on my way home now to change."

"Great, I'll pick you up at six then."

Avery glanced at her watch.

Forty minutes and counting.

Chapter 20

With her father's retirement party in full swing, Avery took a moment to tune out the conversation with Jackson, Mitch, and his fiancée, Kayleigh, in order to search for her mother in the crowded reception hall. Shania Twain's "You're Still the One" played in the background. Servers dressed in starched black-and-white uniforms worked to replace food on the twelve-foot-long buffet table and ensure the punch bowl stayed full, which meant Aunt Doris was holding up her part of the deal. Avery intended to ensure Mama did the same.

Her father stood talking to a group of his former officers. Clearly he was enjoying the attention despite his insistence that he didn't want—or need—a party in his honor.

She finally caught sight of her mother on the far side of the room, wearing a flattering red sheath dress and chatting to the guests. Claire Hunt was in her element, playing hostess with all the southern charm of Scarlett O'Hara. Mama might have her faults, but she did know how to enchant a crowd.

Avery let out a long sigh of relief. If both

women had actually decided to keep their end of the bargain, as far as the party was concerned, they were in the clear. At least until the food was cleaned up and the floor and tablecloths washed. Then, no doubt, the two of them would go back to not speaking to each other.

Avery felt her shoulders droop and let the stress of the past few days begin to dissipate. A few hours away from her paperwork and interviews would go a long way to help clear her mind.

Mitch's elbow brushed against her, pulling her back into the conversation. "So, Avery? What do you think?"

Avery caught Kayleigh's square, one-carat diamond engagement ring flashing beneath the overhead lighting. "The ring is gorgeous."

Kayleigh was all smiles. "Thank you."

Avery continued. "I have to say that I never thought my partner would actually tie the knot. Though, in his defense, now that he has decided to, I don't think he could have made a better choice."

"Thanks, Avery. That means a lot." Kayleigh stared at the rock on her finger, her eyes still sparkling. "Since you've known Mitch a lot longer than I have, I'm counting on you to give me the inside scoop."

Avery returned Kayleigh's grin. "We'll get together for lunch soon, and—"

"Hey, now. Wait a minute. I'm standing right

here." Mitch glanced from Avery to Kayleigh, then back to Avery again as if he'd just discovered that life as a married man was never going to be the same again.

Kayleigh crossed her arms and frowned. "Don't tell me you're already regretting your escape from bachelorhood, Mitch Robertson."

"Not in a million years." Mitch grabbed Kayleigh's hand and pulled her against him, his gaze never leaving hers. "But that doesn't mean that I want Avery spilling all my secrets."

Avery turned to Jackson, whose white shirt and tie and tailored black jacket made him look like Cary Grant about to sweep her off her feet. "I think this is our cue to exit."

Jackson slipped her hand into the crook of his arm. "I could use something to drink and maybe seconds on those crab cakes."

"Lunch, Avery." Kayleigh laughed as Avery and Jackson started to walk away. "Don't forget."

"Oh, don't worry, I won't."

Avery stopped beside Jackson at the punch bowl and waited for him to pour them glasses of the red party punch. He handed her one. "Have I told you how beautiful you look tonight?"

"At least once." Maybe twice.

Somehow, she'd managed to finish dressing, put on her makeup, and slide on her heels with three minutes to spare. But it had been worth the hurried rush to be ready on time and see the look of approval in his expression when she'd opened the door to let him in.

Avery took a sip of the punch, wondering if they could get away with ditching the party for an intimate table for two at some cozy restaurant. "You clean up pretty good yourself. Though as nice as this is, I'm not sure this is what either of us had in mind for a third date."

"We'll have to remedy that soon, but in the meantime . . ." His hand slid down her arm and took her hand. "I plan to simply enjoy being with you tonight."

She took another sip of her punch, certain Aunt Doris must have spiked it. She felt as giddy as Tess sounded talking about a boy she liked at school.

"Considering we've actually made it to date number three despite family issues and a murder investigation, I completely agree."

So what if it wasn't a typical date. What about their relationship so far had been typical? Maybe typical was overrated.

"Do you want another plate of food?"

Avery eyed the buffet line, then shook her head, still full from her first time through the line. "Go ahead. Between my mother's cooking, too much takeout while investigating a murder, not to mention that fabulous donut you brought me, I think I've indulged enough this week."

Jackson started filling a plate. "Speaking of

murder investigations, what did the DA think about my autopsy findings?"

"The DA is reexamining the evidence while we investigate the Sourns and the problems with Tala's paperwork. Which means Monday's arraignment has been canceled and James Philips will walk. For now, anyway."

"And the Sourns?"

"They're claiming they had no idea Tala's paperwork had been laundered and that she, in fact, had conned them."

"Seriously?" Jackson dropped a tart onto his plate and caught Avery's gaze.

"Which means that until we get some more answers, we're back to square one with a murderer on the loose."

Jackson finished filling his plate and nodded toward an empty table. "Maybe the answer is that we forget about murder and autopsies and serial killers for the next couple of hours."

"I'd like that." Avery grabbed a chocolate-covered strawberry from his plate and popped it into her mouth.

He nudged her with his elbow. "So is this what I have to look forward to?"

"You've haven't seen anything yet." Avery's father came up and hugged her.

"Thanks for the vote of confidence, Dad."

The icing on the cake for tonight was seeing her father's smile that had yet to leave his face. He might hate the attention and spotlight, but these were his men and women. They had fought beside him for the past several decades to keep the streets of Atlanta safe. Many of them owed him their lives. He'd been counselor, friend, spiritual adviser, and more.

He reached out and shook Jackson's hand. "How are you tonight, Jackson?"

"I'm fine, sir, thank you. Congratulations on your retirement."

"I'm still not sure what I think about the idea, but I guess a few extra rounds of golf a week never hurt anyone."

"I'm sure you're right."

"If you don't mind, I'd like to borrow your date for a few minutes for a promised spin. She's a hard lady to track down."

"I've discovered that."

Avery returned Jackson's smile, then let her father lead her out onto the dance floor.

"You don't mind, do you?" he asked.

"Of course not."

"Third dates are a big deal."

"Daddy."

Her father smiled. "Did you notice they're playing our song?"

"Unforgettable" played in the background. A rush of emotions surged through Avery.

"Do you remember this song?"

"How could I forget? Nat King Cole and

Natalie Cole—father and daughter singing together. Seems like forever ago."

"Has anyone told you that you look beautiful tonight? Just as beautiful as you did back then. And tonight there's an extra glow in your eyes."

Avery smiled at the compliment, enjoying the jazzy tone of the music. Enjoying even more the time with her father. The last time they'd danced together had been at her wedding to Ethan.

It seemed like a lifetime ago.

"I'm sure it's just the angle of the lights."

"Or a certain handsome medical examiner. I see the two of you made up, which is good, because I like him. He seems stable. Competent."

Unforgettable?

The soothing rhythm of the sax played with her emotions. "I'm still not ready to look too far ahead, but I like him too, and I've decided that's enough for now. Time will tell."

"What does Tess think?" He led her around the dance floor filled with a dozen other couples.

"She likes him. He's met her menagerie of pets and brought her presents."

"Good. You both need a man in your life. Next to me, that is."

Avery rested her head against her father's shoulder, content for the moment just to feel the safe protection of his arms.

"I guess I need to thank you for saving the day and the food," he said.

"Who told you?"

"Emily."

"I'm just thankful that a truce was made. At least for tonight."

"Your mama isn't the only one I've been worried about. Maybe that's why Jackson seems right for you."

"Why are you worried about me? I'm fine."

"Maybe, but you work too hard."

"I learned my work ethic from the best. God and family first, then work hard at whatever I do, because someone once told me that the only difference between try and triumph is a little umph."

Her father laughed, but his smile quickly faded. "I did teach you to work hard, which is why I've been thinking more about what we discussed. I see you spend the majority of your time either working your cases—including Michael's—or with your family. Which made me start wondering. When do you actually make time for yourself?"

"Let's see. A manicure every month or two. Midnight shopping trips for groceries and indulging in a box of Milk Duds from the candy aisle." Avery couldn't help but chuckle despite the hint of worry in her father's eyes. "Do any of those things count?"

"It's a start. A very small start."

She'd taken her father's words to heart, but

even his advice didn't change the list of demands on her time. Like with Jackson, as much as she wanted things to work out between them, a relationship meant rearranging her life, and it was going to take time to figure out how to do it.

And there were other things she simply wasn't ready to give up. Like Michael's case.

A song she didn't know started playing in the background, but she barely heard the music as she followed her father's lead. "I know you're worried about me, but for the most part I really do enjoy what I do. And with Michael's case, all my digging might actually pay off. I found something earlier this week that we missed."

Clearly her statement took her father by surprise. "Where did you find a new lead?"

"It's a possible witness, buried in the paperwork, who was never followed up on. I'm not sure how he slipped through, but I've put out some calls and am working to track him down. It may not come to anything, but at least it's something fresh."

"Avery, I know that your heart is into this, and I want his name cleared as much as you do, but . . ." Her father's words faded.

"Daddy?" Thomas Hunt might have always been her hero, but losing his only son had changed him too. "What's wrong?"

"Jack's wife is here tonight."

Avery couldn't remember the last time she'd

seen the wife of her father's former partner. Probably not since the funeral. "I'll make sure I say hello to her."

"She'd like that, but her being here reminded me of something I've been thinking about for a long time. With your questions about finding balance in your life, I'm wondering if it isn't time I said something." He pulled back slightly and caught her gaze, still moving in step with the music. "I think you should stop investigating Michael's death. I'll hire a private investigator. Someone who isn't so emotionally involved with the case."

"I can understand this coming from Mama and Emily, but from you?" Avery stopped in the middle of the floor, the music and guests still swirling around them. "Besides, what does all of this have to do with Jack's wife?"

"I know what it's like to investigate the case of someone you're close to." Her father took her hand and pulled her off to the side of the room where there were fewer people. "Fifteen years ago, Jack was shot and killed by a gunman fleeing a home-invasion robbery. He was like a brother to me, and I spent the next two years trying to find the man who killed him."

She'd been young, but she still remembered the man who spent most of his days off hanging around the Hunt home. "You found Jack's murderer."

"Yes, but the process consumed me. I neglected my job, my family . . . I was obsessed. Nothing else mattered except finding the man who killed Jack. And for Jack's wife it was even worse. Then instead of bringing closure, finding the murderer only seemed to spawn feelings of anger and revenge. She's never gotten over Jack's death."

"Are you afraid of what we might find?"

"No. I've never doubted your brother's innocence. But I don't want you to suffer any more than you already have."

"I can handle this."

"Can you? You're worried about all the responsibilities vying for your attention. Maybe it's time to let go of this."

"I don't know if I'm ready to do that." The aromas from the buffet table that filled the room enveloped her senses and turned her stomach.

"It's not just you I'm worried about. It's your mother too."

"I'm doing this for her. For all of us."

"I know, but you've seen your mother. Today's blowup with Aunt Doris is a prime example. She's not getting any better, and I'm worried." He shook his head and rubbed the back of his neck. "I'm sorry, I didn't mean to bring this up, tonight of all times, but I don't know what else to do. Some days I feel like I've already lost her. She's not the same woman I married, and this downward spiral keeps getting worse."

The music faded in the background. "I'll be the first to admit that she needs some professional help, but stopping my search for the truth isn't going to help her."

"I know it won't just go away, but every time there's a new lead, or even the hint of a clue in the case, she gets her hopes up, only to have them come crashing down. Honestly, I don't know how much more she can take."

"Mama is stronger than you think. She'll get through this. She told me about going to the counselor . . ."

"She's said she'll go. She has to . . . We both have to come to the realization that Michael isn't coming back. And finding his killer isn't going to change that."

"Mom." Tess appeared in her bright blue party dress, holding a small silver gift bag with a purple ribbon.

"Tess, your grandfather and I are in the middle of—"

"It's important, Mom."

Avery shifted her attention to her daughter. "What is it?"

"That man over there—" she turned back toward the entrance—"I don't see him now, but he asked me to give this to you."

"For me? You must have misunderstood. It has to be for your grandfather?"

He'd already opened a table full of retirement

gifts, everything from gift cards, to luggage tags, to charitable donations. Someone must have come in late.

Avery started to hand the gift to her father.

"No, the man said you." Tess's smile widened. "Which means it's probably from Jackson."

The hint of romance clearly had Tess's attention.

Worry still lingered in her father's eyes, but he managed a weak smile. "I think I like this boy."

Tess nudged her grandfather. "It's romantic, isn't it?"

Avery reached for the attached note. Well, at least she didn't need to worry about what Tess thought about her dating again. She opened the card and started reading.

"Ring around the rosy,
Pocketful of posies,
Ashes, ashes.
They'll all fall down."

Avery's breath caught. She flipped the card over. No signature.

They'll all fall down . . .

"This isn't from Jackson."

She pulled open the bag and glanced inside. A sweet, lemony smell filled her senses.

"Mom, what's wrong?"

Avery's fingers shook. The bag dropped to the ground. Out tumbled a white magnolia.

Chapter 21

Jackson put his empty plate on a tray, then refilled his punch. Watching Avery dance with her father had offered a rare peek into the private life of the woman he was falling for. She'd found a way to take both the good and the bad that life had given to her and allow them to make her stronger. The threads of vulnerability that ran through her only made her more real . . . and made him want to be the one to protect her.

He had his own haunting memories to throw into the mix and, like Avery, knew what it meant to lose someone he loved. Something that gave him a place to connect and understand better where she came from.

Jackson turned back to the dance floor and searched for Avery. She and her father now stood across the room with Tess. A silver bag lay at her feet beside a white flower. She turned and the light hit her ashen face.

Something was wrong.

He put his cup down on a table and crossed the room in long, determined strides. "Avery?"

She looked up at him, eyes wide, and handed him a card.

"What is this?"

"Read it." Avery gripped Tess's hand. "It's him, Jackson. He was here."

"Ring around the rosy . . . Ashes, ashes . . . They'll all fall down."

He didn't have to ask who she was talking about. He knew exactly what she meant. But why? Why send a threatening message to a function where there were dozens of police officers and even the former captain himself?

"Where did it come from?"

"A man gave it to Tess. He knows who I am, Jackson. Knows about Tess, my family, but it's more than that. They'll all fall down. He isn't finished."

Jackson watched the color start to return to her cheeks again as determination settled in. She was right. They had to find this guy and find him quickly. The fact that he'd given the gift to Tess could have been a coincidence, but he didn't think so. And Avery was thinking the same thing, because she'd be looking at the situation both as a detective and a mother.

KATE'S FLOWER SHOP was imprinted on the envelope. Avery turned to her daughter. "Tess, this is extremely important. I need to know everything you can tell me about the man who gave this to you."

"I don't know . . . It was just like I told you. Some guy in a uniform came up to me, handed me the package, and said it was for Avery North. Then he left. I thought it was a surprise from Jackson."

Jackson stared at the flower on the floor. The edges were already beginning to wilt. "Did he leave through the front doors?"

"Yeah, I was standing over there by the food table eating one of these little quiches."

"I need you to tell me what he looked like, Tess."

"Mom, you're scaring me." She reached down to pick up the flower, but Avery pulled her back gently. She'd already have to eliminate finger-prints on the card, but that was okay. She was thinking like a police officer again. "Tess, we need to leave the flower where it is for now."

"It's just a flower."

"Just tell me what he looked like."

"I'll try." Tess let out a sharp breath. "He was an inch or two shorter than Grandpa. Dark brown hair, I think."

"Beard or mustache?"

She shook her head. "No."

"Did he wear a uniform or have a shirt with a logo?"

"I don't know."

"Think, Tess. Close your eyes and think."

Tess closed her eyes and wrinkled her nose. Music played in the background as the party went on around them. Everyone laughing, eating, drinking, with no idea what had happened. Avery ignored it all.

If he could get to Tess . . .

She opened her eyes. "I think he had some sort of logo of a flower on the front pocket. It happened so fast. He gave me the present and made me promise to give it to you."

"Good girl." Avery turned to her father. "Dad, keep Tess with you. I'll be back as soon as I can."

Avery struggled to catch her breath as Tess and her father walked away.

"She's safe for now, Avery, and you'll have plenty of time later to figure out how to keep her safe." Jackson followed her across the room. "For now, the clock is ticking and your priority needs to be to find this guy."

"This shouldn't have happened. Not in front of my daughter and friends and family."

But there weren't rules in this kind of game. And Jackson was right, the clock was ticking. There wasn't time to sit and wish it would simply all disappear.

A minute later she had her team assembled. "Carlos and Mitch, check the parking lot. He's got a head start, but maybe we'll get lucky. Look for a male, Caucasian, midtwenties, dark hair, no facial hair, wearing a shirt with a florist logo. I'm not ready to assume this wasn't our killer."

Mitch and Carlos double-timed toward the door. Avery turned to Tory.

"Tory, get ahold of the owner of Kate's Flower Shop and find out who ordered a single magnolia."

"What do you want me to do?" Jackson asked.

She grabbed a napkin from the nearest table, picked up the glittery bag along with the flower and card, and handed it to Jackson. The moment she let the situation become too personal, she'd lose her focus. "This isn't exactly an official crime scene, but if you could take it to forensics and see what you can find on it? Fingerprints, DNA trace evidence, anything."

"Consider it done."

She hesitated before following Mitch and Carlos to the parking lot. "Jackson . . . I'm sorry. This isn't exactly the evening I imagined."

"As long as you promise me a fourth date, I won't hold it against you."

Avery smiled, despite the seriousness of the moment. "I think I can arrange that."

Five minutes later, Jackson had already headed to the lab while Avery stood in the parking lot beside Mitch. Half a dozen streetlights lit the lot except one in the northwest corner that had burned out, leaving shadows along the back fence. A couple was leaving in their sports car, but no delivery van or signs of the man Tess described. Whoever had delivered the flower was long gone.

"Did you know that the magnolia flower isn't pollinated primarily by bees or butterflies, but instead beetles?"

"Beetles?" Avery looked up at Mitch. "You never cease to amaze me."

"My mother's always been into botany. Used to bore me to death as a child, but you never know when you might need a bit of trivia to lighten the mood."

She laughed, which is what she knew he was after. Something to break the tension in the air, hanging heavier than the humidity. Something to distract her from the reality that there was a killer out there who knew her family.

"It worked."

"You'll have to thank your mother for me." Her phone rang and she answered, praying for anything that would bring them one step closer to their killer. "What have you got, Tory?"

"The shop was closed, but I was able to track down the owner and get ahold of her. She's agreed to meet you at the shop. I'm sending the address."

"Tell her we're on our way. Mitch and I will take it from here."

Avery scanned the parking lot. There was nothing more to do here. A minute later she was driving toward the florist with Mitch.

Mitch tapped his fingers against the armrest. "Sorry you had to leave the party early. I know

196

you looked forward to this for a long time."

"My mother has been the one looking forward to this party, but as long as Daddy knows how proud we are of him, that's all that really matters."

"I think you succeeded."

She'd suggested to her father to let the party wind down naturally and not tell Mama unless they had to. No need for everyone's evening to be ruined. And if Mama asked, Daddy would simply tell her that an emergency had come up in the case Avery was working. Mama had been married to an officer of the law for forty years. Emergencies and late nights weren't exactly a surprise.

"I guess we both had to leave our dates."

"Fiancée," she reminded him.

"It has a nice ring, doesn't it? I asked Jenkins to drive Kayleigh home. She insisted she could get a cab, but with all that's happened tonight . . ."

Avery understood. It was hard not to worry about those they loved. "So what does she think about living with a homicide detective who takes on the world of crime on a daily basis?"

"Her uncle was a police officer in New York, so she's not coming into this completely unprepared."

"Still, it's one thing when you're investigating a murder. It's a different matter when you're the one being threatened."

"How are you?"

"Coping. I'm more worried about Tess . . . and what my mother's reaction is going to be when she finds out. I don't want to make this into something it's not, but I can't ignore the note and its implications."

She'd done everything she could to ensure Tess was safe. One thing Mama had always insisted on was the latest in home security. Depending on how things went over the weekend, school next week might be out of the question as well. While she had no intention of letting this man run their lives, neither was she going to ignore basic precautions.

Mitch broke the silence. "We're not going to let anything happen to you or Tess. Not that I wasn't determined to catch this guy before, but what he's done has made it more . . . more personal."

Avery pulled into a parking spot in front of the corner florist shop. "Then let's go get him."

There was a light on in the store despite the CLOSED sign in the window, and a bell jingled as she swung open the front door. The strong scent of flowers greeted them, along with shadows casting darkness on shelves full of knickknacks.

Avery introduced themselves to the owner, Kate Wright, who sat behind the counter, then gave a brief update on the man they were looking for.

"Sean made the delivery." She checked the log on the computer. "That was his last one for the evening. I still don't understand what the problem is, though. Is Sean in some sort of trouble?"

"No, it's the person who ordered the flower that we're looking for."

"Then you might be in luck. Normally, I don't remember the details around every specific order, but not too many people ask for a single magnolia to be delivered. The request stood out."

"What can you tell me about him?"

"Not much. The man came in yesterday and asked for it to be delivered at eight o'clock tonight at Captain Hunt's party."

"Any other specific instructions?"

"Not other than the fact that it was for . . ." She glanced at the order on the computer screen. "Avery North."

So Tess had just been a coincidence? But he knew who Avery was. Knew she was working on the case. Knew she was still working on the other Jane Doe case.

She would have to deal with implications later. "What about a description?"

"Nothing that stood out. Caucasian, wearing jeans and a T-shirt, baseball cap."

"Any camera footage we could look at?"

"I've got a couple security cameras I've been meaning to fix. Not too many people looking to steal a dozen roses, so it's never been much of a priority. I figure just having them helps ward off any would-be thieves."

"How did he pay?"

"Cash."

Figured.

"I just remembered something." The owner started digging through one of the drawers. "He filled out one of our store's frequent buyer forms that includes name and address."

Mitch leaned against the counter. "What would be the point of paying cash in order to remain anonymous and then fill out personal info?"

"That I don't know." The owner dug through the pile of cards. "Here it is. It's dated yesterday and signed . . . Michael Hunt."

Chapter 22

Jackson glanced at his watch, then quickened his steps down the narrow hall of the precinct toward Avery's office. Five till midnight. He shouldn't worry. Of all the people he knew, Avery was capable of taking care of herself. But even that realization couldn't stop him from driving across town just to make sure. Not when he'd called her cell phone a dozen times—with no answer. If she wasn't in her office, he was going to have to end up putting out a BOLO for her.

He rubbed the back of his neck and felt the

tension spreading. Overreacting wouldn't help, but the incident at tonight's party had everyone involved on edge. It was one thing to lead an investigation by following up on all the forensics, evidence, and a list of suspects. It was another thing when the killer tried to turn things into a game of cat and mouse.

Ahead, a yellow beam of light from Avery's office spilled into the darkened hallway that had been freshly mopped, leaving behind the strong scent of industrial cleaners.

Jackson wrinkled his nose at the odor and stopped in the doorway of her office. Relief swept through him. She sat behind her desk, surrounded by crime scene photographs, forensic reports, and an evidence box, so intent on what she was looking at that she didn't even notice his arrival.

He leaned against the wooden door frame, content to watch her work for the moment. She still wore the black dress from the party, complete with tiny diamond earrings dangling from her ears. She looked tired, but just as stunning as the moment he'd picked her up for the party. Relief mingled with the worry he'd felt over the past few hours, confirming that he was smitten. Funny. He'd once told his grandfather that he'd never get involved with a detective. Their job was simply too dangerous and time-consuming. But none of that seemed to matter right now.

Once, before he and Ellie married, she'd asked

him how he could work with dead people every day. While she'd always encouraged him, he knew she'd be the last one to show up in his autopsy room. He'd smiled and told her that they never talked back like the patients she saw on a weekly basis at their church's counseling center.

Ellie had been his first real relationship, and he'd loved her fiercely. But Ellie was gone. And while he wasn't looking for someone to replace her, he'd never stopped longing for someone to fill the emptiness she'd left.

Avery was managing to do just that. Somehow, she'd found a way to wrap herself around his heart—and at the same time change his mind about detectives. She understood his desire to fight for justice—no matter what the cost.

Which meant they both knew it was worth the risk and the long hours to track down killers. His motivation came from seeing young girls like Tala lying dead on his autopsy table.

The fluorescent lights overhead crackled, pulling Avery's attention toward the ceiling. Her gaze stopped on Jackson. "Hey. How long have you been standing there?"

"Not long. I tried calling your cell, but you never answered."

"I'm sorry." She shot him a sheepish grin and shrugged. "My phone . . . it's somewhere around here, more than likely with a dead battery."

"I was worried."

"I came here after we finished up at the florist, hoping that if I went through everything again, I might find something we'd missed. We've got to find this guy."

"We're going to."

She didn't look convinced. "He used my brother's name to sign some stupid frequent buyer form. Why would he do that?"

Jackson sat down on the empty seat across from her. Except for the cluttered desk, the rest of the room was immaculate. "He's toying with you, Avery. He's trying to get in your head, distract you, scare you, and lead you on some wild-goose chase. That's what serial killers do. They're psychopaths who would like nothing more than to take you down as well."

"I guess finding out who is in charge of the case wouldn't be hard."

Every lead they'd followed up on in the past five hours had seemed to focus on that very fact. The deliveryman, the prints on both the card filled out at the flower shop and the bag, and now Michael's signature . . .

The only thing they could do at this point was continue searching and pray he made a mistake. Which he would. And then they would catch him. Until then, they'd have to keep examining the evidence and trying to turn up new leads.

Avery leaned forward, allowing the dimmed light to catch the fatigue in her expression. Five days working on an intense—and personal—case wasn't just physically exhausting, it was emotionally draining as well. She needed a day off, but since he was sure she wouldn't go for that, at a minimum she needed a good night's sleep.

"You need to go home. You're exhausted."

She shot him a half smile. "So it shows?"

He had no intention of falling into that trap. "I'm not answering that question."

She looked away, her smile quickly fading. "Tell me what you would have me do. I can't ignore what happened tonight."

"But you also can't let him start leading this case. You're in charge of this investigation. You have to find a way to keep the lead."

She shook her head. "That's the problem. I'm not in charge. He chooses his victims. Determines their fate. Kills them in cold blood. I'm not in control of anything. Everywhere I look ends up being the wrong direction, which means all I've done is run around chasing a bunch of crazy red herrings. And to make it all worse, he's made it pretty clear that someone else is going to die."

She shook her head and drew in a deep breath. "Tess came too close to things tonight. What if the killer had been the one delivering the flower?"

"He wasn't."

"Still, it's not right for me to put my family and my child in danger. Which is why sometimes—

like today—I have to ask myself if it's worth it."

Her doubts took him by surprise, or maybe more accurately what struck him was the fact that she had the courage to verbalize them to him. Avery wasn't a quitter, he knew that, but neither was she the kind of person who would put her career above her family. It was a tough balance that many officers in her field struggled to find. And why many of those he knew had given up having a family for their career.

He tried to read her expression. "Maybe it's time to give this case to another team."

"No." A spark of determination was back in her eyes. "But I can't stand by and take any chances when it comes to Tess. I've had run-ins with criminals, threats against my life, but this . . . this was personal, Jackson. It's made me think about just how dangerous my job is, and no matter how much I love it, it's not worth losing someone else I love."

There it was—that irresistible mixture of competence, persistence, and smarts thrown together with a hint of vulnerability that made him want to wrap his arms around her and promise her everything was going to be okay. Except that wasn't something he could guarantee. "It is a risk."

"I don't think I ever told you that Ethan died in the line of duty. A car wreck in a high-speed chase in north Atlanta."

"No. You hadn't told me how he died."

"I don't talk about it much. I guess I figure most people around here know. Do you know how many times I planned to quit after his death? I even typed up a resignation letter and brought it to work."

"What stopped you?"

"A case I was working on at the time. A young girl had been found murdered in one of the neighborhood parks. She was nine years old. The same age as Tess at the time. Like this case, I remember thinking it could have been Tess. I could have lost her too. When we found the man who killed her, he had another girl in the back of his vehicle. She would have been dead in another hour. Knowing that she was going to live, seeing the joy in her mother's eyes, gave me what I needed to keep going. To do everything I can to save one more."

"We live in a fallen world. Death, hatred, jealousy, everything that motivates man . . . none of it was ever a part of God's plan."

She looked up and caught his gaze. "But when you see it day after day, it's easy to wonder if what you do really makes a difference."

"We make a difference to the ones we save."

"And the ones we don't?"

"Do you want my advice? At least for tonight?"

She smiled, but the fatigue was clear in her eyes. "I have a feeling you'll give it to me no matter what I say."

"I know this entire case has become personal, but you need to go home and get some sleep. You're exhausted. You'll be able to think clearer come morning. You're not going to be able to help anyone if you're not able to do your job."

"It is morning, if I'm not mistaken." She rubbed her eyes, then glanced at the mound of paperwork covering her desk. "But—"

"No buts." He stood up and moved to rest his hands against the back of the chair. One way or another he was going to get her out of here and home where she should be this time of night. "Where's Tess?"

"She's at my parents'. For tonight anyway."

"Good. That's where you should go."

"I'm not ready to move out of my house because of this guy, Jackson. I've got an alarm system and my Glock. I'll be fine."

"And don't forget Freddie the frog, a couple rats, and a few other animals that can protect you."

"Very funny."

She switched off the light on her desk, then reached for her purse hanging on the chair behind her. She might still be arguing, but at least she was moving.

"I just want you to be careful. This guy might be smart, but more than likely he's off balance, which makes for a dangerous combination."

"Is that your professional opinion?"

"I might spend a lot of time with dead people, but I've been around enough murder investigations to learn a thing or two."

For a moment he wished for a normal life. One where they didn't have killers breathing down their necks. Where the stakes weren't so high.

They'll all fall down.

More girls? Tess? Avery? They wouldn't know until they stopped him. Which meant they had to find him.

He grabbed his keys out of his pocket as they walked out the front door. "Let me drive you home."

"I've got my car."

Stubborn as always. "Then I'll follow you."

"Jackson—"

"Do it for me. I'll sleep better tonight if I know you're home safe."

"Okay."

He brushed his hand across her cheek. "Just promise me you'll be careful."

She took a step forward, nodded, then slipped her hand into his.

Chapter 23

Avery jerked into a sitting position in her bed, her heart pounding with a flood of adrenaline. Something had awakened her. Beads of sweat formed on her forehead and at the base of her neck. Her light capri pajamas felt sticky against her skin. Maybe it was nothing more than the frightening dreams she'd had all night, but she'd heard something.

She moved to the edge of the queen-size bed, waiting for her eyes to adjust to the darkness. Now that she was awake, the vivid scenes began to vanish. But not completely. The killer had chased her across the medieval courtyard surrounding a looming castle with dark clouds hovering overhead. He'd taunted her, playing a game of cat and mouse where she was no longer the hunter but the prey. She'd been forced to run through the tangled bodies of dead girls—girls she hadn't been able to save. And then, just before she woke up, she'd stopped where Tess's lifeless form lay sprawled out, sticky red blood pooling beneath her.

Avery gulped in a lungful of air. No. None of the images that had played through her head were true. Her dreams were nothing more than warped versions based on a slender thread of reality. Tess was fine. Sensing the elusive killer stalking her as she slept was nothing more than a nightmare—her mind playing tricks with her.

Her breathing began to slow. The last time she remembered waking up feeling panicked had been after Ethan's death. For weeks her dreams had been plagued with nightmares. Every night they would take her back to those final moments. Waiting up for him, the knock on the door, the two officers whose job it was to tell her he was dead. They had apologized and told her how sorry they were. Everyone had been sorry.

Tess had been her only motivation to get out of bed in the weeks and months that had followed. Then slowly, she'd begun to believe again that she could make a difference out on the streets and that Ethan would want her to do that. One day, the haunting dreams finally vanished. She had been free of them until tonight, when this case brought them back.

She flipped on the bedside light and reached for the Glock nestled beneath the extra pillow on the far side of the bed, grasping it tightly between her fingers. She might have allowed the tragic death of a Jane Doe to become too personal, but Tala's death had reminded her of the fragility of life and brought with it fresh concerns about Tess.

Avery wiped the back of her neck with her hand

and listened to the familiar sounds of the house. The hum of the air conditioner . . . the water heater clicking on in the bathroom . . . the squeak of the hamster's exercise wheel . . . the neighbor's yappy dog barking next door . . . The dreams had disturbed her, there was no denying that, but something else had awakened her. She was certain of it.

Someone was in the house.

She shoved the covers aside. The digital clock on the bedside table read 3:37. She wished it were full morning, even though she knew the accompanying sunlight wouldn't completely erase her unease.

They'll all fall down.

The words shot through her. She'd wanted to convince herself that the message scribbled on the card was not pointed at her, but instead was only a reminder that their killer wasn't finished with his death spree. But if that were true, it would also mean that her current fears were irrational and nothing more than her imagination. Whether or not the physical threat to her was real seemed secondary. He wanted to mess with her emotions, and he'd done exactly that.

But what if she was wrong? What if the words had been meant as a personal threat, with implications that they would one day meet face-to-face? She dropped her cell phone from the nightstand into her pocket. She had to be ready. If he had come after her, she would find him first.

Years of training automatically kicked in, helping to deaden the haunting fears the dreams brought with them. Avery started a systematic sweep of the house, turning on lights as she went. Room by room, searching the closets, behind doors, anywhere someone could potentially hide. She looked beneath the frilly pink ruffles of Tess's single bed and was reminded again of how grateful she was Tess was safe with her parents.

She intended to do everything she could to keep Tess away from any danger, both perceived and real.

Avery continued the search, swung open the bathroom door and flipped on the light. With her gun held level, she pulled back the shower curtain. The faucet dripped. Was that what she'd heard earlier?

No. She'd heard more than water pinging onto the porcelain tub. Avery drew in a slow breath and forced herself to focus while Jackson's words replayed in her mind. *He's toying with you. Trying to get in your head. Trying to distract you.*

That's why their killer had sent her the flower. And used her brother's signature. None of it would lead them to him. It would only lead her on the trail of a ghost. And keep her running in circles. Which was exactly what he wanted her to do.

Avery finished checking the second story.

Clear.

She made her way down the stairs to the ground floor, turning on lights that swallowed up the darkness. Jackson had done a sweep of the house when they'd arrived to ensure no one was hiding inside. It had been a futile attempt to reassure both of them that she was safe and to erase the visions of magnolia flowers with their sickly lemony scent. Instead, the haunting words had played over and over in her mind.

Ashes, ashes . . . they'll all fall down.

He was out there. Somewhere. A shiver ran down her spine, playing on her nerves, making her feel vulnerable. Who would be next?

Light from the streetlight streamed through a break in the curtains in the front window of the living room. Avery pulled back the soft ivory fabric, crumpling it in her fingers, and looked outside. Nothing about the quiet, tree-lined neighborhood looked out of the ordinary. No suspicious cars or people hanging around from her vantage point.

Avery squeezed her eyes shut for a moment. She had to have imagined whatever woke her up. Upstairs was clear. The windows were all locked. Nothing looked out of place. The front and back doors were still locked. Security alarm set. She opened the closet near the front door and rummaged through the coats hanging there that wouldn't be used until winter. Empty.

All that was left was the kitchen and basement.

Avery stepped into the kitchen. The refrigerator's motor clicked on. Avery tensed, hating the fact that every unexpected noise had her nerves set on edge. She caught movement out of her peripheral vision near the floorboards. She lowered her gun, aimed, and searched the shadows. Shards of blue glass were scattered across the brown tiles. She flipped on the light as Mrs. Whiskers—with her chocolate-brown and white fur—skittered across the tile floor toward the living room. Tiger, the cat, tensed on the counter, her gaze on the prize.

Avery lowered her weapon an inch and blew out a soft sigh of relief. She didn't have to be much of a detective to figure out what had happened. She'd left one of the cobalt tumblers on the counter last night. Tiger and Mrs. Whiskers—who had a tendency to escape her cage—had a tenuous relationship at best. Tiger had found her, taken chase, and knocked over a glass in the process.

Which only posed one problem besides the mess left behind. Like she'd told her sister, she might chase down murderers for a living, but she didn't deal with rodents. Tiger clambered down from the counter to the bar stool, still stalking Mrs. Whiskers. So what had awakened her was nothing more than a real game of cat and mouse. And it was up to her to catch Mrs.

Whiskers before Tiger did. Something that wasn't going to be easy.

But first, she needed to clean up the broken glass. She grabbed the broom, then paused. The hairs on the back of her neck bristled.

The door to the basement was half open.

Avoiding the scattered glass with her bare feet, she leaned the broom back against the wall. Holding the gun steady in front of her, she walked slowly across the kitchen toward the basement. She'd closed the door last night. She was sure of it. She always shut it as a part of her bedtime ritual.

Check the locks . . . turn on the alarm system . . . run the dishwasher . . . shut the basement door.

It shouldn't be open.

Avery moved forward slowly. The basement was the last place to look. But if someone were still in the house, she could have missed him if he'd slipped into the living room—

He grabbed her from behind.

Avery reacted instinctively. She thrust her elbow back as hard as she could, striking the intruder in the ribs. He groaned and took a step backward. Glass crunched beneath his shoes, but he didn't loosen his grip. Avery fought for control of her Glock. He squeezed her wrist, forcing her to loosen her grip on the weapon, then clasped his other hand over her mouth and nose. Her gun hit the floor as his hands tightened around her face and torso.

Avery fought for air while grasping for the ski mask he wore. She twisted her body and kneed him hard in the groin. He groaned and dropped to his knees, but instead of releasing her, he pulled her onto the hard tiles with him. She cried out at the impact. A shard of glass dug into her arm as he came at her again. Her forehead slammed into the flooring, and everything went dark.

Chapter 24

Jackson shouted Avery's name while Mitch pounded on the front door of her house. They'd watched the lights come on, one by one, from the front seat of his Honda parked in a neighbor's driveway nearby, but they had no idea what she was looking for.

A muffled cry from inside confirmed that whatever she'd found wasn't good.

The sound of splintering wood ripped through the quiet of the night as Mitch kicked in the door. Jackson let his eyes adjust to the light as he stepped through the threshold, the urgency to find her growing.

"Avery!"

He found her sprawled on the kitchen floor, still dressed in her pajamas, with blood running down her arm.

Glass crunched beneath his shoes as he bridged the distance between them. He squatted down beside her. "Avery? What happened?"

Her eyes opened and she looked up at him, seeming disoriented. "Someone . . . someone was in the house. He attacked me."

"Where did he go?" Mitch gripped his gun at his side.

"I don't know."

"Stay with her. I'll check the house." Mitch disappeared down the basement steps, while Jackson slowly helped Avery into a sitting position.

He knelt on the floor next to her and pulled her into his arms, lifting up a prayer of thanks that they'd gotten to her in time. But as much as he wanted to hold her, he had to find out how badly she was injured. He could feel her heart pounding against his chest. Her breathing came in rapid bursts.

He brushed back a strand of hair from her forehead, careful to avoid the goose egg developing, and caught the look of fear in her eyes. "Everything is going to be okay. You're safe. And if someone else is still in the house, Mitch will find them."

"I need to help."

She tried to pull herself up, but he stopped her. "You're not going anywhere. Not until I find out where you're hurt."

She reached up and pressed her hands on either side of her head. Blood ran down her forearm, forming a long jagged trail before dripping onto the floor. "He knocked me around a bit, but I'm okay."

"You don't look okay. Your arm is bleeding, and you've got a lump on your head. Where else are you hurt?"

"I don't know."

Jackson took her wrists carefully and pulled her against him. "What did he do to you, Avery?"

"Grabbed me from behind and left me with a few bad bruises."

"You must have hit the tile when you fell. Stay here for a moment."

Thankfully, she didn't argue as Jackson got up, pulled open a couple of drawers, and found a dishtowel. He soaked it in warm water from the faucet and wrung it out before carrying her to one of the chairs in the dining room, making sure she didn't step on the glass in her bare feet.

Jackson held up her arm to see where the blood was coming from. He pulled out a shard of glass an inch square. "You're lucky. You'll probably need stitches, but this piece could have done some serious damage."

Avery winced as he set the glass on the table

and wiped away the blood from her arm. "You never told me what you're doing here."

"Rescuing you."

"What did you and Mitch do? Spend the night in my front yard?"

"I talked to Mitch, and we both decided that while you might not have wanted to think the card was a threat toward you personally, we weren't willing to take any chances. So we grabbed some junk food and caffeine and hunkered down for the night."

"I suppose I could have offered my couch and a couple sleeping bags."

"We agreed that you might argue over the fact that you needed protection."

"I can't imagine why you would think that."

"I can." Jackson pressed the cloth against her arm, still trying to stop the bleeding. "Besides, I would have shown up this morning anyway. That was a promise I made to your father. He asked me to keep an eye on you and make sure you're okay while he looked out for Tess."

Avery rested her arm against the oak table and sighed. "So what, in the end it's easier to ask forgiveness than get permission?"

"Pretty much." He pulled out his cell phone. "I'll answer all your questions later, but for now, I'm calling an ambulance."

"I don't need to go to the hospital, Jackson."

He caught her gaze and shook his head. "Like

you didn't need the two of us standing guard tonight?"

She reached out and traced her finger along the back of his hand. "I'm sorry. I hate feeling vulnerable, and tonight . . . you were right. He got into my head."

"You have every right to feel the way you do. That's why we're here."

He laced her fingers between his own and, as soon as the 911 operator answered, gave instructions for where to send the ambulance and police backup. It was going to be a long time before he was willing to let her out of his sight.

Mitch came back into the kitchen. "Whoever it was is gone, but he left a huge mess downstairs."

Avery leaned into Jackson's chest, her body language matching the fatigue in her eyes. "Can you tell how he got in?"

"The alarm didn't go off, so we can assume that he found a way to disarm the system."

Jackson wrapped his arms around Avery, careful to avoid the gash on her arm that had finally stopped bleeding. "How would he do that?"

"We've seen it before. Professional thieves gain access to the schematics of particular security alarm systems, either via the internet or an employee of the security company. His entry point was one of the windows in the basement.

doing."

"So much for my high-tech alarm system."

Mitch leaned against one of the bar stools. "Did you get a good look at him?"

"No. He grabbed me from behind, and I was never able to see his face because it was covered with a ski mask. I do know that he was taller than me by several inches. Stocky and solidly built."

"I guess that's a starting point. We'll go through the house and see if we can come up with something else, but this wasn't some low-life thug from off the street. We'll be lucky if we come up with a fingerprint."

Avery checked the jagged gash on her arm. "I want to look downstairs. Clearly he was after something."

While she might be right, Jackson wasn't convinced she needed to do anything but wait for the ambulance. "You can do that later. Your house is secure for now, which means any clues he left behind will be here when you get back."

She shot him a weak smile. "I'm okay. Really. I need to do this. The quicker we can find out who broke in, the further ahead we'll be."

Jackson found himself relenting. "You have until the ambulance arrives, okay?"

"Okay, boss."

Jackson grabbed a pair of flip-flops for her from beside the back door, then helped her downstairs with Mitch following behind. While he hadn't found any other significant injuries, there was a good chance she had a concussion, and that had him worried. Maybe he was being overprotective, but the last thing she needed was to lose her balance on the narrow staircase.

Downstairs, she stopped in front of the window where glass lay shattered across the top of the desk. The burglar's point of entry. Photos had been rummaged through, the crime board marked through with a black marker, and her painting dumped onto the floor.

"Avery?" He watched while she examined the damage without touching anything. "You okay?"

"For the moment. I'll have to deal with my emotions later. For now, we need to figure out why he was here and what he took."

Mitch stood in the corner of the room, hands clenched at his sides and a scowl written across his face. It was clear he didn't appreciate anyone messing with his partner.

Jackson moved to stand beside her. "Tell me what you notice."

"I had three files sitting on the upper left-hand corner of my desk. All three are missing."

"Good. That gives us a place to start. What were the cases?"

"The first one was my notes from our current investigation."

"And the second file?"

"It was related to the Browning case." Her leg started shaking.

Jackson rolled the black office chair toward her. "Why don't you sit down?"

Instead of arguing like he expected, Avery sank into the office chair. "Until about a month ago, it was classified as a cold case. Sarah Browning was murdered in her bedroom five years ago, and even though most of the evidence pointed to her husband, the prosecutor was never able to get a conviction. I pulled out my personal notes from the case a few days ago because some new evidence surfaced recently. Mr. Browning is going to be tried for the murder of his wife, and I was going to be a witness for the prosecution."

"And the third file?"

Avery heard Jackson's question and tried to force her mind to focus. To bring order to the chaos surrounding her so she could make sense of what she had found. But nothing added up. Her head hurt, her ears were ringing, and the cut on her arm ached along with every muscle in her body. But as awful as she felt, she wasn't ready to stop yet. "Michael's case."

"Anything significant?" Jackson asked.

Avery rubbed the back of her neck. "I was following a new lead regarding a witness. He was named in one of the reports, but I never found any record of a follow-up or mention of his name in any of the other reports. His name was . . . Ben. Ben Jacobs."

"Did you tell anyone about this Jacobs?"

She tried to answer Mitch's question, but thinking hurt. "Besides my father, I made a few phone calls trying to track him down. But it's no secret that I've been investigating Michael's death."

"Did you find Jacobs?"

"Not yet, but I do know that he's been in and out of prison, with no evident connection that I've been able to find to Michael's death or his undercover role. I started putting out some feelers. I planned to follow up on any information I could get, which so far isn't much. Which leads us back to our current case. It's the only option that makes sense." She caught the concern in Jackson's eyes while she spoke. "For some reason, he went upstairs, encountered me in the kitchen. If the two of you hadn't shown up . . ."

No. She wouldn't think about what could have happened if the two of them hadn't arrived when they did.

Sirens loomed in the distance.

Jackson reached for her hand. "You're not going to argue, are you?"

Avery shot him a half smile that managed to only make her head hurt worse. "Between you and Mitch, I don't think I have a choice."

Chapter 25

After a thorough exam by the doctor, Jackson drove Avery back home from the hospital, her arm stitched up and thankfully no signs of a concussion. The doctor had suggested she rest the next few days. Right. She'd find time to rest after she found out why someone had broken into her house and attacked her. All she needed now was a hot shower, clean clothes, and she'd be as good as new. Or at least pretty close to it.

Thirty minutes later, she'd showered, dressed, and fed the animals. Someone had already swept and mopped the kitchen floor. There was no sign of Mrs. Whiskers, but Tiger was on her perch, looking content. Too content. All Avery could do was hope it wasn't too late for the furry rodent.

Mitch had stayed to work with the police going over the crime scene, and had just finished rehanging the door they'd kicked in when she stepped back into the living room. Jackson was opening a bag of fast food at the table.

"Find anything?"

Mitch dropped the screwdriver he was holding back into the toolbox. "The CSU team found a couple of things, including traces of blood on the window where we believe the man cut himself.

Hopefully we can find something that will allow us to catch him. Carlos and Tory were here, but returned to the precinct to continue follow-up on leads from last night."

"I appreciate it. Everything."

"I know." He smiled, but the normal banter she was used to was missing. This morning's incident had them all feeling subdued and out of control. "Feel better?"

The hot shower and pain pills had helped, but even they couldn't erase the lingering fear. "Physically, yes, but I can't shake the feeling of knowing someone was inside my house."

"Unfortunately the emotional trauma of situations like this often lasts longer than the physical scars." Jackson held up some orange juice. "But hopefully this will help. I picked up some breakfast while you were getting ready. Hungry?"

"Yeah. Actually I am." That had to be a good sign. And there was no denying she was glad he was here. "Thank you for being here for me. Both of you. If you hadn't shown up when you did . . ."

"We did show up, so you don't have to wonder about what-ifs." Mitch nodded toward the table. "Go on and eat, and I'll join you as soon as I'm finished up here."

Avery's hands shook as she pulled down three plates from the cupboards. She set them down on the counter, then drew her hands back, hoping Jackson wouldn't notice, but he did.

"Maybe you should go lie down."

"The doctor said I'll be fine."

He rested his hands against her shoulders and turned her toward him. "The doctor also said that you should rest."

"I will."

"When?"

"When all of this is over."

"I'm not sure that's soon enough."

"It's going to have to be."

She thought he was going to argue with her. Instead, he pulled her closer and let his lips meet hers. All the tangled emotions of the past few days seemed to come into focus as she responded to his kiss. Fear of commitment, of neglecting someone, of not being able to be enough to everyone—even the reality that someone had broken into her house—none of it seemed to matter at the moment. All that mattered was that Jackson had been there when she needed him, she was safe, and they were together.

The cell phone vibrated in Avery's pocket, then rang. She pulled slowly away from Jackson's kiss and embrace, wishing she could forget the rest of the world for the moment.

"I'm sorry." She glanced at the caller ID. "It's Tess."

"It's okay."

Avery answered the call, then leaned back against the counter, Jackson's arm still protectively

227

around her waist. Between him, Mitch, and her father, whoever had broken into her house better watch themselves. "Tess. Morning, sweetie."

"I just wanted to make sure you were okay. How did you sleep?"

She couldn't mention the break-in. Not yet, anyway. Tess—and her mother—would only worry. "A few bad dreams, but I'm okay."

"How are the pets?"

Avery hesitated while Jackson moved to finish setting the table and laying out breakfast.

"Mrs. Whiskers is loose."

"Loose?"

"I'm trying to find her." Avery shivered. With her luck, she'd find her snooping in her cupboards or crawling across her pillow one morning.

"She's fast, Mom. You remember when Ricky got out of the cage."

"Trust me, I remember."

Tess had been heartbroken. The only thing they'd found was his tail, but they'd still held a memorial service.

"Listen, sweetie, I want you to stay at Grandma and Papa's for now, but how about we plan on dinner? I'll bring some sweet and sour chicken takeout."

"My favorite."

"I know." She'd have to explain her injuries, not only to Tess but to her parents as well.

Something that would be easier done in person.

"You'll feed the animals?"

"Already done."

"Love you, Mom."

"Love you too, baby."

Avery hung up and dropped the cell phone onto the counter, her hand still shaking. "Looks as if I have a mouse to catch . . . that is, if Tiger hasn't already gotten her."

Jackson was shoving his phone into his back pocket. "I just got a call. A match to the partial print off the card you received last night."

He had her attention now. "Who is it?"

"His name is Landon Rice."

"What do we know about him?"

"He's got a few priors, including burglary and assault, though nothing as serious as murder. But he's certainly been on the wrong side of the law more than once."

Until they brought him in and questioned him, everything was simply speculation, but that didn't stop the scenarios from running through her mind. "So either he's our murderer or our murderer had him order the flowers since cash would be untraceable and online he'd have to use a credit card."

"I don't know, but they've put a BOLO out on him."

"Good. I think I'd rather catch Rice than Mrs. Whiskers."

Jackson laughed as he finished distributing the food. She watched him, clearly comfortable in the kitchen. They needed time to discover what was happening between them, but for now, she was content to let things continue to develop slowly.

He threw the empty fast-food bag in the trash under the kitchen sink, then turned back to her. "I got the feeling the last time I was here that you're not as fond of all the pets as Tess is."

"It's only the rodent variety I try to avoid. I was bitten by a rat as a child and haven't been able to get over those evil sharp front teeth."

"Evil?"

"Yes, evil. But I love my daughter and share her love for animals—for the most part."

He took a step toward her, his gaze locked on to hers. "You're a great mother, you know."

"I try." She felt her cheeks blush as she sat down at the table, breathing in the scent of sausage, pancakes, biscuits, hash browns—along with a hint of enchantment. She could get used to being spoiled.

Her stomach growled. When was the last time she'd had a bite of greasy sausage? "I normally eat muesli and yogurt for breakfast, so you certainly win brownie points for this."

"Good, because you need to keep up your strength, and I don't think muesli is going to cut it today. We've got a killer and a thief to catch."

"And a mouse."

She tried not to watch him or notice the fact that he was watching her. Today he was dressed more casually, in khaki shorts and a black T-shirt, rumpled from his stint in the car. There was a hint of a shadow across his jawline and his eyes seemed a richer shade of chocolate.

At the table, he offered a prayer of thanks for the food before they started eating. It almost scared her how natural it felt to be with him. How comfortable she felt to state her feelings, questions, or even express doubts about her life.

He took a bite of his eggs. "I think you need to reconsider going back to bed. You look tired."

"Before the break-in, I didn't sleep well thanks to a few restless dreams after I finally fell asleep."

"Nightmares?"

"Yeah." She had to stop letting this guy get to her.

Mitch entered the dining room and sat down in front of his plate. "Door is hung, and while it might have a few extra dings and scrapes, I'd say it's as good as new."

"I appreciate it, Mitch." Avery bit into the sausage biscuit. She really did appreciate all he'd done, but that didn't erase the fact that it was still another reminder of how, if someone wanted to get into her house, they could.

"That's my phone again." Avery grabbed the phone from her back pocket. Number unknown.

"Hello?"

Avery worked to make out the garbled sounds on the other side of the line. Voices whispered in the background. She couldn't make out any of the words.

The connection went dead.

"Everything okay?"

"I don't know. There was a bunch of noise in the background before the call got cut off."

Mitch took his empty plate to the sink, then turned around and leaned against the counter. "I don't like this, Avery. If it was meant to be another threat—"

"I didn't hear anything threatening." She wanted to brush off their fears—along with her own. "It was probably just a wrong number."

Mitch shook his head. "I don't buy that."

"Me either," Jackson added.

She tried calling the number. No answer.

"You need to get a trace on the caller."

"I'm calling Tory now." Avery dialed the office next and waited until Tory picked up. "Tory, I need you to contact the network operations center and trace a number that just came through on my cell phone. I need a name and address."

Ten minutes later, Tory called back with the information. "The phone is registered to a Mrs. Jade Chu. You might have talked to her while canvassing the neighborhood, because she lives about two blocks from the Sourns."

Avery pulled out her notes from the canvassing. "I remember that house. Mitch and I spoke to a young Vietnamese woman and a little boy. We're going to need a translator."

"I'm ready to go."

"I'll pick you up at the station in fifteen minutes."

Avery ignored the concerned looks as she grabbed her bag off the back of the kitchen chair, but this time her bodyguards were going to have to go along with her plan. Apparently she'd been right about thinking Malaya knew something. And it was time to find out exactly what it was.

Chapter 26

Mason felt the muscles in his chest groan as he turned into the parking lot on the west side of the warehouse, wishing—not for the first time—that his beat-up pickup truck had power steering. At thirty-three, he was already feeling too old for the backbreaking job of manually lifting boxes onto pallets, then stacking them onto trailers that would be shipped across the country. All this while trying to keep up with a half-dozen college-aged kids for a measly ten bucks an hour. But he couldn't complain too much. If everything went as planned, he was about to be promoted.

Inside the open warehouse, he found Owen Jefferson already at work at his desk in the back corner, sweat dripping down his bald head and onto the sides of his neck. The overhead fans did little to alleviate the heavy heat in the warehouse. Mason had never seen Owen lift more than a pile of papers, but the man clearly worked out somewhere.

Mason had received extensive profiles on Owen the first day of work. Ex-military, with combat experience. Two ex-wives and hefty alimony payments. After a few years working security, he now managed a distribution center of imported furniture and knickknacks from Asia.

Whatever Mason might think about the man's personal life, Owen was his way in. And with word from his informant that the timeline had suddenly been pushed up, it was going to take every trick Mason knew to get there. Which was why he'd left Gavin lying on the floor of his apartment in a pile of vomit.

Owen punched off his cell phone and dropped it onto his desk. He frowned at Mason. "You're early."

"You never know how traffic is going to be." Mason poured himself a drink from the water cooler and took a sip, wondering what Owen knew. "Something wrong?"

"Just got a call from Gavin's girlfriend."

"Gavin?" Mason furrowed his brow and pretended to try to place the man.

"Short, stocky, curly red hair. He was supposed to be working today's second shift."

"Oh, yeah. I've spoken to him a time or two. Something wrong with him?"

"He's not coming in today."

Mason took another sip of the cold water. "He sick or something?"

"Something. Girlfriend found the door open to his apartment, went in to investigate, and found him unconscious."

Mason tossed the empty cup into the trash. He must have just missed her. "Seriously?"

"Crazy, isn't it? Ambulance took him to the hospital about an hour or so ago. She said something about food poisoning."

That familiar wave of guilt swept over him. Some of his aunt's preaching still got to him every now and then. *Love your neighbor as yourself. Turn the other cheek.* How did that fit in with all the lies he'd told in the past two years, or the bodily harm he'd inflicted? He was convinced there was a special place in hell reserved for people like him. Unless the good he managed to pull off could make up for everything else.

Owen started punching something into his computer.

Mason weighed his words. "Listen, Finn said you might have some extra work. If you need someone to work Gavin's shift, I could really use the money."

Owen stopped and looked at him hard. This wasn't a man Mason would want to meet in a dark alley, and he had his own experience with hand-to-hand combat. But as long as he played it cool, he could definitely win at mental games.

Owen leaned back and crossed his arms, looking as if he were sizing him up. "We don't normally let our workers take double shifts. I don't like being responsible for my men collapsing on the job."

"I can do it."

"You do pretty well keeping up with the college-age boys you work alongside, but that's for one shift."

The comment hit low, but Mason ignored it.

"Finn told me what you did for him. Saving his life."

"It was nothing really."

"Don't be so modest. He said you took out a cop for him. That's no small feat."

"It seemed to be the right thing to do at the time, and he did get me this job. You know how it is with debt and ex-wives. Can't sit around doing nothing for too long."

Owen laughed. "He also said you're a user."

"Just on the side. You know my record. Never late for work. Always get everything loaded on time."

"Oh, I know that and more. I did a background check on you."

Mason shifted. "I thought the background check was required."

"It is, but I did a bit of extra research on my own."

Mason felt his pulse increase.

Play it cool, man. If Owen had found a hole in his story, Mason would already be gone by now.

"And?"

"You weren't kidding about the debt."

"Just a few . . . gambling issues."

"Finn did talk to me about you. Told me you're looking to make some extra cash on the side."

"Yeah."

"I might have a job if you're interested."

"I am." Mason slowed his breathing. "What's the job?"

"It's worth five grand for a couple days' work."

"More than I make in two months." Mason leaned forward. "So I assume I wouldn't be driving pillow cushions and shag rugs."

"Oh, but you would be."

Mason shook his head. "I'm not a fool. If I take the risk, I at least want to know what I'm getting into. Drug smuggling? Cigarettes with fraudulent tax stamps?"

Owen shifted his gaze toward the back of the warehouse and hesitated. "Weapons."

"Weapons?" Mason furrowed his brow, making sure Owen didn't catch the hint of satisfaction in his eyes.

"With Gavin out, I need a fourth man to drive one of our store trucks from here to Houston. And I need that someone today."

Trafficking weapons across state lines would mean the FBI getting involved. This was no small family business.

"It's the tip of the iceberg. A couple dozen guns every month. Guaranteed extra income for those of us involved."

"Where do they come from?"

"Mainly from China and India. It's easier than you think, and as far as I'm concerned, the demand far outweighs the risks. Did you know that there are craftsmen living in local villages who can clone assault rifles? Within days, they ship them into the country. Guns with no serial numbers and no way to trace them. It's unbelievable how easy it is. From here we send them across the country, to the UK, and of course, Mexico."

"If I get caught, I could get into a lot of trouble for this."

"Don't get caught."

"How are they shipped?"

"Sourn Imports is a legitimate business, remember. So they are shipped inside the pillow cushions and shag rugs. Sometimes, they're broken down into parts and concealed to be sent internationally."

"How do you know I won't simply go to the police with the information you've just given me?"

"You think I'm stupid enough to hire people off the street?"

"No. That's why I'm asking."

"I trust Finn's recommendations, and my background checks are thorough. I happen to know a man by the name of Veno who you owe seventeen thousand to in gambling debts. And I know you're already two months late. Veno and I go way back, and I know how he works. If you don't pay up, he won't kill you, but he'll hunt you down and start breaking your bones, one by one."

Mason swallowed hard. "Then you understand why I need this job and why I'm willing to take on a shady deal or two for some extra cash. When does the shipment need to go out?"

"Later this afternoon."

"Can I see the goods?"

Owen hesitated briefly, then nodded for him to follow him across the back of the warehouse to a locked door Mason had noticed his first day on the job. The older man opened the door with a key from his pocket, then shut and locked it behind him after they entered. The room was large, at least twenty by twenty, and filled with imported items that looked ready to go into the storefront.

Owen pulled open two wooden chests along the wall. Mason eyed the cache of weapons ready. Five or six shotguns, two dozen handguns, three boxes of M-16 rifles, plus ammunition. And that was just for starters.

"Worth at least two million dollars on the street," Owen bragged.

All illegal and untraceable. Mason couldn't help but smile. All his hard work was finally paying off. "Does Mr. Sourn know you're using his warehouse to launder weapons?"

Owen's laugh was back. "Don't worry about your employer."

Mason shifted his stance as Owen shut the containers.

"You're sure you can do this?"

"Like I said, I need the money. Five thousand will go a long way to get Veno off my back, not to mention my ex-wife. I'm more afraid of her than Veno at this point."

"Then we have a deal. You drive your truck to Houston, and I'll help you keep Veno—and your ex-wife—off your back."

Chapter 27

Avery turned into the winding streets of the Chu's pricey neighborhood with Tory beside her in the passenger seat and winced at the movement of her arm as it pulled against the stitches. The doctor had warned her that she'd be sore for the next few days, but also promised that once her arm healed and her headache vanished, she'd be as good as new. A diagnosis that was going to have to be enough for now. Because she wasn't going to step away until she had answers.

She pulled alongside the curb in front of the Chu house, but didn't turn off the engine.

Tory turned to Avery and caught her gaze. "You okay?"

Avery concentrated on the steady blast of cool air from the air conditioner before answering, knowing Tory must have caught the fatigue still lingering in her eyes. Despite the continual roadblocks her team faced in this case—now complicated further with this morning's attack—she nodded. She could do this.

"My head hurts and my arm is still sore, but other than that, I'm fine."

"You're sure?"

Avery shut off the engine and pulled out the keys. "If I'm not feeling better by the end of the day, I promise to rest tomorrow."

"Okay, but I can still call Mitch or Carlos and have them track down this lead with me."

"I appreciate the offer, but let's do this."

Avery glanced behind her as she and Tory exited the car and headed up the drive toward the Chu's brick and stone exterior house. Her latest shadow parked in front of the neighboring house, compliments of the captain. She'd expected Mitch and Jackson to insist on continuing their roles as bodyguards, but apparently they weren't the only ones who believed she needed extra protection. Now it had become official.

She could talk to the captain later about the necessity of spending department resources on her, but if she were perfectly honest, last night's break-in had her flustered as well. And until they could confirm who had broken in and what his connection was, being cautious might not be such a bad idea.

An Asian woman answered the door—thirty-something, thin, and well dressed in a skirt and pleated blouse. But Avery didn't miss the frazzled, almost frantic edge to her appearance, as if she were in a hurry to get somewhere.

Avery held up her badge and introduced them. "Mrs. Chu?"

"Yes? I . . . is there a problem?" Mrs. Chu

reached up to smooth her short, dark hair, her gaze darting behind Avery.

"We're not sure. I received a call about forty minutes ago, and we were able to trace it back to your phone."

She shook her head. "You must have made a mistake. I haven't made any calls this morning."

"Does someone else in the house have access to your phone?"

"No . . . I always keep my phone with me." Mrs. Chu turned and spoke to someone inside the house in Vietnamese.

The little boy who had answered the door on Thursday appeared a moment later with a large bag. Mrs. Chu dug through the contents. "I don't understand. It's not here."

"Mrs. Chu, I was here two days ago and spoke to a young woman. Perhaps she used your phone. I gave her my card and asked her to call if she thought of anything else. She said her name was Malaya."

"You spoke to Malaya?" A shadow crossed the woman's features. "I'm sorry, but she isn't here. It's just my son and I."

"Mrs. Chu, we can't emphasize enough how urgent it is that we speak to her, especially if she was the one who tried to contact me this morning." Avery's voice softened as she took a step forward and attempted to connect with the woman. "If we could come in and speak with you for a few minutes, you might be able to help us."

The woman clutched the purse against her chest. "I don't know."

"If it was Malaya who called, she might have information on a murder we are investigating," Avery continued. "She's not in any kind of trouble. We simply need to ask her some questions. Please, Mrs. Chu. This is extremely important."

This time, clearly, it was fear that flickered in the woman's eyes. "I don't think that would be a good idea."

"Then just answer this, please. Do you know where Malaya is?"

"No, she . . . she's gone."

The little boy, Teo, pressed in against his mother. "You're the police who came here yesterday."

Avery knelt down so she could talk to him at eye level. "Yes, I am, and we are looking for your friend, Malaya. Do you know where she is?"

All traces of the boy's smile vanished as he shook his head. He looked up at his mother. "No, but I know she wanted to talk to you."

"Teo, I don't want—"

"How do you know she wanted to talk to me?" Avery jumped in before his mother had a chance to stop him.

The boy dropped his gaze.

"It's okay, Teo. Malaya might be in trouble,

which means that it is very important that you tell me what happened."

Teo pressed his lips together tightly for a moment before speaking. "It . . . it was our secret. I am teaching her English and how to use the phone—"

"Teo." Mrs. Chu turned back to Avery. "Maybe if you came back later, she would be able to speak to you."

Teo shook his head. "What if she doesn't come back? What if the man took her?"

Avery's stomach cinched. Another young Vietnamese girl was missing. It fit a pattern. The pattern of a serial killer. At least two girls were dead, and if their killer had taken Malaya, the chance of finding her alive was diminishing with every minute that passed. There was no time for search warrants or excuses. They were going to have to get Mrs. Chu to realize the importance of her cooperation.

"Mrs. Chu, I need you to understand that this is a murder investigation. If you know something and withhold that evidence, then you also need to realize that you could be prosecuted. And if that isn't enough to convince you to help us, if someone has taken Malaya, then there is a very good chance that her life is in danger."

"I'm sorry. I told you the truth when I said that I don't know where she is."

"Mrs. Chu, let us come in and talk to you.

Please. I need to know everything that happened."

Tory turned to Avery. "Can I try?"

Avery nodded. Her head pounded, and while Tory spoke to the woman in the clipped sounds of Vietnamese, Avery tried not to imagine the worst-case scenario.

Finally the woman nodded, then turned to her son. "Teo, there are some cookies in the kitchen cupboard behind the peanut butter. Why don't you get three or four, then go color in your room."

"But I—"

"Now, Teo."

Tory turned to Avery while Mrs. Chu tended to her son. "She's scared, but she does know something. I'm not sure if it is related to Malaya disappearing, but something is going on."

A minute later they were sitting in the living room, decorated primarily in reds and yellows with heavy teakwood furniture. "Thank you for letting us in and talking with us."

"I don't want to be responsible for something happening to Malaya."

"What do you think happened?"

"I don't know. I . . . I should have called the police, but I didn't know what to do."

"Just tell us what happened, Mrs. Chu. Did someone take her?"

"I honestly don't know. On Saturdays, Malaya always has breakfast ready between eight and eight thirty, but this morning, when I came downstairs to get my coffee, she wasn't here."

"And that's unusual?"

"Yes. Because I could tell she'd been up for a while. The coffee was brewing in the pot like always, but breakfast wasn't made. On Saturdays, she sometimes fixes an American breakfast like pancakes—something I taught her how to make—but typically it's more traditional, like rice porridge or noodles."

"And today?" Avery probed.

"Today, when I came downstairs, like I said, I couldn't find her. Teo had asked for pancakes, so there was a box of the mix on the counter."

Avery looked toward the gourmet kitchen that opened up to the living room. A box of Aunt Jemima pancake mix sat on the black granite counter beside a bowl and a couple of measuring cups. "Tell me what happened next."

"I heard a crash outside. I told Teo to stay in the house, then I went to see what had happened. I thought maybe the trash can had rolled into the street and someone had hit it. I forgot to bring it in last night."

"And when you got out there?"

"The trash can was out by the street, tipped over on its side, but there was no sign of Malaya . . ."

Avery frowned. "People don't simply vanish."

Either Malaya left on her own . . . or someone had taken her.

247

"I spent thirty minutes walking up and down the street. I couldn't find her."

"Did you see anything? A strange car, or someone walking down the street?"

Mrs. Chu closed her eyes for a moment. "There was a car I didn't recognize when I went outside, but that's not unusual."

"Do you remember what it looked like?"

"It had . . . dark, tinted windows. That's why I noticed it." She shook her head. "Besides that, I don't remember."

"Why didn't you call the police?"

Mrs. Chu dropped her gaze and started picking at one of her dark red fingernails that matched the pleated blouse. The woman was afraid.

"Mrs. Chu?" Avery prompted.

"You won't understand."

"I can try."

"My husband is gone on a business trip. If he finds out that she has run away . . . he will be very upset."

"Why?" Avery asked.

"Having full-time help isn't cheap. And finding someone isn't easy."

"So you haven't told your husband Malaya is missing?"

"No."

"And you believe she ran away?"

"I don't know."

"Where would she go? Does she have friends or family nearby?"

"No family, but friends . . . yes. Of course she has friends."

"Can you give me their names?"

"Maybe." She shook her head. "I don't know."

Avery handed her a business card with her numbers on it. "I need you to try and get me their contact information. In the meantime, why do you think she might have run away?"

"I don't know. I thought . . ." She sounded lost. Flustered. "I thought she was happy."

Avery leaned forward on the contemporary-styled black sofa. "Do you have a photo of Malaya?"

"I think so . . . at Teo's birthday party last month." Her hands shook as she reached for a box sitting on the bottom shelf of the coffee table. "He adores her and asked for her to come."

"How old is Teo?"

"He just turned six."

"He said that someone took her. Why did he say that?"

"He doesn't think she would leave without saying good-bye, so to him I guess it makes sense that someone took her." She opened the box and began flipping through photos. "I haven't had time to organize them. I'm sorry . . . Here."

Mrs. Chu handed the four-by-six photo to Tory, who studied it for a moment, then passed it on to Avery. Malaya stood beside Teo, his arms wrapped around her neck. Thin face, soft features . . . the girl was beautiful.

"So, Malaya isn't family?" Tory continued.

"No . . . I needed some extra help at home, so when my husband heard about a chance where we could get a girl who could work for us, we decided to hire her. I also didn't want Teo to lose his Vietnamese. She speaks to him and takes care of him when I'm out. I spend a lot of time volunteering and doing fund-raising for charity."

"Tell me more about Malaya. How long has she been working for you?"

Mrs. Chu gripped the yellow tassels of the throw pillow she'd pulled into her lap. "For about three months."

"Does she have papers allowing her to work in the country?"

"Yes, of course. My husband took care of everything."

"We will need to see her INS documentation and talk to your husband as well."

"He's on a flight back to Atlanta later this evening. He'll be able to provide you with what you need."

"I assume she lives here with you."

"Yes."

"Do you mind if we look at her room before we leave?"

"I . . ." Mrs. Chu glanced toward the staircase. "Like I said, my husband will be able to provide you with what you need when he returns."

Avery bit back a heated response. If they needed to, she'd come back with a search warrant. "I just have one last question before we go, Mrs. Chu. Does Malaya have a tattoo?"

"Yes, on her shoulder. Some kind of white flower."

A magnolia.

Avery stood and started for the door beside Tory. "If we have further questions, we will be in touch with you. And in the meantime, I would file a missing persons report with the police station."

A minute later, Avery and Tory stepped out of the air-conditioning and back into the humid Georgia air. "So what do you think?"

"That she's more concerned about how her husband will react than the well-being of a young girl."

Avery sensed Tory was right, there was an ugly picture beginning to emerge. "She doesn't want us to look at Malaya's room or documents, doesn't have contact info for any of her friends, no English or phone use . . ."

"Just like Tala. Which means we're probably looking at more than a serial killer case."

Avery nodded. "Girls brought into the country illegally and forced to work."

Long hours. Little or no pay. She wanted to believe that such scenarios only happened in faraway places on the other side of the world, but she knew that wasn't true. The United States wasn't immune to human slavery any more than she was going to be immune to this winter's flu season. But they needed proof to back up their growing concerns.

Tory slid into the passenger seat beside Avery. "If they are keeping illegal girls and using them as domestic slaves, it would explain why the Sourns are lying. Facing the possibility of stiff fines and even prison time gives them more than enough motivation to keep things hidden. What we don't know is why—or who—is targeting these girls."

"Maybe because they are vulnerable and have nowhere to go." Avery started the car and headed back toward the precinct. "Clearly, Mrs. Chu didn't want Malaya using the phone or learning English."

"Do you think she took the phone and ran?"

"Teo could have helped her against his mother's wishes. Knowing how to use a cell phone and speak a few phrases of English could have been her key to escape."

Tory pulled out her laptop. "In the meantime, if Malaya still has the phone, we can try to track her location."

"Do it."

Because if they didn't find her soon, there was a good chance they wouldn't find her alive.

Chapter 28

Malaya couldn't stop shaking. His instructions had been clear when he'd stepped out of the car. If she tried to run or get someone's attention, he would kill her. Just like Tala. He knew she wouldn't run. How many times had they told her what would happen if she tried to escape?

There was nowhere to run.

Malaya breathed in the gas fumes seeping through the crack at the top of the car window as he pumped the fuel. On the horizon, dark clouds gathered, laced with narrow threads of lightning. The coming storm only added to her fears. When she was younger, she used to climb the twisted staircase to the top floor of their house, hand in hand with her father, until they reached the balcony, where they would watch the storms rumble across the sky. From their perch on the open patio, they could see the crowded alley below and smell mouthwatering scents of smoked pork and fresh prawns drifting up from the street corners, and she would forget her fear of thunder-storms.

That was a lifetime ago.

It wasn't the first time she wished she could

get lost in the sea of pedestrians and crowded markets home offered. There was so much she missed—hawkers singing on the streets while selling bread, the tiny café where she used to sip coffee with milk and egg white, and even the incessant honking of motorbikes.

Malaya gnawed on her lip as she studied the unfamiliar scene now surrounding her.

The promises of a better life were empty. Maybe she could hold her breath until everything went dark and she felt nothing. But all she could think about was Tala.

Tala had been promised the same things she had. Freedom, a job, and a new life. As much as she prayed, it wasn't going to be any different for her. Mr. Chu had told her that the police would arrest her if they discovered she was in the country without papers. Prisoners were beaten and left to starve, and he'd given her a taste of what it would be like if they found her.

Rain began to splash onto the black pavement. Malaya shivered despite the heat. She never should have tried to talk to the policewoman. They wouldn't help. Without the right papers, she'd end up in jail.

Unless that too was just another lie.

Despite the risk, she'd kept the card, because when she'd looked into the woman's eyes, she hadn't seen the hate or suspicion she'd expected. Instead, she'd seen kindness. But evil often raised its head disguised as benevolence. Maybe prison wasn't any worse than the beatings and long hours she was forced to work. And then there was the way she'd seen Mr. Chu look at her the past few weeks. One day, when his wife and Teo were out, she knew he'd come for her.

She dug her hand into the pocket of her skirt and wrapped her fingers around the cell phone, surprised her captor hadn't noticed it. She hadn't planned to take it. She was only going to call the woman and Teo had agreed to help. It had been their secret. She owed it to Tala to help find out the truth.

Teo had turned off the ringer so his mother wouldn't hear them if it rang, then slowly dialed the number at the kitchen table. By the time she heard the steps on the staircase, it had almost been too late. In a panic, she'd dropped the phone into her pocket before Mrs. Chu entered the room, then slipped out the side door. If she got caught, she'd planned to tell Mrs. Chu she was bringing in the garbage can from the street. It was the one time she was allowed outside the house.

That was when he'd grabbed her. She pressed the phone closer against her chest, praying he wouldn't discover her only link to freedom.

She looked at the clock on the dashboard. Another minute had gone by. He'd left the car running while he stood out in the hot sun, pumping gas, his hat pulled low so no one would recognize him. Drips of perspiration ran down the back of his neck, under his arms, and through the shirt.

A fat man with a red cap on came near the car. She could hear him yelling at someone across the parking lot. She wished she could understand the words. What if she signaled him somehow? Got his attention?

The man turned and jumped into his beat-up truck, never noticing her.

Malaya's heart pounded in her throat. She had to call before he got back into the car, but without Teo she only had a smattering of English words she could use.

Another minute passed. He would be coming back soon. She was running out of time. The woman wouldn't be able to get here in time. And she might never have the chance to call again.

Malaya peeked out the window. There was a row of buildings in the distance. What if she ran to the building and hid behind it? She was strong and could run fast.

The door was unlocked. She pressed her fingers against the metal handle, weighing the risks. He was going to kill her anyway. She'd seen it in his eyes.

Malaya pushed open the door, slid from her seat, and ran.

Chapter 29

Avery pulled her sedan against the curb, then put the vehicle into park, her protection detail still trailing a hundred feet behind her. She turned to Tory. "How much time to locate the cell phone?" They couldn't waste time looking in the wrong direction.

"Not long. Give me a few minutes, and I should be able to locate her within fifty meters or so, thanks to the density of the mobile traffic in the area."

"We don't have a few more minutes. If he's got her, he's going to kill her."

Avery grasped the steering wheel while Tory worked, wishing they knew more about their killer's pattern. How long had he kept the girls before he killed them? Where did he take them? There were too many questions. Too many unknowns. And no time to make a mistake. She put in a call to Mitch and Carlos and told them to be ready as soon as they had a location.

"I've got her." Tory pointed to the gridded map on the computer screen. "The triangulation pinpoints the phone's location to a gas station seven miles from here. And at the moment, it's not moving."

Seven miles.

"We can assume that the distance was too far for her to have walked on her own."

Which also upped the odds that someone actually had taken her.

Avery pulled out into traffic. "Let Mitch and Carlos know where we're going, then give our protection squad an update. We could use the extra backup."

Six minutes later, Avery pulled into the parking lot of the gas station and stopped beneath the huge overhead canopy, praying they weren't six minutes too late. Exiting the car with Tory, she studied the scene. If her captor had brought her here, he'd probably chosen the busy station on purpose, where it would be easy to get lost in the crowd. Where no one would remember his face.

Or the face of a young, kidnapped Vietnamese girl.

Rows of pumps—most of them filled with customers—spread out to her left. The station's convenience store ran parallel behind it. There were side entrances and delivery doors in the building, giving them a lot of ground that needed to be covered.

Avery turned back to Tory. "Any movement on the cell phone?"

"Nothing."

She had to be here.

Avery's focus narrowed. An old man stood

beside his pickup truck, pumping gas. A woman came out of the store with two children eating ice cream. A car of teenage boys messed around while filling their tank. All of them were oblivious to a possible life-and-death situation taking place around them.

Where was she?

Mitch and Carlos pulled into the parking lot right behind them and jumped out, joining officers Kelly and Taylor.

"Where do you want us, boss?" Mitch asked.

Avery laid the photograph Mrs. Chu had given her on the hood of her car and started handing out instructions. "If our serial killer is involved, we're going to need to work as quickly as possible. Mitch and Carlos, join Kelly and Taylor and start searching all the cars in the lot. We might not have a search warrant, but we definitely have probable cause. Tory and I will search inside. If she's here, I want her found."

Avery and Tory ran past the dozen cars fueling up with gas toward the convenience store. "Has the signal moved?"

Tory glanced at the computer screen in her hands. "The signal's still not moving."

Avery flashed her badge and announced their presence to the manager on duty before she and Tory split up to search inside the huge building. Avery headed toward the bathrooms past rows of junk food, a long line of fountain drinks, and for those feeling a bit more health conscious, a selection of fresh sandwiches and salads.

But there was no sign of Malaya.

Inside the white-tiled bathroom, she shoved open the door of the first stall with the toe of her shoe, letting the metal door slam against the wall. The woman standing at the counter applying a layer of lipstick paused, her eyes wide.

Avery held up her badge along with Malaya's photo, then moved on to the next stall. "I'm Detective North. I'm looking for this young woman."

The woman's gaze dropped to Avery's gun peeking out beneath her jacket before shaking her head and heading toward the exit. "I'm sorry. I haven't seen her."

Avery moved on to the last stall. It was empty.

She pushed open a cramped closet filled with mops, brooms, and the strong industrial smell of cleaning products. Nothing.

Avery turned to leave, stopping when she caught her profile in the mirror. Her face was pale and there were dark shadows under her eyes from lack of sleep. She hesitated. He'd tried to get into her head and won. The card, the flower, Michael's signature, the break-in . . .

All of it was nothing more than a game to him.

But he wasn't going to win this time. She was going to track him down and find Malaya before he did anything to hurt her. And then ensure that he spent the rest of his life in a high-security prison.

Which meant every second counted.

Avery stepped back into the brightly lit storefront. Tory was making her way down the chip aisle toward her.

"Anything?"

Tory shook her head. "I checked the men's restroom and the delivery entrances. She's not there and no one has seen her."

"She's not in the back either."

Where was she?

The front door opened. Mitch entered, holding up a black cell phone, with Carlos trailing a step behind. "I found the phone."

"Where?"

"Against the curb near the west entrance of the parking lot."

"But no sign of Malaya?"

"Nothing. I instructed the other officers to expand the search, but there's no sign of her so far."

Avery felt the air rush out of her lungs. Without the phone in Malaya's possession, they had no way to trace her.

God, where is she? We need another miracle.

She fought to put the pieces of the puzzle into some sort of semblance. Logic said that Malaya's kidnapper—a theory she was going to assume true at this point—had stopped to get fuel for his

261

vehicle and left as quickly as possible. Somehow in the process, Malaya had lost the phone. But that still didn't put them any closer to knowing where she might be.

"He could have discovered the phone and dumped it." Tory rested her hands against her hips, clearly as frustrated as the rest of them. "They could be halfway across the city by now."

"I realize that, but there is also the chance—slim as it might be—that she tried to run and is still here. Tory, verify Mrs. Chu's story about her husband being out of town, so we can eliminate him as a suspect. As soon as you're done, you can help me check all the transactions that have gone through over the past hour and see if anyone came through here who is related to the case." Pushing aside any emotional attachments to the case was the only way she was going to be able to focus. "Carlos and Mitch, get with the manager and go through the video footage for the last hour to see if Malaya is on there. I want to know every person who has passed through here, especially if we can somehow link them to this case."

Avery started toward the front of the store, praying that the miracle that would point them in the right direction was here. A minute later, she was sorting through the receipts. Most were credit card transactions, and none of the names raised a red flag. After verifying that Mr. Chu had indeed left for New York three days ago and was scheduled to return tonight as his wife had told them, Tory started cross-referencing names in order to find any connections with the case or those with a criminal past.

"We've got five cash transactions." Avery held up the receipts. "Let's run the time stamp on the receipts against the times on the videos and see if we can get a match and identify the customers."

They were one step closer.

Avery mentally sorted through what they had, trying to see the situation through their killer's eyes. He'd picked one of the busier stations in the area, presumably hoping no one would remember his face. Paying cash meant risking a face-to-face encounter with the cashier, but it was less risky than using a credit card that would leave a paper trail. If taking Malaya had been a crime of opportunity, then he was making things up as he went along, which in the end, gave them a slight advantage. All he had to do was make one mistake. But they needed his identity.

Avery stood at the video monitor beside John, one of the cashiers helping them. "You were working out front?"

His hand trembled as he reached up to scratch his face. "Yes."

"I need you to tell me anything you can remember—anything about these cash transactions while we watch the customers on the video."

"I'll try, but we have so many customers going through . . ."

"Anything you can tell us will help."

"Okay."

Mitch began cuing up the time frames on the video that matched the cash receipts. They watched the first match. An older woman, seventy, seventy-five, paid cash for her gas.

John nodded. "She paid her bill in quarters and pennies."

"Doesn't look nervous and certainly doesn't fit any profile." Just slow. "Next."

John didn't come up with anything until the fourth customer. "Wait. I remember him. He had his hat pulled low. Mumbled, seemed in a hurry. Nervous."

The video feed was grainy. "Can you give a detailed description?"

"I don't know. Midfifties. Asian, I think."

Avery's mind started clicking. It had to be him. "You're sure about that?"

John nodded his head. "Yeah . . . yeah, I'm sure."

"Okay. Mitch, see if you can get a clear shot of his face, then find the corresponding video from outside so we can identify him getting into his car."

Two minutes later, Mitch paused the tape again. "There isn't a clear shot of his face inside the store, but take a look at this."

Their suspect unlocked a dark sedan with tinted windows. "That's him."

Tory tapped on the screen. "The car matches the description Mrs. Chu gave about a vehicle she spotted in the neighborhood when she went out to look for Malaya."

"Rewind the video thirty seconds, before he exits the store, and slow it down to half speed." Avery held her breath while Mitch rewound the video. "There . . . there she is. Malaya exited the vehicle right before he returned from paying for his gas."

Avery watched the gray-scale video flick by frame by frame. Their suspect pulled open the driver's door, cap pulled low, then looked around and noticed Malaya was gone.

"How much time has passed?"

"Thirty minutes, which gives us an approximate radius of two miles."

Avery tried to put herself in Malaya's shoes. With no circle of friends, whether she was in the country legally or not, she probably had no idea where she should go or where to turn for help. "She won't go far. She's feeling scared and vulnerable and doesn't see any viable options."

Tory nodded. "Which means she's looking for a place to hide."

Avery mentally ran over the block surrounding the gas station. It was filled with shops and apartment buildings, and there would be dozens of places to hide. Which gave them a lot of ground to cover. But first . . .

"We need an ID on this man."

"Wait a minute." Mitch forwarded the video a few frames, stopped, then zoomed in on the man's face. "He must have panicked when he noticed she was gone because we've got him."

Avery felt her breath catch at the familiar face. "That's him."

Robert Sourn.

But there was no time to celebrate. "Tory, I want a warrant put out for Mr. Sourn's arrest. Carlos and Mitch, watch the rest of the surrounding footage to ensure we didn't miss anything. Tory and I will coordinate with the other guys and help expand the search. You can join us as soon as you're through here."

Mitch grasped her arm. "Be careful, Avery. He's still out there."

Avery nodded at her partner, then headed outside.

"What do you think he did?" Tory hung up her phone, then hurried to keep up, a step behind Avery. "Went looking for her specifically, or was it simply another opportunity?"

"I don't know, but if he thinks she can identify him, he's not going to let her go without a fight. He knows she's out there."

Sourn had a lead on them, which meant that he could have already found her. Avery shook off the fear of that thought, refusing to believe that they had come this far only to lose her.

They quickly coordinated with the other officers, then headed north on foot. Lightning struck in the distance, and Avery caught sight of dark clouds moving across the city. It had become another game of cat and mouse. Of who could find her first. And Avery's job was to save Malaya from the man who hunted her.

They made their way up one of the dozens of side streets in the area. Avery quickened her step with Tory right behind her, then stopped midstride. Something had caught her eye.

It was a shoe.

Avery felt her heart sink as she closed in on the figure. If they were too late . . .

They found her there. Hovering behind a Dumpster. Alive.

Avery called on the radio to the rest of the team. "I've got her. Tory, call in an ambulance."

Avery knelt down beside Malaya, who sat curled up in a ball, unmoving, her arms wrapped tightly around her legs. Blood ran down her face from a cut on her forehead.

But she was alive.

"Malaya?"

Big brown eyes looked up at Avery.

Avery knelt down beside Malaya, then turned to Tory. "Tell her she's going to be okay now. Tell her the nightmare is finally over."

Chapter 30

Malaya sat on a hard metal chair in the small room. Gray walls threatened to close in on her. The clock on the wall told her it had been only fifteen minutes since they had brought her here, but it already seemed like hours.

The woman with the red hair and pretty smile placed a sandwich and drink in front of her, but Malaya's stomach turned at the thought of eating. All she could think about was that Tala was dead and a man had grabbed her, threatening to kill her the same way. Somehow she was still alive, but the woman had been wrong. She'd never wake up from this nightmare.

A second woman sat down across from her, the one who spoke her language.

Her voice was soft, but even the familiarity of the words did little to calm her racing pulse. "You've been through a lot today. How are you doing, Malaya?"

She shook her head, unable to answer. Fear had crept in and taken over. Every dream she'd ever had shattered. Trust wasn't easily earned. Even when she had no choice.

"Do you remember Detective North?"

Malaya nodded at the woman's words and watched her smile, but her own words still wouldn't come.

"I'm Detective Lambert. My mother grew up in Hanoi."

The name brought back a rush of familiar images, scents, and longings of a place she believed she'd never see again. But if she closed her eyes, those vivid images from her childhood surrounded her, almost as if she were still there. Merchants standing outside their silk shops beneath the shadow of ornamented temples. The scent of rice noodle soup being sold at the street-side cafes. The rumble of motor scooters passing by . . .

"I want you to know that you don't have to be afraid anymore. You're safe."

Malaya's eyes blinked open. She wasn't sure she'd ever feel safe again. Hadn't she believed her father's words? Promises that life would be better for her in America. She'd believed the man who had taken their money at the employment agency. Believed that once she arrived in this country, everything would be different.

Why should she believe them now?

Detective Lambert leaned forward. "I know this isn't easy, but we need you to tell us what happened today."

The reminder of the past few hours ripped through the memories from Malaya's past and changed them into a nightmarish hue. For a moment, she couldn't breathe. It was as if she were slowly drowning and all the air within her was being sucked away.

"Malaya?"

She reached for the drink in front of her, tried to steady her hands, then took a long sip.

"I know this is hard for you, but we need your help. We don't want what happened to you to happen to another girl. Anything you can tell me will help us catch the man who took you. Did he tell you where he was taking you?"

Somewhere a seed of strength emerged. Tala had visited Malaya's dreams—her face white and bloated. The same thing would have happened to her if these people hadn't found her. She'd known it the moment he'd grabbed her from the Chu's driveway. She would have been his next victim.

She shook her head.

"That's okay." Detective Lambert pushed a button on a tiny machine and set it on the table between them. "You're not in trouble, but we need to gather evidence against him to ensure he never does something like this again. I'm going to record what you say. Do you understand?"

Slowly, Malaya nodded her head. If she was ever going to see her family again, she was going to have to trust someone. Maybe stopping the man who had taken her was the first step.

"I had gone outside to bring in the trash can

when he grabbed me. He shoved me in the backseat of the car." She closed her eyes again for a moment. It was the voice she wanted to forget. "He spoke to me in Vietnamese."

Rough. Authoritative, like he was used to telling people what to do.

"Had you ever seen him before today?"

Malaya searched her memory, but she already knew the answer. She shook her head. He might not have the same face as the others, but he was just like them. Out to hurt her. Out to control her and get whatever he wanted without ever considering the cost to her . . . and to other girls like Tala.

"Did he make any stops before the gas station?"

Malaya shook her head. "No, we were driving in circles. Like . . . like he didn't know where he was going."

"Let's talk for a minute about when you first came to this country. How long ago was it?"

Time had begun to run together like her mother's spicy dipping sauces on their white dinner plates, some days moving slower than others. But Mrs. Chu had a calendar that hung on the kitchen wall. It was filled with notes about parties, appointments, and Teo's swim classes, and with it, Malaya had silently marked off the days.

Malaya took another sip of her drink. "It was . . . about three months ago."

"How did you get here?"

"On a boat."

"Do you remember the name of the boat?"

Malaya shook her head, then watched Detective Lambert's pen scribble across the yellow page, taking notes even though the tiny machine was recording her words.

"Did your parents pay to send you here?"

This time Malaya nodded, wishing she could erase the guilt that resurfaced with the memories. "My family . . . they are not as poor as many, but my parents worked hard to provide, and there weren't many jobs. We met a man. His name was Nien. He was a nice man who promised me a new start in the United States and a job where I could earn enough money to send to my family. My parents had saved for many years for such an opportunity and gave him everything they had."

The detective looked up from her paper. "Were there other girls on the boat with you?"

"Yes." She could still see the tangled web of girls sleeping inside the vessel and smell the soured stench of their unwashed bodies. She'd spent the last three months trying not to think about where they were. Or what horrible things had happened to them since she'd last seen them.

"How many?"

"Twenty . . . maybe twenty-five."

"How long were you on the boat?"

"I don't know." Malaya tried to focus on the

question, but the days on the boat had stretched into weeks, leaving her with nothing more than vague impressions of the passing days. "We stopped a few times, in isolated spots, with warnings from the captain that it wasn't safe to leave the boat. One of the men would buy fuel and supplies while the other ensured we followed the instructions. At the time, we believed it was simply for our safety that we were told to stay on board."

In the end, she'd realized that even then they had been prisoners.

"What happened once you arrived here?"

"I was told I was a fool to believe that a new life awaited me in the United States. That I no longer had any rights, and I would have to do what I was told."

"What about Tala?"

"After we left the boat, I never saw her again."

Until the photo. How could Tala have been living so close without Malaya knowing it?

"Why didn't you call the police, Malaya?"

She looked to the other detective, who sat quietly at the end of the table, then back to Detective Lambert. "I don't speak English, except for the words that Teo taught me. They told us if the authorities found out we were in the country illegally, we would be arrested. I know what prison is like in my country. And they watched me. Mr. Chu beat me if I did anything wrong. Even if I decided to run away, where would I go? I don't know anyone in your country except for the Chus."

"You're very brave to have escaped the man who took you."

"I am not brave." Malaya ducked her head and wiped the condensation that had collected on the table from her drink. "I only did not want to end up like Tala."

Detective Lambert set her pen down on the pad of paper. "What about the magnolia flower tattoo? Did they give that to you as well?"

Tears filled Malaya's eyes as she pulled the sleeve of her shirt from her shoulder to reveal the small flower. "When we were on the boat, they . . . they told us that we belonged to them now, and there was nothing we could do. If we run, they will find us. And when they find us, they will kill us."

Chapter 31

Avery popped two Tylenol into her mouth, then chased them down with what was left of her lukewarm water sitting on the edge of her desk. She'd made a second pass through the notes from Malaya's interview that Tory had transcribed into

English. The swell of nausea had yet to leave. They'd focused their resources on searching for a murderer and in turn had stumbled across something that expanded far beyond the ordinary MO of a serial killer and the tragic death of a couple of girls.

"I didn't want to be right." She shook her head and looked up at Tory. "But we're not just talking about the harboring of one or two illegal aliens."

"I know." Tory leaned against the edge of Avery's desk, her thumbs circled through the front belt loops of her dress pants. "And we've got to figure out how everything ties together."

Avery nodded as she dropped the notes onto her desk and leaned back in her chair, her mind—and stomach—still churning from the interview with Malaya. "They're trafficking young girls, treating them as though they were nothing more than pieces of property. How can anyone do that?"

No matter how many cases she worked on— how many horrific crime scenes she witnessed— she'd never be able to understand how humans could mistreat one another. Or how the value of life could be dismissed as insignificant.

"There's still one thing I don't understand." Tory's frown deepened, her somber expression mirroring the emotional impact that Avery felt. "Granted, these girls weren't involved in the sex trade, which would bring in a more steady income, but still, why murder the merchandise?"

"I don't know."

Avery pushed her chair away from the desk and stretched her back, trying to loosen the knotted muscles lining her spine. Tory's question was one she'd asked herself a dozen times since the interview, and to make it worse, more than likely the girls they had encountered were only the tip of the iceberg. With billions of dollars generated every year, human trafficking had become the fastest-growing criminal industry in the world. And it was no longer a situation that affected someone else on the other side of the world. These girls—as they'd discovered—were right here in their own backyards.

Tory dropped into the chair across from Avery and caught her gaze. "Can I talk to you about something?"

"Of course." Avery caught the frustration brewing in Tory's eyes. "Are you okay?"

"I don't know."

"These last few days have been hard."

"It's more than that." Tory leaned forward. "One of the reasons I wanted to join the department was so I could be an advocate to my people, but now . . . it's my people who are responsible for this."

Avery shook her head. "That's where you're wrong. The Vietnamese community is a part of this, yes, but for one thing, that involvement doesn't include everyone. And secondly, you know as well as I do that it doesn't stop here with what we've found in this specific case. There are many, many others involved."

"I know but—"

"We're talking global profits into the billions, Tory, and nearly every country and economic class feeding into this trafficking network in some way." Avery understood Tory's anger, but nothing about what had happened could be placed at the feet of one group of people. "This isn't about race or color or status, it's about injustices being forced on those who have no voice. It's human beings violated and sold as property."

"I know, but I just can't shake this feeling of horror over what's happening." Tory fiddled with the silver ring on her finger. "When I worked in white-collar crime, it was easy to look at a case as simply numbers and dollar amounts. Listening to Malaya tell her story and realizing that there are other girls out there just like her . . ."

"That's exactly why I need you on this case, Tory. Not only are your language skills proving to be essential, so are your people and computer skills. You're going to help us take down those behind this atrocity and potentially save the lives of dozens of other girls."

"But it's become personal. I'm afraid it's going to affect what I do."

It had become personal—too personal—for all of them. Which was all the more reason to find the truth and put a stop to what was happening. "This case has affected all of us in one way or another, and being emotionally involved to a degree is a part of the job. But I need you to stay focused and with me on this one."

Tory pressed her lips together and nodded. "You're right. We're going to get this guy. We're going to get all of them."

Carlos entered the room and dropped two bags of takeout onto Avery's desk. Mitch followed a couple steps behind, carrying a tray of drinks.

"Lunch is served, ladies."

"Thanks, guys." Avery pulled the drink marked "sweet tea" from the cardboard holder and took a sip from the straw while the rest of the team grabbed their lunch, overdue after a long morning.

She breathed in the savory smells of seasoned lamb, onions, and garlic sitting in front of her, but even the guys' offer to pick up her favorite takeout while they were out had done little to restore her appetite. She understood all too well the conflicting emotions Tory was dealing with at the moment, because she was struggling with them herself.

Mitch helped himself to one of the wrapped gyros and a bag of fries, along with a large drink, before taking one of the vacant seats. Avery watched him take a bite. Nothing got in the way of Mitch and his appetite.

She dropped her food onto a paper plate on her desk. Hungry or not, she'd worked enough cases to have learned the importance of keeping up her own energy level while in the middle of an investigation.

Carlos unwrapped one of the gyros, then sat down next to Mitch. "Tory briefed us on the interview with our victim. We've somehow gone from serial killer and the possible harboring of an illegal alien to human trafficking?"

"That pretty much sums up the situation. So much for a more advanced and intelligent society."

Human trafficking was alive and well with everything from domestic slaves, to sex slaves, to agricultural laborers. But tracking down the girls who had been brought over with Malaya was going to be difficult, if not impossible. How did you track down girls who had been sold like merchandise to the highest bidder?

Avery looked up at the crime board. "Let's go over the facts again."

Carlos put his hands behind his head and leaned back in his chair. "We've got girls brought here by recruiters who promise them the world, and once they're here, if they're given anything at all, it's laundered identities, including fake high school diplomas, driver's licenses, and immigration papers."

"Besides that, the fear and the threat of violence

is what keeps them from running away." Tory toyed with the edge of her napkin. "These girls fear that the authorities will arrest them because they aren't in the country legally. They're impressed with the belief that there's no escape."

Avery shook her head. "Which allows their 'owners' to do with them what they please without the fear of them going to the authorities for help."

"And makes people like the Sourns and the Chus far from being the innocent victims they claim to be," Mitch added. "Instead of finding freedom in the US, these innocent young girls become indentured servants, forced to work for little or no money."

Avery looked at Mitch and Carlos, who had spent the last two hours tracking down the man forensics said had signed the gift card she received with the magnolia from the flower shop. "What did you find out about Landon Rice?"

"We met with his parole officer and found out that he missed his last check-in."

"Which means on top of everything else, we still need to track down another fugitive." Avery nibbled on a fry and felt her stomach rumble. Maybe she was hungry after all. She turned to Mitch. "Have the Chus been brought in yet for questioning?"

Mitch nodded. "I checked on the way here. Mrs. Chu was brought in a few minutes ago, and officers just met Mr. Chu at his gate at the airport."

"Guess that was an unwelcome surprise greeting. What about the Sourns?"

"So far—like our Mr. Rice—both of them have dropped off the grid. Nothing has come back yet on our BOLOs."

Avery reached up and rubbed the back of her neck. "Mitch, I want you to get me a search warrant for Robert Sourn's home and business. If we can't find them, then let's find something that will tie them in to all of this, including the murder. Tory, keep trying to track down Mr. Rice and the Sourns. Check on phone records, banking records, as well as airports, train stations, whatever it takes. Hopefully forensics will be able to pick up something from the break-in at my house as well."

"I'm on it."

Mitch and Tory gathered their lunches and headed for their desks. Since it was a transportation hub, Atlanta was easy to disappear from. They needed to find these people and find them quickly.

"Carlos, I'll sit in on the interview with you and the Chus . . ."

Avery let her voice trail off. Jackson appeared in the doorway, looking like the anchor she'd been searching for in the middle of a storm.

She nodded at Carlos, hoping to mask the relief

she felt over Jackson's arrival. "Give me a minute, okay?"

"You got it, boss." Carlos shot her a knowing look, then left the room, leaving her and Jackson alone. So much for her trying to hide her interest in the handsome ME standing in the doorway.

If Jackson noticed the interchange between them, he didn't show it. "I'm sorry if I'm interrupting."

"No. It's okay." She felt some of the tension in her back and shoulders melt as she stood and skirted the desk. "It's been a long day, and it's barely noon. I could use the distraction."

"I only have a minute. I'm on my way to talk to the chief about another case, but I wanted to stop and check on you before I went up. How are you?"

Avery's hand automatically reached up and touched her forehead. "I'm okay."

"And now for the honest version?"

She smiled. "Honest. The painkillers have done their job of taking the edge off the pain, and things have moved so fast, I haven't had time to think much about how I feel."

Or her new feelings for the man standing in front of her. She was still waiting for the moment when she had enough time to savor the idea without any distractions.

"Just don't forget that you're never going to be able to take down this guy if you're not in top form yourself." He nodded toward her desk and the uneaten gyro and fries still sitting there. "Like eating your lunch for starters, young lady."

He always knew how to make her smile. "Yes, Mother."

Jackson took a step toward her. "I like your mother, but being compared to her isn't exactly what I had in mind."

Avery laughed. "You are nothing like my mother, and while I love her, that's a good thing."

Because the idea of him—of the two of them together—was sounding better every day. She couldn't stop thinking about how he'd guarded her house all night, stopped an attack on her life, kissed her in the middle of her kitchen . . . Or how he was always able to bring things into focus for her and still somehow make her laugh.

She sighed, wishing he could kiss her again right now and allow her to forget at least for a moment all the frustration and stress of the case that had piled up. When all this was over . . .

"Now that we've established that I'm nothing like your mother, how is your arm?"

"Just sore when I move it."

He reached out and grasped her hand, then ran his thumb across her fingers. "And what about you? How are you coping with all that has happened?"

Avery felt the lightness of his touch as the past twenty-four hours rushed over her. Even without the physical evidence reminding her what happened, it would be a long time before she was able to forget. "I can't say that any of this has been easy, but as soon as we catch those involved, I'll be able to move on."

"Honest?"

She caught the doubt in his eyes. "Honest."

"Good, because I was hoping that when all of this is behind you, you'll feel up to going out again. If I remember correctly, I think you owe me a date. The last two were cut short."

She studied the hint of shadow across his face where he hadn't shaved in the past twenty-four hours or so and caught the fatigue in his eyes. The week had been just as tough for him. "I'd like that."

"And maybe . . . maybe we can find time for the two of us to figure out exactly where all of this between us is going."

Avery felt her heart flutter. A quiet dinner for two, no cases, distractions, or talk about forensic evidence. The thought left her smiling. And surprised that she felt ready to take the next step. "I'd like that as well."

"Good."

His thumb rubbed the back of her hand again. "So what's left today? I heard that you found Malaya, and that there's an arrest warrant out on Mr. Sourn as the man who kidnapped her."

Thoughts of a romantic night began to fade.

"Malaya is lucky to be alive. Right now we're starting interviews with the Chus while waiting on a warrant to search the Sourn residence and business. Hopefully we can find evidence that will tie the murders in with the trafficking of young girls and put Mr. Sourn—and whoever is running this ring—away for a very long time."

"What happens when you're done saving the world?"

Avery laughed. The last thing she felt like today was a superhero, but maybe her sister had been right—she didn't have to take on the world. All she had to do was help one person at a time. Losing her heart in the meantime to Jackson Bryant wasn't a bad way to go. "If we can bring in Sourn today, I plan on picking up takeout from the Jade Palace near my parents' house and spending some time with Tess before crashing."

He leaned against the desk beside her, still holding her hand. "And if things do settle down tomorrow, I'm hoping there's a day off in sight for you?"

"I'm hoping for church with Tess and my parents, lunch somewhere so I don't have to cook, and a long afternoon nap."

"If it works out that you can, I could pick up you and Tess?"

"I'd like that." Her smile widened. It might not be the perfect date for the two of them to be alone, but she'd take joining him for worship as a close tie. They both needed the spiritual renewal. "I'll call you with an update later, but I promised my parents I'd stay at their house tonight, so Tess and I will both be there."

"Perfect."

"Which means you can get a good night's sleep too."

"I have to admit that sleeping in my own bed is more appealing than hanging out in Mitch's Dodge Shadow."

She took a step closer, needing to feel his nearness, along with the assurance that everything was going to turn out okay.

"I need to go." He looked down and caught her gaze. "Call me when you can with an update."

"I will."

He let go of her hand, and she watched him walk away. Long, steady stride, confidence in every step, with a down-to-earth realness that made her want to get to know everything about him. He was providing that calming balance in her life that she craved.

Fears of overcommitment still simmered near the surface, but she was slowly learning to shove them aside. She needed someone who didn't make her life more complicated, but who could help her pick things up when they got messy.

Jackson was looking more and more like that person.

Chapter 32

By the time the judge signed the search warrants, Avery had ensured that their teams had detailed instructions and were geared up to carry out the search. There were two planned raids coordinated with SWAT. Tory and Carlos rode with the team to the Sourns' private residence, while she and Mitch joined the second team headed for the complex that housed the warehouse and the import company's main offices. They might have video evidence that linked Sourn to the kidnapping of Malaya, but Avery needed more—a connection to the human trafficking ring they'd stumbled across and, if Sourn was their killer, answers to Tala's murder.

She sat in the back of the van transporting their team and tried to keep her mind focused. The combination of the dull ache pulsing in the back of her head and the reality of the risks involved in executing a raid had her distracted. She'd warned Tory of the lethal combination, but sometimes, the opposing strains of responsibility were hard to ignore.

She shifted in her seat and felt a bruise on her hip she hadn't noticed before. She let out a low sigh. This morning's attack wasn't the first time she'd found her life in danger. Sometimes her need to pursue justice clashed with her concern for Tess, making it hard to justify the former. They ended up being two desires that simply weren't compatible. But counting the cost was not a foreign notion. Serving her community through the police force had become a family tradition and was how she'd learned firsthand about both sacrifice and the pain of loss.

God, you know the risks to take down men like this, and while part of me doesn't understand why you don't just wipe them off the face of the earth, I also know that you allow us to make our own decisions. It's just hard to see the fallout when girls like Malaya are paying the price for someone else's greed. Which is why I need your protection today. For my team, the SWAT guys, for the girls out there we still need to save . . . for everyone involved in this game.

"We're going to get this guy, Avery," Mitch said.

"I know." She stared out the window at the oncoming traffic. "He's already gotten away with too much."

He'd taken these girls' lives, taken away their hope, and left them in a wake of despair with nowhere to run. No one deserved that.

"I don't think I'll ever understand what makes these guys tick." Avery pressed her fingertips together. "Power, control, sex, greed? How do they look in the mirror every morning, straighten their tie, and head off for work like nothing's wrong?"

"That's a good question and one I don't have an answer for."

"Sometimes I just wish I could find the victims before they end up nameless in some back alley."

"Life can't be controlled. Life can't be bottled."

Avery raised her brow.

"Superman versus Brainiac."

She chuckled softly and shook her head. "You have an answer to everything, don't you?"

"Think what you like, but there is truth there. You can only control a small fraction of what goes on around you. But every criminal we help convict puts us one step closer toward making this world a better place."

Avery shoved away the conflicting thoughts and tugged on the bottom of her bulletproof vest as the vehicle pulled into the parking lot of the warehouse. Through the tinted window, she refocused her mind and studied the scene. Outside was quiet. A few scattered cars in the parking lot, trucks pushed up to the loading docks, but no sign of workers on this side of the building. No sign of Sourn.

The van door slid open. Avery took in a slow, deep breath and checked her weapon. Ideally, she preferred waiting until after dark or early in the morning for a raid, but the risk that Sourn would destroy evidence relating to the case was too great.

She jumped out of the van ahead of Mitch, and as her team members filed into position, she mentally rehearsed the plan she'd laid out to each of them. Their initial entrance had to be both quick and precise as they relied on designated teammates to ensure the perimeter was contained, leaving no avenue of escape for anyone inside. They'd conduct their preliminary search, detain and cuff everyone, then search for evidence that would aid in Sourn's conviction.

Avery felt the familiar rush of adrenaline spread through her as the SWAT team burst through the heavy side door of the warehouse ahead of her. The wooden frame groaned at the impact, then splintered as the metal hinges popped lose.

The moment they stepped inside, chaos erupted.

Someone shouted from across the room. Weapons pointed at her team. Gunfire exploded. A bullet smashed into the wall behind Avery before she had a chance to react. They'd landed in the midst of an ambush.

There was no time to figure out what had gone wrong. Avery took aim at one of the men and shot. He dropped his weapon and grabbed his arm. A bullet whizzed past her ear, pinging against a metal plate on the wall. She ducked behind a row of crates.

It was over as quickly as it started. Someone

shouted for them to stop shooting. Three men on the other side of the warehouse were surrendering. They stepped out into the open, then froze with their hands held high.

Avery was barking an order to the team when she saw him. The gunshots had ceased, but Mitch lay on the ground in a pool of blood.

"Mitch!"

Avery was only vaguely aware of what was going on around her as seconds ticked by in slow motion. Someone called for medical backup, while the SWAT team rushed to secure the warehouse.

Silence filled the aftermath of the gun battle. She crossed the cement floor to where Mitch lay and dropped onto the ground beside him. Everything around her faded until all she could hear was his raspy breathing. If the bullet had punctured a lung . . .

Oh God, please . . . No . . . no . . . no . . . Not now. Not this way . . .

"Mitch?"

This should have been a routine raid. Take the search warrant, secure the premises, and find their evidence. No one, especially not one of their own, was supposed to have gotten hurt.

She leaned closer and started searching for the bullet hole. "Mitch. Talk to me."

He looked up at her, his pupils dilated. "I . . ."

"Listen to me, Mitch. The bullet hit your vest.

291

You're just stunned. You're going to be okay." Why was there so much blood? If the vest had stopped the bullet, there shouldn't be any blood. Avery fumbled to find the bullet hole. "We've got an ambulance coming. We'll get you to the hospital, and they'll patch you up."

"Kayleigh . . ."

"Stop it, Mitch." She found where the bullet had entered his side, pulled on the Velcro closure to loosen the vest, then pressed her hand against the wound, trying to stop the bleeding. She searched for an exit wound with her other hand. Nothing. Her mind struggled to compute what had happened. The vest hadn't stopped the bullet, and there was too much blood. "You're going to be fine."

Mitch caught her gaze. "Please. Tell her how much I love her."

"I said you're going to be fine."

"You're a lousy liar, Avery. But a very good partner."

Not if she let him die. How could she forgive herself if he died after she let him walk into an ambush? She shook her head. She wasn't ready to give up. Because he had to be okay.

Tears burned her eyes. She blinked them away, pressing harder against the wound, her hands shaking, and started praying. "What was it that Spider-Man said to Mary Jane? You have a knack for—"

"For . . . for getting into trouble."

"Which is why you're going to have to tell Kayleigh that yourself. Just hang in there."

"Tell her, Avery . . . tell her that I'm so sorry."

Sirens wailed in the distance. All they needed was a few more minutes and there was a chance he could make it.

Someone from the SWAT team knelt down beside her and handed her a pressure bandage. "The ambulance is almost here. We've secured the scene, and your team has begun their initial search."

Avery nodded her thanks, then turned back to Mitch, but something in the background pulled her away for a split second. Her mind struggled to focus. Mason Taylor stood against the back wall, hands cuffed behind him. The man who'd betrayed her family. The man responsible for her brother's death.

She couldn't breathe. She shook her head and turned back to Mitch. Mason shouldn't be here, but for the moment it didn't matter. Taking down Sourn, Mason's presence, and everything else swirling around her seemed insignificant. None of it mattered compared to losing Mitch.

Chapter 33

Avery stormed down the hall of the precinct after spending fifteen minutes changing her clothes and trying to get rid of all the blood covering her hands. Soap and water might work to erase the stains on her skin, but she'd never be able to get rid of the images of Mitch lying on the ground.

And that hadn't been all she'd seen. Avery felt the knot anchored in her stomach dig deeper. Why had the man responsible for her brother's murder been at that warehouse?

Revenge might be yours, Lord, but surely you don't mind some help every now and then. I can't let him get away with this again.

No matter what explanation he came up with, Mason Taylor had to be responsible for the ambush at the warehouse, and this time she would prove it.

Carlos stood outside one of the interrogation rooms, talking on his cell phone.

Avery cut him off. "Where is he?"

"Just a minute." Carlos pressed the phone against his chest. "Who?"

"Mason Taylor."

"He's in interrogation room one, but—"

"Alone?"

"For the moment. I'm waiting for Captain Peterson to—"

She didn't have time for explanations. Avery shoved open the door to the room. Three chairs, one long, narrow table, and Mason. "I want to know what happened back there at the warehouse—"

"Avery." Carlos was right behind her.

The metal door slammed shut behind them. "I just want five minutes, right now."

Mason stood, uncertainty marking his face, but he didn't fool her. He never had. Dark blond hair that needed to be cut, day-old beard, and muscular frame. Her brother had trusted this man with his life. That had been Michael's first mistake. Mason might as well have pulled the trigger on him.

"I don't think that's a good idea."

"Sit down, Mason." Ignoring Carlos, Avery leaned forward, her hands braced against the table between them, waiting until he complied. Mason looked back at her, more confusion than defiance in his eyes, then finally sat down. "I was just told that my partner probably won't make it out of surgery alive, and I want to know why. What were you doing this time? Playing the role of the inside man? The mole in the department we never found? They let you explain away my brother's death, but if Mitch dies . . . this time

I'm going to make sure you don't get so lucky."

Mason managed to find his composure and shook his head at her. "I didn't betray Michael, and I didn't betray this department today."

"Really. Then explain it to me. Because the way I see it, you have everything to do with it. You were there at the warehouse. What else needs to be explained?"

"I was your brother's best friend. When are you going to realize that I had nothing to do with his death?"

"When the evidence stops pointing in your direction."

At one time, she'd considered him a friend as well. He'd spent almost as much time at the Hunt dinner table as her brother had. But Michael's death changed everything. And as much as she hadn't wanted to believe the compelling evidence of Mason's guilt, neither could she ignore it.

"You knew Michael was walking into a trap. I have phone calls and a paper trail, all pointing to your involvement, and just because the department cleared you doesn't mean I'm going to stop looking for the truth. You can't tell me you didn't know. And now Mitch?"

"Michael wasn't supposed to be there that day, and you know it." Mason's voice rose, tinged with anger. "I warned him that he needed to stay away. I don't know why he didn't follow my instructions. I guess we'll never know."

"Which is all very convenient for you, isn't it?"

"Avery, we've gone over this a hundred times."

"And we can go over it a hundred times more until I finally get the truth from you. And this time, you can add why my partner is now fighting for his life."

"I had nothing to do with what happened today."

"You can't be serious. You were there. You've been arrested for harboring arms and as an accomplice to attempted murder."

"Avery?" Captain Peterson stood in the doorway. Arms crossed. Anger evident across his ebony features. "To my office now."

"I—"

"Now."

She followed the captain down the hall, furious for the interruption. They could yank her off the case, but that wouldn't change anything. She would find her brother's killer.

With only a few weeks on the job, the captain hadn't had time to decorate his office. All that hung on the wall were a couple family photos of his wife and two grown children and a few awards. No clutter, frills, or excess, simply direct to the point like he always was. She missed the hands-on, fatherly approach her father had always taken with the officers. Captain Peterson was here to get things done. Nothing more.

He pointed at the open chair and took the one behind his desk. "Sit down."

Avery hesitated. Standing would make her feel more in control, even if it went against the older man's request.

"Mason Taylor is responsible for what just happened. We were ambushed at that warehouse, and now Mitch is probably not going to make it through surgery."

"I understand how hard this is for you, and because of that I'm giving you a little slack for your behavior, but that doesn't mean a screaming match between the two of you is justified—"

"My behavior?"

"Detective." He pointed to the chair again.

Avery closed her mouth and sat down.

"I'll start. Then, maybe, I'll let you say your piece. Like I said, I realize that you just witnessed your partner getting shot. Something that is extremely traumatic, which is why I'm not sending you home on disciplinary leave, but don't ever try and take over an interrogation like that again."

Avery balled her hands into fists. "This isn't the first time I've had to deal with trauma. Maybe now you'll believe the evidence I have against Mason Taylor in my brother's case. We all know that there's a mole in this department, and his presence at the warehouse proves—"

"It doesn't prove anything. He's not under arrest."

Avery felt the air gush out of her lungs, suddenly glad she was sitting down. "What do you mean he's not under arrest?"

"Taylor has been working undercover. He infiltrated a ring of smugglers working at that warehouse and has already handed over a growing amount of evidence all tied to money laundering, fraud, weapons selling, and now apparently, human trafficking. Mason Taylor isn't your bad guy. He's in one of the interrogation rooms so no one on the outside realizes he's undercover."

The room spun around her. "He was responsible for my brother's death, and now Mitch . . . I don't believe this is just a coincidence."

"I've read the file and your complaints against him, and while I can see where the evidence might point to him, there has never been enough to back up your theory. And despite what you think about the man, he's always performed his job in an exemplary manner."

"But what about today? His presence at the warehouse wasn't simply a coincidence. Surely you don't believe in coincidences any more than I do."

"I told you, this wasn't a coincidence. He was undercover."

Avery tried to make sense of what he was telling her. "Then why didn't you tell us before we went in there that he might be in the middle of this? Mitch wouldn't be in surgery right now. And if Mason really is working on our side, why didn't he stop the ambush from happening?"

Captain Peterson leaned forward. "Mason's been working undercover, helping the FBI with a gun-trafficking investigation first discovered by our department. But even I wasn't privy to all the details, including today's meeting with the buyers. Mason tried to stop it once he realized what was happening. Which means that if Mason hadn't been there, more of you could have been hurt."

Avery still didn't buy it. "They met us with open fire."

"They thought it was a raid on the weapons they were getting ready to transport. The reason more people weren't hurt is because of Mason. He told them to stand down once he realized what was happening."

But by then it had already been too late.

The captain's arguments did nothing to convince her of Mason's innocence. Too many things simply weren't adding up. "What if I get you the evidence you need?"

"How are you going to do that?"

"I've found another witness that slipped through the cracks—or as I'm beginning to believe, was purposely covered up."

"You do it on your own time and don't let it affect your work. And don't bring anything to me until you can back it up with hard evidence."

"Yes sir."

"I need you to stay on this case, because you're one of the best detectives I've got, but I won't hesitate to pull you off if you can't put your feelings aside. If you can't do this—"

"I can."

"And you'll do it with Mason's help."

Avery bit back the angry retort that surfaced. "You expect me to work with him?"

Captain Peterson ignored her question. "He's been working for the Sourns, and he has information he's been gathering that might help with your illegal alien case. Maybe between the two of you, you'll be able to put Sourn away for good."

"This isn't just a case of illegal aliens. Girls are being trafficked across the country, and Sourn is our biggest lead right now."

"This is exactly why I want Mason working with you. And why I need you to put aside any personal feelings you might have and work with him to solve these cases. Right now we've got two murdered girls, a police raid gone bad, and one of our own that might not make it through the day—not to mention the gun running and everything else Sourn and his people are involved in. I want this case closed and put behind us before anyone else gets hurt."

"Yes sir."

"And in the meantime, I want you to take the rest of the day off—"

"I can't—"

"You don't have a choice, Detective North. You won't be following up on what happened today, anyway. I'm putting Rogers's team in charge of wrapping up what happened at the warehouse, though I'll let Tory and Carlos join them if that makes you feel better. You'll be working with Mason on tying Robert Sourn to the trafficking and weapons smuggling. But not today."

There was no use arguing that she wanted to be the one to take down Mitch's murderer as well. From day one, Captain Peterson had run the precinct like a military general and made it clear that just because she was the daughter of the previous captain, there would be no special treatment.

"What about the Sourns?"

"I'll make sure someone lets you know when they're brought in, but for now, I want you to rest. I'll see you on Monday morning at oh seven hundred hours for a meeting between you and Mason. Maybe by then you'll have cooled off a bit, so you won't end up killing each other."

Chapter 34

Avery paced the carpeted floor of the hospital's waiting room. She'd forgotten just how much she hated being enclosed within the walls of a building, engulfed with sickness and dying. Because no matter how prepared she thought she was to face death in her job, its presence always came as a surprise. Especially when it was one of her own.

Too much blood loss . . . Hit an artery . . . We don't expect him to make it through the surgery . . .

She'd chosen to hang on to the last shred of hope until five minutes ago when the surgeon had spoken the words she'd prayed she wouldn't hear. *I'm sorry, but we lost him.*

Mitch was dead.

Avery stopped at the large window overlooking a row of oak trees that lined the hospital's landscaped grounds. They had attempted to create a relaxing atmosphere using natural sunlight and nature, but none of their efforts helped to ease the grief and frustration inside her. Instead, the doctor's final words had shattered the remaining hope she'd held on to. She now had to tell

Mitch's parents, who were flying in from Orlando, as well as his fiancée, who was driving to the hospital right now, that Mitch was gone. And then somehow find a way to help them all put the pieces back together again. This wasn't supposed to have happened.

Avery sank into a chair and studied a row of yellow marigolds starting to wilt from the afternoon sun. Mitch's vest was supposed to protect him from bullets, but instead the rifle cartridge had hit the seam and penetrated his chest. There was nothing the doctors could have done to save him. Nothing, she'd been assured, that any of them could have anticipated and stopped from happening. But no matter how many times she replayed the scenario, all the assurances fell short. They should have been able to secure the building and anyone inside in a matter of seconds, but instead they'd been hit with gunfire. There had been little time to react beyond running for cover.

For Mitch it had been too late.

"Avery?"

She turned as her father dropped his cell into his pocket. She'd been so lost in her own world, she hadn't even realized he'd been talking to someone. He'd insisted on staying with her, a gesture she'd appreciated more than he knew, while her mother—and two police officers—stayed home with Tess until they had a handle on what had happened at the warehouse. The last thing she wanted was her family caught up in the fallout of this case. Enough people had been hurt already.

"Tory just called and wanted to know how you're doing. They're finishing up at the scene and will report back to you as soon as they're done."

Avery nodded. "Thanks."

He sat down beside her on one of the hard leather chairs. "I told her you were handling things as well as could be expected."

"Which is a nice way of saying I've completely fallen apart?"

"Considering the circumstances, I think you're handling things quite well." He'd been through this with her before. "It's okay to hurt, Avery. Mitch was a huge part of your life."

"Which is why I can't stop thinking about Kayleigh." She pulled back, glad for his presence, while at the same time feeling an irrational frustration that her father didn't have the power to make it all just go away. "I don't know how to tell her Mitch is gone."

She felt a heaviness in her chest as reality began to sink into her own mind. "I've heard the words 'your husband isn't coming home.' 'Your brother was killed serving his country.' I know what it's like to have your entire world shatter in an instant."

"Which is why Kayleigh is going to need you. You've been where she is right now."

Avery tried to swallow, but her mouth felt as if it were full of sand. She reached for her drink and fumbled with the straw. The ice had long since melted, watering down the tea to a flavorless liquid, but at least it was wet.

She set the drink back down, stood, and started pacing again. Intellectually, she knew he was right. She did understand all too well what Kayleigh was about to face, but the thought of telling her that Mitch was dead still seemed too surreal . . . How had things turned into such an ugly nightmare that she couldn't wake up from?

"I still don't know if I can tell her."

"You can. Because Mitch would want you to be the one to tell her."

Avery stopped and dropped her gaze to the black-and-gray pattern on the carpeted floor, knowing he was right. Perspiration beaded at the base of her neck. The air conditioner was struggling to keep up with the hot Georgia afternoon. Like the day Ethan had died.

The memory swam through her mind. She'd been at her mother's that day. They'd sat on the front porch together, sipping iced tea and waiting for the next breeze to float by while the repairman fixed the air conditioner that had gone out during one of the hottest weeks of the summer.

Michael . . . Ethan . . . Mitch . . . She'd lost all

of them. And they'd all been protecting the people of this city. Sometimes life was so unfair.

"Mitch should be here right now." Tears began forming again. "He should be alive and planning a wedding with Kayleigh. He called me a few nights ago and told me he'd bought a seven-day cruise package for their honeymoon as a surprise, but he was afraid he'd end up telling her. He never could keep a secret."

"You're right." Her father moved in front of her and rested his hands on her shoulders. "Just like Ethan and Michael, he should still be here, but we both know all too well that's not always how life works."

"Sometimes I don't know if I want to do this anymore." Tears formed in her eyes. "What if we take down Sourn? There'll just be someone else to take his place. I solve one crime, and there's always more waiting for me. It never ends."

Her father took her hand and led her to the row of chairs overlooking the hospital grounds. "It's hard whenever someone makes the wrong choice that affects others around him, but you can't let that change who you are."

"My head knows that." She sat down beside him. "But my heart . . . Is there ever a time when it's best just to walk away?" The idea wasn't new, but today, the reality of her choices engulfed her like a raging storm. "I have a daughter to think about, a family who cares about me, and a relationship to explore with Jackson. How do I know that tomorrow I won't walk into a situation like today, and I'm the one who doesn't come home?"

"We can't know, Avery. None of us do."

"It just hurts so bad."

"I know."

Her father gathered her into his arms and let her sob. The strain of the past week, every moment of despair and heartache she'd witnessed, flooded through her. Sometimes life simply wasn't fair. Sometimes the good guys didn't win. Sometimes none of it made sense.

He reached down and grabbed a handful of tissues from the square side table, handed them to her, then waited for her to blow her nose.

Avery dropped the used tissues into the trash. "Thanks for being here."

"You know I'm always here for you."

Kayleigh would be here any moment, which meant she had to get control of her emotions—at least for now.

"One last thing." Her father took her hands in his. "You do what you do, because while it might not save the world, what you did today matters to Malaya, and it will matter for the rest of the girls when you find them. What you do matters, and that is why God has given you the courage to get out of bed every morning and face evil head-on."

Avery nodded, trying to draw strength from his

words. It might not be enough for right now, but later, when she had a chance to step back from the situation, his encouragement would give her something to hold on to. She blew her nose again, then took a deep breath.

Five minutes later, Kayleigh entered the room, the fatigue from the drive up from Columbus where she'd been visiting her brother coupled with worry about Mitch evident on her face.

"Kayleigh . . ."

"I got here as quickly as I could. My brother's parking the car. How is he?"

Avery walked toward her, struggling for the right words, but she already knew Kayleigh could see it in her eyes.

Kayleigh shook her head. "He's gone, isn't he?"

Avery nodded. "I'm so, so sorry. They did everything they could to save him, but in the end . . . it just wasn't enough."

"His vest?" Kayleigh dropped onto one of the chairs. "I told him to wear his vest."

"He was wearing it, and while they save many lives, sometimes it just isn't enough." Avery knelt down in front of her, knowing all too well what Kayleigh was experiencing. The shock numbed you, then the pain hit. Anger, depression . . . it could be a long time before acceptance finally settled in. "I'm so sorry. Mitch was like a brother to me. He was family."

"I know." She laughed in spite of the tears. "I

was so jealous of you at first, he seemed to bring you up in every conversation. He looked up to you."

"And he loved you."

"I just can't believe he's gone." Kayleigh stared at her hands twisting in her lap. "I found the perfect wedding dress online last week. I hadn't even shown it to him yet. It had the most beautiful neckline with tiny beads sewn in . . . He'll never see it. Never see me in it."

"I'm so, so sorry, Kayleigh." Avery felt a lump of emotion lodge in her throat. "He . . . he asked me to tell you how much he loved you before he died."

"Thank you." She grabbed for the box of tissues beside her, took one, and blotted her eyes. "It's crazy, but in some ways I think he tried to prepare me for this day. I just always assumed that he'd be around for us to enjoy our honeymoon and, at the least, a few years of wedded bliss. He was a good guy who believed in what was good and right."

"Which is what made him a good cop."

Kayleigh blew her nose. "What about his parents?"

"They're on a flight from Florida right now."

"I never met them. We were planning to visit next month—Mitch had requested a week off. We thought we'd spend a day at Disney World, maybe a few days playing golf so I could get to know them. I was terrified, actually imagining one of those horrible meet-the-in-laws disasters. I told him that once. Now I'd do anything to spend that week with them."

"They're great people. I met them once. You'll like them. They'll be there for you, and I think that together you'll be able to work through things."

"I don't know what to feel." She shook her head. "I'll meet Mitch's parents and figure out what happens the next few days, then go stay with my brother and his family."

"You'll need them close."

Kayleigh nodded.

Avery struggled for the right words. Nothing she could say could fix the situation. "Please, don't hesitate to call if you need someone to talk to."

"You'll pray for me, won't you?" Kayleigh fiddled with the strap of her purse. "I . . . I've never really gone to church, but right now I need something . . . anything."

"I already have been praying, along with our prayer team at church."

"Kayleigh . . ." Her brother stopped in the doorway, the resemblance obvious.

Kayleigh started toward the door, then turned back to Avery. "I've got to go talk to my family. Thank you. For everything."

Avery watched Kayleigh walk out of the room

with her brother's arm around her. Mitch was gone, and nothing any of them could do would bring him back. But she could find out the truth about what happened at the warehouse. Which for starters meant digging deeper into why Mason had really been there.

Chapter 35

Jackson found Avery at the neighborhood park not far from the precinct. She sat on one of the wooden benches, hands in her lap, staring straight ahead, her gaze lost somewhere along the horizon. He watched her for a moment, taking in her now familiar features and marveling at how her entrance into his life had changed something inside him. It had brought back that spark of life he hadn't even realized was missing.

Knowing it could have been her he'd lost today in that warehouse swept through him. He stopped beneath the shade of an oak tree, a dozen paces from where she sat. The reality that she could have been the one to take the bullet had shown him one thing—that he wasn't ready to lose her. Seeing her now with his own eyes was the only thing that could assure him that she was okay. Alive.

He slid onto the seat beside her, wishing there were something he could do to make the hurt and pain she was feeling disappear. But that wasn't going to happen today. "I got the call about Mitch. I'm so sorry."

She looked up at him, the faint hint of a smile masked by tears. "I needed some time off alone to clear my head. At least according to the captain."

"If you want me to leave—"

"No." She reached up and clasped his hand. "Please. Stay."

He laced her fingers together with his, then pulled her closer. She leaned against him, nuzzling her head against his shoulder. It had been so long since he'd felt this way. Since he'd felt comfortable with another woman. Avery had walked into his life, surprising and unexpected, and while he might not know what the future held, he did know that he wanted them to face it together.

He looked around, all too aware of the open space surrounding them and of her vulnerability. Too much had happened in the last twenty-four hours for her to be taking risks. If someone was after her . . .

"Does Captain Peterson know where you are?"

"Don't worry. My shadows are over there."

He could see it in her eyes. She wasn't going to let whoever was behind this rob her of her freedom, especially after what she'd lost. He might not agree but also knew that she wasn't the kind of woman to run and hide from a situation. Confining her would only make things worse.

"Do you want to talk?"

"I'm not sure I would know where to begin. With everything that's happened . . . It's still so unreal at the moment." She leaned back and looked up at him. "I've learned, though, that once you start having to tell people about a tragedy, trying to believe you imagined it all doesn't work anymore."

"I know."

It had been that way with Ellie. How many times after she died had he walked into their bedroom, forgetting for that split second that she wasn't there anymore? Every time he broke the news to a family member or friends, the reality that she was gone forever came crashing in on him. He didn't think he'd ever get past the gut-wrenching pain of losing her. Until one day he woke up and realized he had to move on. But the day-to-day process had never been easy. Never short-lived. And the long-reaching fingers of pain and loneliness still tried to grasp him when he least expected it.

He leaned back against the bench, shoving aside his memories of loss. This wasn't the time to dwell on his own past. "Tell me what happened."

"It was supposed to be a routine search." She

pressed a tissue to her eyes that were still puffy from crying. "I had the search warrant. The teams were set up in the front and in back. But the moment we stepped into that warehouse, everything fell apart. It all happened so fast, like they were expecting us."

"An ambush?"

"Not according to the captain." She shrugged, clearly still mentally processing what had happened. "But they were armed and started shooting before any of us could react. By the time I turned, Mitch was already lying on the floor. Blood everywhere. They killed him, Jackson. Shot him in cold blood as if his life wasn't worth anything."

"I know how close the two of you were."

"I realize that death is always a possibility with this job, but when it happens right in front of you, it seems unreal. I had to tell his fiancée that there wasn't going to be a wedding. His parents that their son wasn't coming for a visit next month."

"I don't know. It's never easy, no matter how prepared you think you are."

"Did you know that Kayleigh quit her job to move here from New York a few weeks ago so she could be closer to Mitch? And now . . . and now there isn't going to be a wedding. Mitch loved her. I mean really loved her, and that's saying something for him. In all the time I knew

315

him, he was nothing more than a player until he met her, then everything changed."

He pulled her closer to him, letting her head rest against his shoulder again. "Tell me about Mitch. Before last night, I'd only talked to him a couple of times. He always seemed like a nice guy."

"He was. Hardworking. Honorable. A bit of a goofball, but not when it came to his work. He was good at what he did. He loved the Falcons and followed them religiously, had a crazy passion for trivia and superhero quotes, and ate sushi, of all things." Good memories brought with them the hint of a smile in her eyes. They would be something to hold on to in the coming days and weeks. "We talked a lot about faith during our all-night stakeouts. Mitch always told me he hoped I was right about there being a God who loved him, but he'd seen too much in this life to believe that there was a God who really cared."

"It wasn't a choice you could make for him."

She lifted her head and glanced at him. A shadow crossed her expression again. "I know."

"I have to say, though, I understand where he was coming from." How many times had he stood over a homicide victim and wondered where God was? But God wasn't the one to blame for man's actions. "Sometimes it's hard not to question. We spend our lives taking down the bad guys, trying to bring order to a world where injustice wins out more often than not. But neither can we blame God for man's choices. That's what always seems to help me hold on to my faith. The reality of God is bigger than the failings of man."

"It's still hard to accept," Avery said. "And honestly, it makes me want to think twice about everything I've always believed about heaven and hell. But I also know I can't pick and choose what I believe about God."

"Because God stays the same no matter what we believe about him."

"I know that despite what I do or think, God is still sovereign. I don't want a watered-down faith, but sometimes it just hurts so bad . . ."

Jackson tightened his arm around her. "So what happens next?"

"The captain expects me to go home and take the rest of the day and tomorrow off."

"Good."

She shook her head. "I don't know if I can. My partner was just murdered. I have to find out how this could have happened."

"Do you really think you're emotionally ready to be in there questioning the suspects?"

"Now you're beginning to sound like the captain." She looked up at him and frowned. "I know the routine, Jackson. This isn't the first time I've lost someone I cared about. I know the steps of grief and the process. But this is something I have to do. This isn't just about a serial killer anymore. I need to go back to work and find out why this happened. Because there's something else at play now as well."

"What do you mean?"

"Mason Taylor was in that warehouse. He was arrested along with the other men who shot at us. According to the captain, Mason was working undercover to bring down a ring of arms dealers Robert Sourn is allegedly involved in."

"And I take it that isn't what you think."

Avery shook her head. "I think there's a whole lot more involved than trafficking weapons."

"I know you think Mason's involved with the department leaks."

"Yes, but while I admit that I'm looking at things from a somewhat biased angle, everything is still too convenient. They were there, waiting for us with their loaded weapons."

"When Ellie died, I wanted—needed—to blame someone, but what was there beyond the disease that took her away from me?"

"I can't let this go."

"Then don't. But maybe you need to focus on one case at a time. Find the rest of the girls involved in this trafficking ring, but don't give up on your brother's case."

"And if there is a connection somewhere?"

"Then one will lead to the other." Jackson hesitated, then decided to go ahead and tread carefully on ground he knew she would fight him on. "I do think that the captain is right about one thing."

"What's that?"

"Take the next thirty-six hours to get some rest. If you don't take care of yourself, you won't be able to think clearly and solve this case. Spend some time with Tess and your family. Spend some time praying and asking God for direction."

"Why do you always come across as wise and discerning . . . and put me in my place? I guess asking God for help is where I should have started."

He squeezed her hand. "You'd better watch out, or you're going to give me a big head."

"I'm serious. Today reminded me that we don't know what the future holds, but I do know that I need the kind of balance you bring to my life."

"Good, because I don't plan on going anywhere."

Chapter 36

Avery sat curled up in her father's leather chair beside the office window, reading her Bible and trying to extend this morning's worship time. The late morning light filtered through the sheer curtains. She'd needed today. Corporate worship with a church family she'd grown to love over the past few years, and now the chance to seek God's comfort in the silence. Finding all the answers still seemed out of reach, but for now she was clinging to the moment of rest from the battle.

"Avery?"

Avery looked up from her Bible and smiled at her father. He'd changed from his normal suit-and-tie Sunday attire to one of his Atlanta Braves T-shirts and sweatpants. "Hey."

"I didn't know you were still here. I thought you went with Jackson and Tess to feed the animals."

"They insisted I stay here and rest." She'd started to protest but, with the two of them, realized it was a losing fight. And besides that, she knew they were right. She really did need the rest and time alone. "This could almost feel like old times, you know. All we need now is some of that double fudge ice cream."

"Now that sounds good. Your mother always got on me for indulging, but it was worth it."

It had become a tradition growing up. When Daddy wasn't working, Sunday afternoons had been their time. While Mama and Emily napped, and Michael played video games, Avery had hung out with her father, and they'd talked, laughed, and simply enjoyed their time together.

"If you need to work, I could leave . . ."

"You know you always come before any work I might have." He nodded toward his desktop computer. "I just thought I'd check my Facebook account."

"Facebook? I never thought the day would come when I'd hear my father hangs out with friends online."

"Just wait until you retire. I've connected with friends I went to elementary school with. I'm also reading Hemingway, Jack London, Thoreau . . . all books I promised myself I'd read years ago but never found the time to."

"We'll have to get you an ebook reader for Christmas."

"Let's not push things too far. I'm not sure I'm ready for that. I still like the feel of a real book."

Avery laughed, trying not to dwell on the pang of guilt for smiling when so much had been lost. Mitch would want them to go on with their lives. To laugh and be happy again. But those feelings were going to be few and far between in the coming weeks.

Her father caught her gaze. "It makes me happy to see you relaxing, with a smile on your face."

Avery felt her stomach cinch. "For now. The storm's about to hit."

"I know."

Which was one of the reasons she needed to soak up the sense of peace and protection she'd always found in the home she'd grown up in. It was days like today when she wished she could transport twenty years into her past and return to that place of safety and innocence she'd always felt as a child. Where hot summer nights running around outside with her cousins, BBQs on the back porch, and Sunday potlucks eating Nana's turnip greens and sweet potato casserole were the norm. And the bad guy was no more dangerous than the imaginary boogeyman under her bed.

But life didn't work that way, and she'd learned years ago that it was impossible to hide from the realities of the world. Which was why refueling her spirit had become so essential.

Her father sat down in the matching leather armchair next to her and leaned back, his legs crossed. "I told you this last night, but I want you to know again how sorry I am about Mitch. I know what it's like to lose a partner. It's not easy at all."

"I know you understand, and it helps that I'm not going through this alone."

"You're never alone, Avery. Not in this family, anyway."

Avery let out a soft chuckle. She'd agreed to take last night off and had managed to keep herself distracted by enjoying a quiet family evening with Tess, Emily, and her parents. They'd ordered takeout, played a few hands of cards, then sat around the table eating popcorn and talking about everything except what had happened. She'd have plenty of time to deal with the emotions surrounding Mitch's death in the coming days, but after a week that had pushed her emotions to the brink, she quickly realized just how much she needed the break. She even laughed a few times at Tess's attempts to lighten the mood as they all tried to pretend—at least for one evening—like things were normal.

But trying to forget had only worked for so long. She ended up sleeping little, reliving instead the shootout in the warehouse over and over, while her mind tried to figure out what had gone wrong. And what she could have done to stop what happened.

"So how are you doing? And I want the honest gut answer, not a flippant 'I'm fine.'"

"The honest answer? I feel . . . lost." She ran her finger down the crease of her Bible. "I've been sitting here, reading my Bible, and trying to find answers. Looking for a why to what happened yesterday."

"And what answers have you found?"

"Not answers as much as the familiar reminder that even though life is tough—sometimes even dark and horrible—that doesn't change who God is. He's still in control."

It was something easy to say but hard to truly grasp hold of and put into practice in her day-to-day life.

"That's something all of us need to be reminded of daily. What else?"

She tapped her finger against the page she'd started reading. "I've never thought about comparing myself to King David, but in Psalm 18, he talks about pursuing his enemies. David was fighting a battle, and it struck me just how much I can relate."

She looked down at her Bible and glanced at the passage she'd been studying the past thirty minutes. "David talks about calling out to God in distress and crying for help."

"It does sound all too familiar, doesn't it?"

"Yes, considering yesterday I was ready to walk away from all of this."

"And today?"

"Part of me still is."

"It's the guilt for Mitch dying and your living. Guilt for what you could have done to save him. Anger toward the killer who's still alive."

"That sums it up pretty well. But then I started looking at David's reaction. He said, 'You armed me with strength, you humbled my adversaries, you made my enemies turn their backs.' David completely relied on God to be his shield and salvation when his enemies were hunting him down, when his life and the lives of others around him were at stake. I need to take this guy down, Daddy, and I realized today—not for the first time—that I can't do it on my own."

"None of us can."

Avery slid the cloth bookmark into place, then closed the Bible. "There's something else I'm struggling to do on my own. I didn't tell you this, but Captain Peterson has ordered Mason Taylor to join our investigation."

"And you don't want his help."

"I still believe he could be responsible for Michael's death."

"Maybe, but that's not the way the department sees it."

She shook her head. "Do you think he's a dirty cop?"

"He might have bent the rules a time or two, but he and Michael were close friends, and I can't see him betraying Michael. For now, I think you're going to have to trust him, especially if the captain has placed him on your team."

"I don't think that's something I can do. Trust has to be earned."

"Then you need to keep your head up and be on guard, but give him a chance. He's admitted that wrong choices were made that day. But you know as well as I do that it's a whole lot easier to make decisions in hindsight. You're going to have to come to the place where you can forgive Mason."

"That's going to be a tough place to find."

"Sometimes forgiveness becomes more like a daily choice. It's messy and often continues rearing its head like the bindweed your grand-father could never get rid of."

"I'm not sure I even know how."

"You can't. Not on your own. You've lost a lot. We all have, but the bottom line is that it's human to want vengeance and justice in a situation. And if we can't have that, we want the answers. Forgiveness is a messy process that takes time to sort through, but think about the alternative. You let bitterness take hold of you and it will ruin you. Your mother has let her loss consume her. I've had to think a lot about it over the past few months. I think there's a good reason why Jesus told us that there shouldn't be a limit to our forgiving."

Avery turned her father's words around slowly in her mind and tried to process them. She knew he was right, but forgiving Mason seemed comparable to David slaying Goliath at the moment. "I can't make any promises, except that I'll try."

"I know you will, and in the end you'll be a stronger person for it."

Her father pressed his fingers against the arms of the leather chair. "While we're confessing, something you said the other night made me realize that I need to take my own advice regarding my retirement."

"What do you mean? Personally, you might still not be ready to embrace the idea of retirement, but I think it's doing you good. You look far less stressed."

"I might not admit that in public, but you're right, even though the first couple of weeks I thought I was going to go crazy. But I spent some time talking with your mother and Pastor Philip and a lot of time praying. What you and I talked about the other night confirmed some things I've been thinking about. I'm looking at starting a second career."

"A second career? Wow. I think that sounds great." Avery curled her feet beneath her. "What exactly did you have in mind?"

"I've been talking to the captain about working for the department again, but this time as a chaplain. Pastor Berg is moving to Texas to be closer to his grandchildren, and they're looking for someone to take his place. It would mean I stay busy and feel as if I'm making a difference."

"You would be, and I think it sounds perfect for you."

"Well, you're the one who reminded me that I'm not too old to start something new besides golf. You found room for Jackson. I'm going to find room for a new career."

Avery smiled at her father's confession. "The challenge will be great for you."

Her father laughed. "I figure your mother and I have been volunteers with Downtown Rescue Mission for some twenty-odd years, so between all of the mentoring, counseling, and seminary classes I've taken on the side, I actually have experience in ministry that could be put to good use. I've already agreed to come in on Monday to be there for those involved in the shooting."

Avery felt the sting of the reminder. "Starting with your daughter?"

"You know I'm always here for you." Her father's gaze dropped. "Which brings me to the next thing I wanted to talk to you about. I realized that just like it wouldn't be right for me to ask you to walk away from Mitch's case, neither is it right for me to ask you to walk away from Michael's case."

"You have every right. Michael was your son—"

"I know, but it's also clear to me that you need this closure. And I respect your need to find out the truth about what happened to Michael."

"I promise to keep what I find quiet until I have some solid answers."

Avery's phone rang. She hesitated before checking the caller ID. Unless it was from Tess or Jackson, she wasn't going to answer.

"Go ahead." Her father nodded toward the phone. "Maybe it's good news."

A moment later, Avery hung up the phone and grabbed for her shoes sitting beside her chair. "You were right. It was good news. We might have just gotten the break we needed in the case.

A couple of officers just picked up Mrs. Sourn and had her brought back to the station."

Avery slipped on her shoes and was picking up her car keys and bag from the foyer when Jackson and Tess stepped into the house.

"Hey." Jackson's gaze drifted to the keys dangling from her fingers. "You're leaving?"

"They just called me in. They found Mrs. Sourn."

"Mom. I thought you were supposed to be resting."

Avery pulled Tess against her in a big hug. "Sorry, sweetie. We just got a break in our case, but I promise I'll be back as soon as possible."

"She's right," Jackson began. "You should be resting."

Avery frowned. "I need to go, Jackson. You know that."

"Then we'll compromise. Let me drive you. We can pick up lunch on the way."

"You've already done so much—"

"No arguing." He took the keys out of her hand. "And besides, I'm volunteering."

Her father stood in the doorway of the study. "Listen to the man, Avery."

"Okay. I will." Avery laughed, then hugged her father and Tess good-bye before slipping out the front door with Jackson.

"I appreciate your taking Tess to the house. I really did rest."

"I'm glad."

"Did you find Mrs. Whiskers?"

"We did, and she's now safe and sound back in her cage."

"She's lucky. Where did you find her?"

Jackson hesitated on the last stair and shot her a sheepish grin. "She was sleeping inside one of your slippers."

"Eww. She had to choose my room?"

"We made sure she didn't leave any . . . presents behind."

Avery laughed. "For that I'm grateful."

Jackson slipped into the driver's seat and started the engine. "Are you sure you're up to this?"

"Yes. Just worried that we don't have enough evidence to keep her."

Jackson's phone rang. He put the car back into Park and took the call.

A moment later, he turned to Avery. "I might have the evidence you need."

"What is it?"

"The lab. Our CSU guys found blood on what they believe is the murder weapon from the Sourn house. They want me to come in and see if I can match it to our victim."

Chapter 37

Avery entered the precinct, needing to hear Mitch's loud voice spouting off some stupid bit of trivia or a witty Marvel quote.

Apparently you really are the one with the knack for getting into trouble, Mitch.

A dose of Tylenol had taken the edge off her headache, but had done little to ease the roller coaster of emotions as the reality of her partner's death began to close in around her.

Carlos and Tory sat at their desks, working silently, while Avery stood in the middle of the room for a moment, searching for something to say. Anything that might help ease the haunting reality of what had happened.

Tory spoke first. "Hey. The captain called us in, but I thought you were supposed to be off until tomorrow morning resting."

She caught the concern in Tory's eyes, the same worry she'd seen in her father's and Jackson's eyes, but being back at the station had only proved to remind her that she wanted—needed—to be here working this case. "The captain wants me to be in on the interview with Mrs. Sourn."

Tory dropped her pen onto her desk. "How are you feeling?"

Avery fought back the tears. "Like something's missing. I'm ready for Mitch to walk through that door and say something crazy that makes me laugh."

Carlos let out a low chuckle. "He was always good for a laugh."

She studied Mitch's empty desk. An unfinished pile of reports lay stacked haphazardly on the edge. The dirty Spider-Man mug with a coffee ring around the top sat beside the computer keyboard. In front of it was the half-empty glass jar of Milk Duds he kept especially for her. Nothing here had changed since the moment he walked out of this office the last time.

For the rest of them, everything had changed.

Tory pushed her chair back from her desk a couple of inches and pressed her palms against her thighs. "Avery?"

Avery tried to ignore the lump swelling in her throat. It was either that or start crying again. "I'm just trying to process the fact that he's really gone."

"We . . . we all are." Carlos's voice broke. "Have they settled on a date for the funeral?"

"Yeah, I talked to Kayleigh this morning. It'll be Wednesday morning, in order to give family time to get here. My father will deliver the eulogy."

Tory shook her head. "I hate funerals. They always make me wonder why we don't say all those nice things to people while they're still alive."

"You're right, you know. It's too easy to take each other for granted." It was hitting each of them differently, but it was up to her to keep them focused. "We were . . . we are a good team. And if Mitch were here, he'd want me to tell you both that."

"And he would want us to close this case before anyone else died," Tory added.

Carlos stared at Mitch's desk. "He'd tell us that there's a hero in all of us, that keeps us honest, gives us strength, makes us noble. And finally gets us to die with pride. May Parker. *Spider-Man 2*."

The quote struck a chord. Honest, strong, and a hero. Mitch had been all those things. "I guess Mitch rubbed off on us more than I realized."

Movement in the doorway caught Avery's attention. The ache threatening to engulf her morphed into irritation. "Mason?"

"The captain called me in." Mason walked slowly into the room, as if he knew he was stepping into enemy territory. "Listen, I haven't had the chance to tell you how sorry I am about Mitch's death. I know that all of you were close."

Just like you and my brother used to be.

She squelched the thought.

She dug for a grain of forgiveness, but came up lacking. Sometimes it was just so hard. "It's going to take some time to realize that he's really not coming back."

"And," he continued, "I know that you're only letting me work with you on this case because of Captain Peterson's orders, but I really think I can help."

"I hope you're right."

"Carlos and I were planning to go get some coffee." Tory signaled to Carlos. "Can we get either of you anything?"

"I'm fine." Avery nodded her thanks. No matter what she thought about the situation, she was going to have to include Mason in the investigation. But before they got started, there were things that needed to be said.

Tory looked at Mason.

"I'm good. Thanks."

Avery waited until Carlos and Tory left the room. "I guess it's time we attempted to clear the air between us."

"Your feelings toward me since Michael's death have never been a secret, and I'm going to assume that nothing has changed in the past twenty-four hours. So let's get it out in the open. Ask me whatever you want, and I'll give you an honest answer."

"Okay. Let's start with why you were working

undercover in the Sourns' business, and what you know that might help my case."

"I was working on the case in conjunction with an ongoing FBI investigation." Mason caught her gaze. "We were looking for evidence that would bring down a major arms network working primarily out of Asia and the Middle East that we believe has connections to Sourn's business. My role as an undercover employee was to tape conversations, track the guns, collect whatever evidence I could, and eventually help to take down as many as we could."

Operation Stronghold.

She'd spent a couple hours last night going over the files and reports she had, but she needed to hear things from Mason firsthand. "What were you doing at the warehouse yesterday?"

"We found out that there was a shipment of illegal weapons going out, and I was able to arrange to be one of the drivers. Two million dollars in M-16s, handguns, and ammo from India and headed for Mexico. I was planning to make the run in order to take down both the sellers and the buyers."

"Why were the guns loaded?"

"An associate of the buyer showed up unexpectedly to inspect the guns to ensure that his boss was getting what was agreed on. He was in the process of doing that when you arrived. If I had known a raid was being planned . . ."

So Mitch's death was reduced to nothing more than a series of unfortunate events?

Avery leaned back against her desk. Trust was something earned. Forgiveness a messy process. But what if everything about Mason's story added up? What if she'd been wrong about what happened at the warehouse and Michael's death?

For now, she had no choice but to shove the lingering doubts aside. Mitch was dead, and they had a job to do.

"As for Sourn," Mason continued, "I've spent the past few months getting to know the players and getting them to trust me. I know who's involved, which means you need me as much as I need you. We have a chance to take down this entire network if we work together."

"What do you know about what's happening right now?"

"A couple of hours ago, two uniforms pulled Mrs. Sourn over for speeding, about a hundred and twenty miles northeast of Atlanta on I-85 toward Charlotte. They realized that there was a BOLO out on her and brought her in."

"Why was she heading for Charlotte?"

"She hasn't said. She insisted on speaking to her lawyer first."

"She could have been planning to meet her husband, or maybe just trying to get across state lines."

Carlos and Tory stepped back into the office, coffee in hand.

Avery fought the nagging frustration gnawing in her gut. "The four of us are going to have to work together if we're going to bring down Sourn and his people. Tory, I need you to try to track down any land or property belonging to the Sourns or their company."

"I'm on it."

"Carlos, what about the forensic evidence from the searches of the Sourns' property? As of this moment, I'm walking in there with little or no solid evidence that will tie Mrs. Sourn to the crime. Follow up with the lab and see if you can get us some leverage—"

"I might have something." Tory sat back down at her desk and clicked on a file. "When you came in, I was digging through some of the city's surveillance videos. I've been waiting to hear back from a contact."

Tory printed out something, then handed Avery a black-and-white photo. "This was taken Monday morning just after two."

"This just might do it." Avery smiled and stuck the photo into her file before heading toward the door. "Let me know if you hear from forensics. And in the meantime, we'll hope this gives us the leverage we need to gain a confession."

Avery walked toward the interrogation room with Mason, wondering how she'd come to the place where she was working a case with a man she'd been trying to convict for the past few months.

Mason strode down the hallway beside her. "I hope you know that I want to take down Sourn as badly as you do."

Avery stopped to face him. "Why?"

"Because while I've been working undercover, I've seen what this man is involved in. You've got a dead girl, and a dead partner. Robert Sourn has figured out how to skirt the law, and up until now, no one has ever been able to gather enough evidence to convict him."

Avery gauged his expression. "This is personal somehow, isn't it?"

"I had a little brother killed in a drive-by with an illegal weapon. He was seven years old. They found the gun but never found out who pulled the trigger."

"I don't ever remember you talking about that."

"It was a long time ago."

Whatever she thought about him on a personal level couldn't erase the reality that she understood the pain he felt. "I'm sorry."

"Like I said, it was a long time ago, but even so, that doesn't change the fact that men like Sourn have to be taken off the streets. Too many people have already been hurt."

"Then let's do whatever it takes to put this guy behind bars."

Avery's phone rang as she started walking again. She checked the caller ID. "Jackson. Hey, I hope you've got something for me, because I'm headed into an interview with Mrs. Sourn."

"I've got exactly what you're looking for."

She stopped in front of the interrogation room door and waited for him to continue.

"A match on your murder weapon."

Chapter 38

Avery dropped the file folder onto the table, then sat down across from Mrs. Sourn. They might have done this once before, but this time things were going to turn out differently.

"Before you begin, Detective, my client doesn't have anything to say."

Avery ignored the lawyer's sour face and focused on Mrs. Sourn, who clearly hadn't slept much in the past twenty-four hours. "Then this won't take long, will it?"

The shadows under her eyes had deepened, and her hair was disheveled on one side. Even the belted, plaid dress she wore looked wilted.

"I just have a couple of questions I need to ask you, Mrs. Sourn. Where were you going this morning?"

Mrs. Sourn clasped the handle of her purse in her lap and avoided making eye contact. "I needed to get away for a while, so I decided to go for a drive."

"You were pretty far from home for a Sunday morning drive. Did your husband tell you to leave town?"

"No." Mrs. Sourn sat still, her fingers slowly clenching and unclenching the leather straps of the purse.

"Can you tell me where your husband is right now?"

"I'm . . . I'm not sure. He's working."

"Is it common for you to not know where he is?"

"He's had a lot of things going on these past few months, as we are in the middle of expanding our business. I can't keep track of everything he does."

"Detective," Mr. Blackburn broke in, "I've tried my best to be patient, but I'm not sure I know what we are doing here. I thought the last time we met we made it clear that my clients are the victims in this investigation."

"You did make it clear, Mr. Blackburn, but in case you were not aware, there is a warrant out for the arrest of Robert Sourn for the kidnapping of a young woman yesterday morning, and for using his business as a means for arms trafficking."

"I am aware of the charges that have been brought against my client, but unfortunately, like Mrs. Sourn, I have no idea where he is."

"I—"

Mr. Blackburn held up his hand for Mrs. Sourn to be quiet. "Do you have any evidence that Mrs. Sourn was involved in any of the aforementioned crimes, Detective North?"

"Right now, I simply need a couple of inconsistencies clarified by Mrs. Sourn." Avery turned back to the older woman. "Starting with last Monday morning. You told us that between one and four, you and your husband were home asleep, isn't that right?"

Mrs. Sourn pressed her lips together. Avery could read the fear and panic that mingled in her expression. But now was not the time for her to shut down. They needed a confession.

Mason slid into the seat across from Blackburn but kept his gaze focused on Mrs. Sourn. "May I remind you that this is a murder investigation, and withholding evidence or lying to the police is a serious offense?"

"So I'll ask you again," Avery continued. "Did you or your husband leave the house during that time?"

"No."

"That's interesting." Avery pushed the black-and-white ATM photo Tory had given her across the table. "Because we have video from an ATM showing that your husband withdrew cash at two forty-seven Monday morning."

"No . . . There must be a mistake."

"Would you like to change your story, Mrs. Sourn?"

"It . . . I don't know. It's possible he had a meeting with clients that ran late. I might have lost track of the days."

"So you were in the house alone during that time period."

"Yes. I suppose."

Avery slid the photo of Tala's swollen body across the table next. Mrs. Sourn flinched. "Mrs. Sourn, as you know by now, Saturday morning a judge granted us a warrant to search both your house and your business. Forensics found traces of Tala's blood in your house—on the banister, in some of the carpet fibers, and on a bronze lamp base that has just been identified as the murder weapon. And according to your last statement, you were the only person in the house at the time of her death."

Mrs. Sourn shook her head, looking trapped.

"Mrs. Sourn"—Mason leaned forward—"it would be to your advantage to tell us what happened that night. It's one thing to harbor an illegal alien, but add murder to the list, and you're looking at a lot of time behind bars."

"Mrs. Sourn, you don't have to say anything." Blackburn grabbed his briefcase, then reached out to help Mrs. Sourn stand up. "We're leaving."

"That's fine." Avery started picking up the photos. "Because we're finished here. I have enough evidence to arrest your client for the murder of Tala Vuong, and that is just the beginning. We also have additional evidence that we plan to hand over to the DA that includes harboring of an illegal alien, slavery, and forced labor."

"And don't forget the smuggling of illegal weapons in conjunction with the family business," Mason said. "We already have a growing amount of evidence tying your import business to illegal trafficking."

"No. Wait a minute." Mrs. Sourn sat back down. "I'd like to make a deal."

"Mrs. Sourn," Blackburn began. "This isn't an episode of *Law and Order*—"

"What kind of deal?" Avery dropped the photos back onto the table, ignoring Blackburn's scowl.

"I'll tell you what happened that night, but you get the DA to lessen my sentence. In exchange, I'll give you all the evidence you need against my husband."

"Mrs. Sourn, as your lawyer, it is my duty to inform you that you are making a huge mistake—"

"Stop." Mrs. Sourn pushed back the chair beside her, letting it smash into the wall. "I'm tired of the games and the lies and the secrets. It's over."

Avery leaned forward. "Why do you want to give up your husband, Mrs. Sourn?"

"Because . . . because he was sleeping with her." Mrs. Sourn's shoulders slumped as she brushed away tears with the back of her hand. "Mr. Blackburn, I want you to leave."

"Excuse me?"

"I said I want you to leave. You're fired."

Mason jumped up and opened the door. "Thank you for coming by, Mr. Blackburn. I'm sure we'll be in touch regarding Mrs. Sourn's husband soon."

Avery turned her focus back to Mrs. Sourn while the lawyer stomped out of the room. "We'll start with Tala's murder, then move on to your husband. Tell me what happened that night."

Mrs. Sourn sat still, elbows on the table, hands in front of her mouth, shaking her head.

"Mrs. Sourn?"

"This wasn't supposed to happen, but I can't . . . I can't keep lying about everything."

"Tell me what happened."

"It was an accident. I swear I didn't mean to kill her. I just . . . I just wanted to scare her. I was so angry."

"But instead of scaring her, you killed her."

"She was young and pretty." Mrs. Sourn stared at the wall. "I knew he was going to her when I was gone, and she admitted it was true. It didn't matter to me at that moment that he was forcing her, threatening her."

"How did you kill her?"

"We fought, I hit her on the head, and she fell down the stairs. Robert came home a few minutes later. I didn't know what to do. She was lying there, not breathing. Robert was furious. He told me he couldn't afford to have another police investigation, and that we were going to have to cover up her death."

Mason still stood at the end of the table. "What did he do?"

"He decided that we would throw off the police by making her death look like the girl killed a few weeks ago."

"What do you know about her death?"

"Nothing, I swear, and I don't think Robert does either. But he had seen the report on the news of her death."

"So he decided to make Tala's death look like someone was murdering young Asian girls. A serial killer."

Mrs. Sourn nodded. "He took her in his car and dumped her in an alley next to a Dumpster for someone else to find. He assured me they would never be able to trace her back to us."

"Then why call in a missing persons report if you didn't think she could be traced back to you?"

"I was cleaning up that morning. Making sure there was no trace of what had happened the night before. I was so upset that my hands were shaking, and I knocked my jewelry box off the dresser. As I picked everything up off of the floor, I noticed that the ring was missing. I couldn't find it, and I knew Tala must have taken it. But by then her body had already been discovered, and it was too late for us to search her."

"And because it was custom-made, you knew that if she did have the ring, once we found her body, we could tie her to you."

Mrs. Sourn nodded. "Robert decided that the only answer was to claim she was our niece."

The tension in Avery's neck began to spread down her spine. One lie led to another, which led to another, which soon became too many to cover up. Finding the truth might solve a case and even bring closure, but it could never erase the damage.

"Keeping the story straight wasn't difficult. Four years ago, a family friend came to live with us after high school for a couple years. It was easy to pretend that Tala was Bian. We'd even kept her room the same after she left, but it didn't take long for everything to begin falling apart."

Ashes, ashes. They'll all fall down.

Mason leaned forward, his hands against the table. "So Robert panicked. Paid someone to send the flower to Detective North and break into her house, then kidnapped Malaya, all in an attempt to ensure we kept running around chasing a bogus serial killer."

346

"I'm not sure what all he did, except that he panicked. He knew he couldn't have the police looking into the business. He thinks I don't know anything, but I do. He's involved in trafficking guns, drugs, the girls . . ."

"How much did he receive for each girl?" Avery asked.

"Five thousand dollars on average, depending what they were going to be used for."

Which made it a lucrative business. Steep fees paid by the parents of the girls, then by the clients who bought them.

"So people paid the fee, and then they were free to do whatever they wanted with the girls."

Mrs. Sourn turned her head. "I didn't have anything to do with the trafficking. You have to believe me."

"But you didn't try to stop him either." The whole thing made her stomach turn. "And what about Tala? Having someone clean and cook for you sixteen, seventeen hours a day, never bothered your conscience? And I'm sure she didn't sleep in that nice bedroom upstairs except for the times she was sleeping with your husband."

Mrs. Sourn clenched her fists in front of her. "No . . ."

"You kept quiet in order to save yourself, but what are you left with now? Tala is dead and dozens of other girls are scattered across this country living as slaves because you didn't speak up."

Mrs. Sourn pressed her hand against her mouth and dropped her gaze.

"What else do you know?" Avery prodded.

"I . . . I don't have any details."

"Just tell us what you know."

"There was a boatload of girls due to arrive this weekend. It was why Robert was so upset. He knew it might be his last chance to get to the girls before the authorities did."

Avery leaned forward. That was something she couldn't let happen. "Where is he, Mrs. Sourn?"

"I honestly don't know. There's a secret route they use, like the Underground Railroad from the Civil War. Except instead of smuggling freed slaves, they . . . they traffic the girls. They call it the Magnolia Passage."

Avery felt her breath catch. These girls had been bought, branded, and sold. "Where are the girls?"

"I don't know."

"Mrs. Sourn—"

"I think it might be off the coast somewhere on one of the islands, but if he never told me about the girls, do you think he'd have told me about the routes he uses? He believed that the fewer people who knew, the better. But I do know one thing. If you don't find the girls before he moves them again, they'll end up scattered across the country. And then you'll never find them."

Tory walked into the interrogation room and signaled for Avery to join her in the hall.

"What have you got?"

"I've been watching from behind the observation mirror. I think I might know where Sourn is."

"Where?"

"Remember a few days ago I told you that I was able to link the Sourns to a number of nail salons? Through a bunch of digging and cross-referencing, I discovered that Mr. Sourn also owns a piece of property near Jekyll Island. Ten acres of secluded land with a house, a large storage shed, and a boat ramp with water access to the Atlantic."

"Bingo." Avery started for her office. "I'll contact the Coast Guard. Make sure our team is ready to leave in ten minutes."

Chapter 39

Tess was nine the last time Avery had been on the water off Georgia's sandy coastline. They'd rented a house with an ocean view along one of the barrier islands and spent the week playing in the sand, feasting on shrimp, and searching for sea turtles.

Avery studied the shore through a pair of Coast Guard stabilizing binoculars. Today they were searching for something far more sinister than a wildlife nest. She lowered the binoculars, still gazing out the window of the pilothouse of the Coast Guard's forty-five-foot response boat. Getting a judge to sign a warrant to search the island property had been difficult. Finding and arresting Mr. Sourn even more difficult.

"How close are we?"

Petty Officer McMillan glanced at the screen of his navigation station. "Looks like the property is just around the bend. You might want to hang on, though. This response boat—or RB-M as we call it—gives a smooth ride most of the time, but the pass between the two islands can get a bit rough."

Avery wrapped her fingers around the aluminum grab rail beside her as the pilot made his way between the two islands. Many of the islets lining the Georgia seacoast had become exclusive hideaways for the rich and famous as well as cheap vacations for families who wanted to get away from it all. On any other excursion, she'd have enjoyed the vast marshlands, glimpses of wild horses, and sand dunes glimmering beneath the sunlight in the distance, but for the moment all she could see was that Robert Sourn had found the perfect hideaway to stash his merchandise until he was able to sell and distribute them to the highest bidders.

Avery caught a glimpse of a structure and turned to Petty Officer McMillan. "Looks like there's a house and outbuilding ahead to the left. That has to be it."

By the time McMillan and his crew had secured the boat to the dock, they were ready to go in. They split up on the shore into two groups, ready to cover both the front and back of the house and the large shed that sat a good fifty feet from the shore.

Avery could almost touch the eerie quiet that hovered in the afternoon air as she made her way across the sandy beach strewn with driftwood and seashells. Beyond the house, outcrops of pine and oak trees filled the terrain before giving way to the inland watery marshes in the distance. No one would expect to find dozens of stolen girls hidden away on this isolated spot.

God, just don't let us be too late. Please . . .

She slowed down as she approached the large wooden door of the structure and tried the handle. Unlocked. The hinges creaked as she pushed the door open, weapon in hand.

They spread throughout the open warehouse-like storage space, searching behind the boxes of supplies and large pallets that filled the room.

"Clear."

"Clear."

"Clear."

There was no sign of the girls.

"They've got to be inside the house." Avery signaled her team, and they made their way back into the afternoon sunlight and started toward the house.

"Avery." Mason dropped his weapon to his side, put his finger to his lips, and jutted his chin toward the shore.

Sourn was escaping toward the dock—and he had a hostage.

Avery glanced toward the small motorboat docked ten feet from the Coast Guard's RB-M. "I'll get him talking. See if you can get behind him and block his access to the dock. Carlos, go to the house, make sure it's secure and that everyone stays back unless I say otherwise. I want this to go down without any bloodshed, but dead or alive, Sourn is not getting off this island. Tory, you're with me."

Avery made her way quickly toward the dock and called out Sourn's name, her gun drawn.

He turned, grasping the girl's arm with one hand while holding his gun to her temple with his other hand. "Stay back, Detective."

"You don't really think we're going to let you leave this island, do you? Let the girl go and end this before someone gets hurt."

Avery caught the look of terror in the young girl's eyes. She couldn't be more than sixteen or seventeen. An image of Tala flashed in front of her. This had to end. Today. Right now.

Sourn glanced toward the shore, then back to Avery. "Call your men off and let me go."

"You know I can't do that."

"I will kill her."

"I don't think you're going to do that."

"Don't be so confident, Detective. I've killed before, and I'll do it again."

Avery chose her words carefully. "We got a full confession from your wife today. We know you didn't kill the other girls, and I don't think you want to add murder to your list."

"Does it really matter? If you talked to my wife, I'm sure by now you have enough to put me away for the next hundred years." Sourn kept walking backward toward the shore, dragging the girl along with him. "The way I look at it, I don't have anything else to lose."

"Think about it, Sourn." Mason had made his way to the shore and was now slowly moving toward Sourn from the other direction. "Detective North is right. We can tie you to arms dealing and human trafficking, but murder has never been your MO. Let the girl go."

"So what are you telling me? If I let her go, you're going to cut a deal so I walk away from all of this?"

"You know that can't happen, but you don't want to make things more difficult on yourself. I can promise you that the DA will look at your situation in a different light if you let her go right now rather than kill her in cold blood."

Avery clicked on her radio while Mason kept talking to the man. "Tell me what you've got up there, Carlos."

"We found the girls. About twenty-five of them locked in one of the bedrooms in the house. Rice, who clearly was working for Sourn, is now in custody. He surrendered without any fight and he's talking."

"What's their physical condition?"

"I'd say the emotional trauma far outweighs the physical, but most seem malnourished and dehydrated."

After weeks confined on a boat with little food and water, the situation could have been worse. "Have the medic treat the girls. Be ready to move, but stay in the house until this situation is resolved. We're going to need to call in another boat to transport them back to the mainland."

"I'm on it."

Avery turned her attention back to Sourn. Here was a man who had worked hard his whole life to get ahead until he forgot the defining line between right and wrong. The value of human life and dignity. This situation wasn't the result of a onetime decision; instead, multiple decisions had led him to this moment.

Avery took another step forward. "What's her name, Sourn?"

Sourn backed toward the dock. "Does it matter?"

"It matters to me."

Avery turned to Tory. "Ask her what her name is. Tell her we're going to do everything we can to make sure she's okay."

Tory spoke in Vietnamese to the girl, who stood shivering beside Sourn in her thin, pink dress.

She glanced up at her captor with wide, almond eyes, then back to Tory before she finally spoke.

"Her name is Mia," Tory translated. "She has a family back in Vietnam, and she—"

"Stop." Sourn waved his gun in front of him. "You're stupid if you think that this is going to convince me to let her go. I've been doing this for too long now to turn back simply because I feel sorry for her. Do you know how much money I can get for each of these girls?"

"Can't you see it's already too late, Sourn?" Mason said. "The girl doesn't have to be involved in this."

"And what happens if I let her go? You'll just let me go as well, because you're so nice?"

Avery held her gun steady. "Like I said, let the girl go, then we can talk about what happens next. No one has to get hurt."

Sourn took another step toward the water. "I'll tell you what happens next. I'm going to get on that motorboat docked beside your fancy Coast Guard rig with the girl, and you're going to let us both go."

Sourn was now less than six feet from the dock.

Avery evaluated the situation. If Sourn managed to get away, there were a hundred places he could vanish in these chains of islands alone. And Avery had no doubt that he had access to money somewhere offshore. Disappearing wouldn't be difficult. If they didn't bring him in now, they might not get a second chance.

"You follow me onto the boat, and I swear I'll kill her."

"Don't let things end this way, Sourn."

"It's already over." Sourn grabbed Mia's hand, pulled her toward the boat, and untied the line. The motorboat rocked beneath them as they stepped into the bow, but he managed to keep his balance, using her as a shield.

Avery jumped onto the Coast Guard boat in front of Mason and Tory, then addressed Petty Officer McMillan. "Follow as close as you can without putting anyone on this boat in danger."

A bullet hit a metal post behind them.

The Coast Guard boat veered to the right as McMillan moved away from the dock and out of range from another bullet. Avery's shoulder slammed against the aluminum pole, the boat's movement almost knocking her off her feet, but she blocked out the pain. She'd deal with it later. For now, they had a girl's life to save.

Sourn pushed the electric start button on his outboard motor, his left arm wrapped around Mia while still gripping the gun. The boat had already drifted a dozen feet into the water, but the motor wouldn't catch.

Avery shouted across the water. "It's over, Sourn. Let the girl go."

"Let me take a shot, Avery."

She glanced at Mason, knowing if anyone could make the shot, he could. "Wait until you can guarantee you won't hit the hostage."

Their RB-M kept its distance but was still close enough for Mason to hit his target. Sourn continued to drift away from the shore as they hit the rougher waters between the two islands. A swell hit the side of Sourn's boat. He reached for something to grab on to and lost his grip on Mia.

"Now," Avery ordered.

Mason fired, hitting Sourn in the shoulder. The boat hit another swell, but this time Sourn couldn't absorb the jolt. He grabbed for Mia. His gun dropped onto the floor of the boat as he fell backward, pulling her into the Atlantic with him.

Avery watched them plunge into the water, arms flailing, and a trail of blood from Sourn's wound drifted to the surface. The petty officer maneuvered the RB-M into the water beside them. Time clicked by in slow motion, frame by frame, but it only took Avery a fraction of a second to react. Mia floundered in the water, gasping for breath. She had no idea how to swim.

Avery set her weapon down and dove over the side of the boat into the ocean. As she surfaced, she saw Mason and one of the Coast Guard crew members swimming toward Sourn's body. Avery felt the searing pain of the stitches in her arm rip as she reached for the girl. Panicked, Mia pushed Avery away, then went under again. Avery grabbed for the life preserver someone had thrown into the water. Holding on to it, Avery coughed up a mouthful of seawater, then pulled Mia into her arms.

A moment later, it was all over. The RB-M was beside her. Someone pulled them out of the water. Wrapped blankets around them. Told her to lie still and breathe.

Tory hovered over her. "Mia is going to be okay."

Avery felt the movement of the boat beneath her as the RB-M headed back toward the shore. "What about Sourn?"

"He'll live. And I just heard from Carlos. He said Rice is squealing to make a deal. Which means that along with Sourn's wife's testimony, we have enough hard evidence to put Sourn away for a very long time."

Avery struggled to sit up, then started wringing the water out of her hair, her arm still throbbing. "Why bring the girls here?"

"According to Rice, new boats arrive with weapons or young girls. From here they can split up their cargo, then transport them to different landing sites on the mainland, making it easier for them to reach their final destination."

Avery pressed her hand against her chest, waiting for her heartbeat to return to normal. Waiting for her mind to believe that it was all finally over.

Mason sat down beside her. "You okay?"

"Yeah."

"You did a good job out there today."

"Thanks. You didn't do too bad yourself."

"I guess it's too much to think we could be friends again."

"Today was a start."

"That'll have to be good enough for now."

Avery looked up at him. "Why does it matter to you if we become friends or not?"

"Because losing Michael changed me like it changed you. I think we have more in common than you think."

She wasn't ready for the comparison but knew at the same time that her father had been right. She might not be able to forget, but not forgiving would only hurt herself in the end.

"Your arm's bleeding." Mason grabbed a long strip of gauze from the medical kit sitting on the bench beside him as the RB-M stopped alongside the dock. He pressed it against her arm. "You're officially off duty, Detective North. I want you to go see a medic."

Avery looked toward the house. "I will, but first I want to see where he kept them."

Officers were already transporting the girls to the second RB-M that had arrived moments before. The scene was being processed as Avery walked into the house where twenty-five girls had been crammed into a room not much bigger than her bedroom. Besides a small kitchen and a few chairs, the house was empty.

They'd been left with no escape, miles from home, completely defenseless. Raw emotions washed over Avery as she walked into the bedroom filled with a pile of dirty mats to sleep on. Girls sat against the walls, looking dazed and confused. She breathed in the stench of unwashed bodies and backed-up sewage from the bathroom and felt the room begin to spin.

She wished that Mitch were here to help her pick up the pieces. Wished Jackson were here to hold her and tell her all of this wasn't real.

But the faces of the girls being escorted past her one by one toward the dock were all too real.

Tory stopped beside her. "How do you ever get over something like this?"

Avery shook her head. "I don't think you do."

"I've told them they are safe now, but I can tell they don't believe me."

"Why should they? They've been lied to, treated like animals, threatened . . . Another day or two in these conditions, though, and we'd be looking at an entirely different situation."

"In a few more hours they would have been gone and we'd never have found them all. North to DC and New York. West to Houston . . . There's no telling where they would have ended up. How many would've survived the next few months in some back-alley brothel or illegal factory?"

Avery leaned down beside one of the girls still waiting to be taken to the boat. "What's your name?"

Tory translated the question.

The girl ducked her head. "Kim-ly."

Avery reached out and let her fingers brush the still-red edges of a magnolia tattoo branded on her shoulder, then slowly helped the girl to her feet. She took a blanket from one of the officers, wrapped it around Kim-ly's shoulders, and started back with her toward the boat.

Sourn wasn't the last predator they would face, and this wasn't the last girl whose life would be affected, but for today, for these girls, what happened today mattered.

Chapter 40

Malaya sat on the mattress with its soft blue bedspread and pulled the pillow against her chest. The walls of the bedroom were painted yellow and pretty lace curtains hung on the walls, but even here she didn't feel safe.

Sleep should bring relief from the constant fear, but instead it brought with it its own terrifying dreams that jolted her awake in the middle of the night. At first she'd been afraid that she'd wake up in the small, windowless room on a dirty mat on the floor, but now a new fear had settled over her.

He'd promised he'd find her if she escaped.

"Malaya?"

She jumped at the sound of her name and pressed her body against the wall behind her as Detective Lambert entered the room.

Malaya let out a small breath of relief. "Detective Lambert."

"It's okay." She sat down on the edge of the bed and smiled. "I just wanted to come by to see how you were doing."

Malaya drew her legs up to her chest, not sure how to answer the question. This morning she'd woken up in a room with three other girls with similar stories to her own. Everyone told her she was supposed to feel happy and safe here. Instead she felt lost. Nothing could protect her from the evil lurking in the shadows.

She forced a smile. "Everyone here is nice. I have my own bed, a bathroom, and plenty to eat. But I don't know how to not be afraid."

"You've been through a lot, Malaya. The feelings you have are normal. It will take time, but the fear and the sadness will fade one day."

Memories from the past few days swept over Malaya until she could barely breathe. It might get better, but things would never be the same.

"I thought you might want to know that we caught the man who kidnapped you. He's not going to hurt any more girls."

"What about the other girls that were with me on the boat? Did they find them?"

"Eight of the girls were working in a factory and picked up yesterday."

"Only eight?" That wasn't even half of the girls.

"We're going to keep looking for the rest of them."

Malaya squeezed her eyes shut for a moment. "I can't forget their faces, and knowing they're still out there . . . People can do such terrible things."

"I know."

"And Teo. What will happen to him?" She

looked up at the detective. He was the one person she didn't want to leave behind.

Detective Lambert shook her head. "He'll go live with someone else. A family who will take good care of him."

"I hope so."

"I wanted to give you something before you left." Detective Lambert pulled something from her jacket pocket. "I thought you might want this picture. Tala had it with her when she died. I thought it might be something for you to remember her by."

Malaya ran her thumb across the photo and felt a tear roll down her cheek. "We had the pictures taken a few days before we left for the United States. We thought we were the luckiest girls in the city that day."

Detective Lambert's brow rose. "You're the other girl in the photo."

Malaya looked up at her and nodded, her eyes still rimmed with tears. "We were cousins, but we grew up as best friends. It was her father, my uncle, who found out about the opportunity to send us to the States. He convinced my father that we would have a better life, and that maybe one day, our families could join us."

"I'm so sorry, Malaya. For everything." Detective Lambert reached out and squeezed her hand. "Are you going to be okay?"

"I don't know. I don't know how to forget what

happened here. How to forget that she's dead, or how I will tell my family that she isn't coming home."

Guilt mingled with joy from the knowledge that she was going home. She was one of the lucky ones who'd survived and would see her family again. Malaya stared at the photo, her stomach aching over the reality of her loss. If only Tala had been so lucky.

Chapter 41

Avery's feet dangled beneath her on the front porch of her parents' home. She'd sat in the same spot for the past hour, escaping the stress of the past few days with a good book and a tall glass of iced tea.

For the past five minutes, she'd stopped reading to study a hummingbird hovering at her mother's nearby bird feeder for a late afternoon drink. For Avery, the ruby-throated flyer had become yet another needed confirmation of God's presence in a world that lately seemed to be spinning out of control.

Today had ushered in the new week with a mixture of both relief and regret. Relief that her case was closed and justice would soon be served. Regret because justice had come too late for Tala and Mitch, and had left in its wake a jagged hole in her own heart. Healing might come slowly, but it would come. For the moment, though, it was the support of family and friends that was keeping her going. That and the growing anticipation of a relationship with Jackson.

She looked up at the sound of an approaching car. Jackson pulled into the driveway, invoking the familiar ping of her heart for the man who'd managed to stir something within her she'd never thought could happen twice in a lifetime. But it had, and if anything, it had become clear over the past few days that she was ready to give her heart a chance. Life could be over in the blink of an eye. She wasn't going to waste precious time worrying, only to lose him forever.

She watched him exit the car, then head up the driveway, dressed casually in gray cargo shorts and a rusty red crew-neck T-shirt. Perfect.

"Hey."

"Hey back at you." He took the stairs up to the porch, then stopped in front of her. "I was told you were following doctor's orders, but I have to say I wasn't sure it was true."

"Book in one hand, a tall glass of iced tea in the other . . . I don't think you'll ever see me more relaxed than this." She set the drink down on the wicker side table, then smiled up at him, savoring the feeling of completeness and balance he brought when he was with her. "Besides, I was told if I didn't take the next few days off, I'd end up with a mandatory two-week leave."

"Why am I not surprised that it would take the threat of *not* working to get you to slow down?" He sat down beside her, smelling like citrus, the outdoors, and a hint of antibacterial cleaner. "There's even a bit of color in your cheeks again today. A little sun and rest have gone a long way."

"I needed it." She wouldn't mention that the color in her cheeks was more because he was sitting beside her, filling in the pieces of her life that had been missing for so long.

"What did you do today?"

Avery dog-eared the page in her book to mark her place, then dropped it into her lap. "My mother took Tess and me to get pedicures, then I actually took a nap." She couldn't remember the last time she'd taken a nap. It had felt good, reminding her how simple things could make such a big difference. "What about you?"

"Unfortunately, my boss made me come in to work today, which meant I spent my day in autopsy."

"You poor thing." There was a hint of teasing in her response, but she couldn't dismiss the grim reality in the reminder of what they both did for a living.

He nudged her with his shoulder. "I'll

remember your lack of sympathy when you're hard at work on my next day off."

"I don't know." She looked up at him and caught his gaze. "I was hoping we might be able to arrange a couple of days off together."

"I'd like that. A lot. And speaking of days off," he continued, "I spoke to my grandfather before coming over here, and I have a message for you from him."

"What did he say?"

"I told him you had a couple days off, and he's invited you over for dinner tomorrow night."

"Dinner? I'd be honored. I'm looking forward to meeting him."

"He's going to love you. Both of you. Tess is invited as well."

"So which one of you will be doing the cooking? As I recall, you told me you could whip up a fairly decent meal, but for some reason I've yet to see that side of you."

"That is one of my many hidden talents, but you'll have to wait a bit longer to experience it. In the meantime, I suggested a tray of Papps's favorite peanut butter and bologna sandwiches, but he insisted on making his famous gumbo."

"Peanut butter and bologna?"

"It's a long story."

Avery laughed. "I definitely vote for the gumbo."

"I thought you might." Jackson's gaze shifted toward the house. "Where's Tess?"

"Inside getting ready. You'd think we were going to prom, not bowling for the afternoon."

"You never know what cute boys might show up."

"Ah . . . now you are starting to think like a twelve-year-old, almost-teenage girl. Though looking back at my own childhood, I'm afraid that this is just the beginning. Before you know it, the boys are going to start showing up at my front door. I'm not sure I'm ready for that."

He put an arm around her shoulder and took her hand, slowly rubbing his thumb across the back of her fingers. "You'll be ready when the time comes and get through it just fine."

"I hope so."

She leaned her head against his shoulder and closed her eyes, content to enjoy the warmth of his arm around her and the rare, quiet moment of just the two of them together. And allowing herself to imagine what it might be like for the three of them to be a family.

The buzz of a lawn mower started up across the street. She opened her eyes and let her gaze focus on a clump of bright pink flowers sitting in a pot on her mother's porch.

"What's the latest from the DA regarding your case?" Jackson asked.

"I got a phone call from his assistant earlier today. Mr. Sourn's arraignment is set for tomorrow morning."

"Once again, justice prevails."

"I'm just thankful it's over. There are still a few lingering unanswered questions, like who killed our first Jane Doe, but Malaya and the others are safe, and thanks to Rice and Mrs. Sourn in particular, those responsible for trafficking them are now in custody."

"What happens to Malaya now?"

"She'll stay at the safe house along with the other girls until the DA is finished getting their testimonies. Then immigration will schedule flights for them to return home." She looked up at him. "We make a good team, Jackson."

"Yeah, we do."

"If you hadn't figured out the reason behind Tala's enlarged spleen, we might still have the wrong person behind bars. And all of those girls might have never been found."

"I don't even want to think about that. What about Bear, our homeless man? What's going to happen to him?"

"My father's recommended him to a rehabilitation program he's worked with over the years. If things go the way I think they will, he'll get counseling and hopefully a job. It's a small step, but at least a step in the right direction."

"I'm glad."

"Me too. The man's been through a lot."

"There is one more loose end that still needs to be worked out."

Avery swallowed hard under the intensity of his gaze. "What is that?"

"Us." He pulled her hand against his chest. "With the case closed, we might actually find some time to spend together . . . so we can figure out where our relationship is going."

Her smile widened. "Oh, I plan on making some time."

"Good, because I don't think it's a secret that I'm falling in love with you, Avery North."

Avery's breath caught. "Love's a big step."

"I know. I also know that life and love are never simple. We've both loved and lost, and while the experiences left scars, I think we're stronger because of them. But just because we've lost in the past doesn't mean we can't enjoy what's ahead . . . together."

"Then where do we start?"

"How about with this . . ." He cupped his hand around the back of her neck and pulled her toward him.

All the frustration and fears she'd held on to over the past week evaporated in the sultry Georgia air, leaving her to enjoy the taste of his kiss, the warmth of his touch, and the realization that this moment was only the beginning for them.

"Mom?"

Avery pulled away, his kiss still lingering on her lips. She pressed her fingers against her mouth and looked up at her daughter. "Sorry."

Tess stood in front of them looking more amused than upset. They were going to have to find a way to fumble through this together.

"I'll pretend I didn't see that." Tess dropped her purple canvas backpack onto the porch beside her. "Not that I'm not happy about the two of you being together, don't get me wrong, but all this kissy stuff—"

"Tess."

"All I'm saying is that while I might not mind the fact that my mother is dating, I do have a young and impressionable mind."

Jackson laughed. "We get it."

Tess reached for Avery's glass and downed the last of the tea. "Are you ready to go? Aunt Emily called to say she'd meet us there."

"I'm ready." Avery stood up, her mind still on Jackson's kiss that had left her longing for a few more uninterrupted moments alone. Her phone rang in her pocket. "Just a second."

Avery stopped at the top of the stairs and took the call.

"Avery, this is Tracy from the lab. You asked me to pass on to you any evidence we came up with regarding the break-in at your house last week."

"Mom?" Tess shot her the familiar please-don't-tell-me-you've-got-to-work look.

"Just a second." Avery held up her hand then

turned back to the phone. "Yes, what did you find out, Tracy?"

"We were able to get a DNA match on a spot of blood on the glass from your broken window."

"Who was it?"

"We were able to match it to a man by the name of Ben Jacobs."

"Ben Jacobs . . . Are you sure?" Avery's mind spun. There had to be some kind of mix-up. Jacobs was the missing witness she was looking for in connection with Michael's case.

"Yeah, his DNA is in the national database, so finding a match was pretty easy."

"Listen, I appreciate your calling, Tracy."

"Anytime."

Avery hung up the phone and let the information sink in. So the break-in and attack had nothing to do with the Sourn case. But if that were true, what had Jacobs been after?

"Avery." Jackson ran his fingers down her arm. "You okay?"

"Yeah." Avery shoved her phone into the back pocket of her jeans and shook off the mounting questions swarming through her mind. "It was just the lab calling with some DNA results I'd asked for."

Bringing with it the possibility that at some point, someone had intentionally tried to remove Jacobs's name from Michael's case files, but why?

Tess frowned. "Please don't tell me you have to go in to work, Mom."

"No, sweetie. This is something I can deal with later." She picked up Tess's backpack off the porch and handed it to her, ignoring the tug pulling her back to her brother's case. "Right now, I'm ready to take you on."

"You'd better watch out, because this time I'm planning to win."

Avery laughed, then laced her fingers with Jackson's before heading to his car behind Tess. Maybe it was simple. Girl meets boy, girl falls in love, they get married and live happily ever after.

Maybe sometimes it really did happen.

Acknowledgments

I'd like to give a huge thank-you to Ane Mulligan and Kristi Ann Hunter for their insight into life in Atlanta, and to retired police officer Linda Crum for reading through my manuscript early on to ensure that the police aspects worked. And Ellen Tarver, your insights into bringing it all together are always spot-on. Any mistakes are my own!

To Andrea Doering and the team at Revell for giving me the opportunity to write this story that has been on my heart for a long time. I'm very grateful!

And to my sweet, sweet family who constantly supports me as a wife, mom, and writer. You guys are the best.

Reader Questions for *Dangerous Passage*

1. Through the story, Avery struggles with balancing life so she wouldn't neglect her daughter and family. How did she try to handle this struggle?

2. On a more personal note, how do you handle your struggle to balance things in your own life?

3. What practical things have you discovered in your own life to help find a better balance?

4. The issue of human trafficking is a major theme of this story. What do you know about this tragedy?

5. Are you surprised to discover that it is an issue in the United States as well as in other parts of the world, and if so, why?

6. Malaya was willing to do almost anything for the hope of a better life. Do you take your freedom for granted? Why?

7. What would you do if those freedoms were taken away?

8. What would be the hardest thing for you to give up?

Author's Note

Dear Reader,

If I were to be perfectly honest with you, I'd have to confess that Avery and I share some of the same fears. It's that reality of feeling over-extended, neglecting one relationship to feed another, and being pulled in too many directions.

I think most of us can relate. Because between kids, spouses, work, and ministry, it's easy to feel like all we do is run. I could give you lots of advice on what you should do. Say no more often, get organized, or start exercising so you have more energy. The Bible, though, has some advice you might find surprising.

"Be still, and know that I am God."

We can run from one appointment to the next, accomplishing all the urgent tasks on our extensive to-do list, but if we don't stop to find out who God is, to really start to know him and build that relationship, what have we gained? How can we know God when we don't spend time with him?

We will never be like God—or perfect—but we were created in his image. Paul says in

Philippians 3 that we haven't obtained being everything God created us to be. But then he encourages us to forget what happened yesterday, or last month, or last year and instead look ahead toward spending eternity in heaven.

Man, in turn, has taken something good and broken it to use for his own gain. That's one of the reasons why the plight of human trafficking rips at my heart. No woman deserves to be forced to sell her body. No child deserves to be forced to work with little or no pay, along with inadequate food, water, and sanitation.

Here are some of the facts:

FACT: Human trafficking takes place around the world, including the United States.

FACT: Human trafficking includes prostitution, involuntary servitude, debt bondage, and serving in armed conflicts.

FACT: About 27 million people are enslaved around the world. Human trafficking is the second largest illegal and profitable enterprise in the world!

FACT: About half of these victims are under eighteen.

FACT: There are more slaves today than ever before in history.

FACT: The FBI estimates that there are currently over 100,000 children and young women being trafficked in the US.

What can we do? One, we can pray for those involved in this horrible crime. Two, we can inform ourselves about what is happening both around the world and where we live. Three, we can go where God sends us to reach out to those around us. It might mean getting involved with a group that is specifically fighting human trafficking. Or it might be reaching out to a hurting neighbor down the street, a lonely teen in your church's youth group, or a forgotten elderly person in your apartment building.

May we each find the courage to step out of our comfortable world and make a difference in the lives of those around us. To see the hurting, the lonely, and the helpless, and learn to stop and make a difference in their lives. The amazing thing is that, in turn, our own lives will be made richer because of it.

Be blessed!
Lisa Harris

About the Author

Lisa Harris is a Christy Award finalist and the winner of the Best Inspirational Suspense Novel for 2011 from *Romantic Times*. She has over twenty novels and novella collections in print. She and her family have spent the past ten years living as missionaries in Africa where she has homeschooled, led women's groups, and runs a non-profit organization that works alongside their church-planting ministry. The ECHO Project works in southern Africa promoting Education, Compassion, Health, and Opportunity and is a way for her to *"speak up for those who cannot speak for themselves . . . the poor and helpless, and see that they get justice"* (Prov. 31:8).

When she's not working, she loves hanging out with her family, cooking different ethnic dishes, photography, and heading into the African bush on safari. For more information about her books and life in Africa visit her website at www.lisaharriswrites.com or her blog at http://myblogintheheartofafrica.blogspot.com. For more information about The ECHO Project, please visit www.theECHOproject.org.